Praise for
TESSA BAILEY

"Tessa disarms you with a laugh, heats things up past boiling, and then puts a squeeze inside your heart. The tenderness, vulnerability, and heat I am always guaranteed with a Tessa Bailey book are the reasons she is one of my all-time favorite authors."

—Sally Thorne, bestselling author of
The Hating Game

"Her voice feels as fresh and contemporary as a Netflix rom-com...Bailey writes banter and rom-com scenarios with aplomb, but for those who like their romance on the spicier side, she's also the Michelangelo of dirty talk."

—*Entertainment Weekly*

"Bailey crafts an entertainingly spicy tale, with humor and palpable sexual tension."   —*Publishers Weekly*

"Tessa Bailey writes pure magic!"

—Alexis Daria, bestselling author of
You Had Me at Hola

"When you read a book by Bailey, there are two things you can always count on: sexy, rapid-fire dialogue, and scorching love scenes..."   —*BookPage*

"[A] singular talent for writing romantic chemistry that is both sparkling sweet and explosively sexy...one of the genre's very best."

—Kate Clayborn, author of *Love at First*

Romancing the Clarksons
Too Hot to Handle
Too Wild to Tame
Too Hard to Forget
Too Close to Call (novella)

Bellinger Sisters
It Happened One Summer
Hook, Line, and Sinker

Hot & Hammered
Fix Her Up
Love Her or Lose Her
Tools of Engagement

The Academy
Disorderly Conduct
Indecent Exposure
Disturbing His Peace

Broke and Beautiful
Chase Me
Need Me
Make Me

Made in Jersey
Crashed Out
Rough Rhythm (novella)
Thrown Down
Worked Up
Wound Tight

Crossing the Line
Riskier Business (novella)
Risking It All
Up in Smoke
Boiling Point
Raw Redemption

Too BEAUTIFUL TO BREAK

TESSA BAILEY

FOREVER

NEW YORK BOSTON

Copyright © 2022 by Tessa Bailey
Excerpt from *Too Hot to Handle* copyright © 2016 by Tessa Bailey

Cover art and design by Caitlin Sacks. Cover copyright © 2022 by Hachette Book Group, Inc.

Forever
Hachette Book Group
1290 Avenue of the Americas, New York, NY 10104
read-forever.com
twitter.com/readforeverpub

Originally published by Forever in September 2017
First trade paperback edition: October 2022

Forever is an imprint of Grand Central Publishing. The Forever name and logo are trademarks of Hachette Book Group, Inc.

The publisher is not responsible for websites (or their content) that are not owned by the publisher.

The Hachette Speakers Bureau provides a wide range of authors for speaking events. To find out more, go to www.hachettespeakersbureau.com or call (866) 376-6591.

ISBNs: 978-1-4555-9422-1 (mass market), 978-1-4555-9420-7 (ebook),
        978-1-5387-4185-6 (trade paperback)

Printed in the United States of America

LSC-C

Printing 1, 2022

For Belmont
(The real one)

ACKNOWLEDGMENTS

People often ask me where my book ideas come from. "Everywhere," is my answer. But Belmont's story has to be the most unique case of plot bunny-itis. My grandmother has always told me stories about her older brother, Belmont. He was the strong, silent protector type. I paid attention to these stories, but one anecdote in particular floored me. Belmont was a difficult child and continually ran away. One day, my great-grandparents handcuffed him to the sink (I don't condone this in any way) to make a point. So Belmont got up a head of steam and *ripped the sink out of the wall.*

As soon as I heard this story, I was hooked. Needed to know everything about the man this young child became. I plotted an entire series around him—and really, Peggy, Rita, and Aaron are *very* important, but they orbited around Belmont, didn't they?

Weeks after I plotted the series and started writing it, I came to find out that real-life Belmont had a different father, too, just like the fictional Belmont, which was possibly where his angst came from. I never knew this fact about his parentage and it was something my grandmother hadn't spoken to me about. So I've spent the last year convinced real-life Belmont and I have a cosmic, beyond the grave connection. In Peggy's book, she describes Belmont as, "More substantial than time," and I couldn't agree more. Belmont and Sage are going to stay with me forever. I hope they do the same for you.

Thank you to my editor, Madeleine Colavita, for your expertise, time, and love of the series. It was truly a pleasure going on this journey with you.

Thank you to my grandmother for telling me the sink story and getting the juices flowing. I'm so grateful that storytelling (and good hair) runs in the family!

Thank you to my husband, Patrick, and daughter, Mackenzie (and Molly the cat), for being the most patient, loving, and understanding people on the planet. I love us.

Thank you to my friends who continue to support me. Jessie and May, the fact that you harassed me for each book in this series made me so happy. Jillian, I'll never forget you crying in the restaurant when I told you I sold this series and how the story ended. And all the Bailey's Babes who have been Belmont girls since book one— thank you.

Too BEAUTIFUL
to BREAK

PROLOGUE

Miriam, January 28

Belmont. Sweet Jesus, already. Lighten up.

I kid.

Belmont was my first baby. But—and this is hard to explain—he never really behaved like one. Sure, in the beginning, he cried and squirmed and royally screwed my sleep schedule. Somewhere along the line, though, his eyes turned grave. I didn't try hard enough to hide my sadness during that period of my life, and thus, Belmont was born a second time.

Born into sadness.

Belmont's father was my one. I might be a French chef who believes food has a soul and tiramisu done right can inspire baby making, but I am the furthest thing from romantic one can get. And yet, I fell in love with my oldest son's father the moment we crossed shadows. I was not his one, however. I didn't know how to be his one...and still retain Miriam. Like Belmont, he was the kind of man who demanded all or nothing. With or against. Love or die.

So I chose to die a little and regenerate. But my son—my giant, beautiful, stormy, aching, ageless boy—he seemed to court the favor of sadness. It shoved him down into a well, robbed him of words and the ability to relate to people the way society dictates he should. There's a place inside him no one has ever reached and therein lies secrets. Turbulent truths. The ones he tried to express across my kitchen table with his eyes but couldn't find the right words for.

Watching my three children orbit the dark planet of Belmont gives me hope, though. Rita, Aaron, and Peggy are the smartest people I know—apart from myself, of course—and the way they cease all movement when Belmont speaks and treat his words like commandments, tells me others will one day do the same. If the demons don't get him first.

CHAPTER ONE

Shaking Belmont Clarkson wasn't going to be easy for Sage Alexander.

For several reasons.

One, she didn't want to.

To an outsider, the dependency Belmont had on Sage appeared to be one-sided. Over the course of the road trip from San Diego to New York, she had fielded several sympathetic looks lobbed in her direction. To the other Clarkson siblings, none of whom were left in the rattling Suburban as it lumbered down the highway, it probably seemed as if Belmont merely used Sage as a crutch for his anxiety. Every time he teetered a little too close to the edge of his comfort zone, Sage would get bundled up in Belmont's big arms and rocked until he relaxed. They didn't see Sage's need for reassurance, too. They didn't realize she stockpiled those moments in Belmont's arms like a hoarder, memorizing the sensation of being anchored, the feel of his hard chest beneath her cheek, his heart laboring in her ear.

When she was growing up, those moments of solace had been nonexistent, so she'd allowed herself to accept Belmont's. Until now. Now she had to stop. Unfortunately, cutting off the growing dependency they had on each other meant welding shut Belmont's escape hatch...in order to escape herself. And ripping off this particular Band-Aid would take ten layers of skin along with it. Right down to the bones he'd invaded.

They were only five miles from the train station now. Five miles to convince Belmont to pull over and leave her there. Continue driving to New York alone, where he and his siblings would fulfill his mother's last wish by jumping into the freezing water of the Atlantic on New Year's Day. Something she desperately wanted to witness, but knew all along she wouldn't.

Sage closed her eyes and went to her happy place. Long white satin aisle runners, strewn with pink and red rose petals. Proud fathers walking their daughters toward the altar, faces freshly shaven. The joyous strains of organ music cueing the congregation to stand and marvel over the bride. If she squinted, Sage could see herself in the back hall, clipboard in hand, marking off her checklist.

No more, though. No more fairy tales and flower arrangements and flowing gowns. Had she earned the right to escape inside those things? Just beneath the polish of her new life, the real Sage, a grimy-faced girl from Louisiana, never stopped reminding her of the answer. She had a responsibility to attend back home. One she'd neglected long enough. In order to make it right, she needed Belmont gone.

Panic lifted like an elevator in her sternum, lodging against the base of her throat. Would he be all right? Would *she*? Ever since that first wedding she'd planned for Peggy, Sage and Belmont had fed each other's need for contact. Severing it would be like choking off a mighty oak's water supply. There was no other way, though.

If Belmont knew where she was headed—and why— he would go berserk. There would be no calming him down to explain. There would be no talking him out of helping. And she knew Belmont better than anyone. She knew the kind of help she required would kill him.

"Belmont," Sage whispered. "Can you take the next exit, please?"

As always, he'd gone on high alert the second she spoke, hands tightening on the wheel, back straightening. So intense. So much. His energy spun like spiked boomerangs around the Suburban, all of them careful to avoid her. "You're hungry," Belmont said, slowing the vehicle.

"No." She twisted handfuls of her dress in her hands, even though Belmont's eyes were sharp to catch the movement and remain there. "No, I need you to take me to the train station."

Back in Cincinnati, right before they'd left Peggy be-hind, she'd almost confessed everything. Almost exposed all her skeletons. But the two of them maintained a bal-ance. He'd been too off-kilter after losing his third sibling in a matter of weeks, and hesitating to confess had bought Sage enough time to come to her senses. Thank God. But she couldn't shake the feeling Belmont had been watch-ing, waiting, for this moment. The man saw everything.

Sage just hoped she'd prepared better than him.

Belmont's eye twitched as he pulled off the highway. "What are you doing, Sage?"

She couldn't help but take a moment to appreciate him once more, his brutally powerful silhouette outlined in the sunny driver's side window. If this was the last time she'd see Belmont, she needed an image to bring along. A perfect vision to tuck into her memory and keep safe, where no one could touch or tarnish it. The place she was headed could muddy up almost anything, but it couldn't reach into her mind. She wouldn't allow it. She never had.

Belmont was attractive. Yes. That much was made obvious by the way women got a certain look in their eyes as he passed. He evoked a chemical reaction that started in your stomach, as if he'd tucked his coarse index finger into your belly button and twisted. His height might have made him rangy, if it weren't for all the muscle, honed from hours working on his salvage boat. His skin had an all-weather texture, bashed with salt water and sunshine, but his inner glow kept it from dulling in the slightest. Dark hair skirmished around his face and collar, no style to speak of, but thick and inviting and gorgeous in its disarray. The first time she'd set eyes on Belmont, she'd thought of far-off places. Grassy moors and mist and trench coats. Things she'd never witnessed, but read about in books. He was the only one of his kind. For some reason, he'd chosen her to crowd into corners, to worry about, to beg for eye contact. And now she had to destroy their connection to keep him alive.

"I'm going home," Sage said, forcing her fingers to stop fidgeting. "There's nothing for me in New York. I want to see my family."

"I'll come with you." His voice was calm, but she knew

if he turned his head, she'd get burned by the sparks coming from his eyes. "I'll find a place out of your way. You don't have to introduce me to them. I'll just be there if you need me."

Sage shook her head, cursing the red light where they were forced to stop and wait. The longer this took, the more impossible it would become to keep up a front. Already the foundation was cracking. What she wouldn't give to have Belmont come with her. *God*, what she wouldn't give. "I..." She barricaded herself against the rushing river of guilt. "I need some time away from you, Belmont."

The Suburban rolled forward a few inches, as if he'd lost the power to keep it braked. "I won't ask you why. I already know I've been...needing you so much lately." He said the next part to himself. "I could see it was too much."

It *wasn't* too much. It was exactly what she craved. Which was part of the issue. "It is. It's too much, the way you rely on me." She rolled her lips inward and tasted the bitterness of her memories, the self-hatred at hurting the man she'd fallen deeply in love with. "My father...he does the same thing to my mother. And vice versa. Depending on one another for support until they have no energy left to worry about themselves. Or desire to accomplish anything. There's no encouragement, only excuses for what *is*." She shook her head. "And I don't want to be like that. I'm not a stuffed animal you can pull off the shelf whenever necessary."

His face was stricken as he turned. "Sage..."

"You don't treat me like a woman," she blurted that genuine insecurity, heaping as much fuel as she could on the fire. "When men hold women, it's usually because they have romantic inclinations. But you drop me and walk away so fast, I feel like a freak sometimes."

Behind them, a car beeped and Belmont applied the gas too hard, jerking the car forward. She'd visibly shocked him, bringing up their physical relationship. Or lack thereof, rather. They must be the only two people on the planet to log hundreds of hours in each other's arms, without kissing even once. She cared about Belmont. She didn't know where his pain originated, but she respected and sympathized with it. Sometimes, she swore they shared a fractured pulse. But she was a red-blooded female and the man treated her like a fellow monk. Intentional or not, it hurt.

Stop. Stop trying to solve problems that won't exist five minutes from now. The ache in the middle of her chest intensified. "What matters is…it's wearing me out. Not knowing when you'll demand I drop everything to…be held by you. Or calm you down." She resisted the impulse to cover her face. To hide the lies. "I can't do it anymore. You're suffocating me."

By the time she'd finished speaking, Belmont's hands were shaking on the wheel. Sage turned away so he wouldn't see her misery. So she wouldn't be tempted to demand he stop driving so she could crawl into his lap and beg his forgiveness. "Once we get back to California, I'll get myself back under control. It's just all the change happening." His throat muscles shifted. "I don't do well with change."

"I'm not going back to California."

It was a good thing she'd braced herself, because Belmont slammed on the brakes, skidding the Suburban to a stop mid-avenue. Just a few blocks ahead, she could see the train station. A three-minute walk at best. She just needed to get out of this car and make sure Belmont didn't follow her. Was it even possible? "Sage," Belmont began, his impatience beginning to bleed through. She could almost see his rope fraying through the window of his eyes. "You've been scrapbooking. There's glue all over your fingers. And paper cuts. I *hate* the paper cuts. But I knew I was crowding you, so I didn't pull over and bandage them. Even though that's all I've wanted to do for the last two hundred miles."

Would she ever breathe again without experiencing the sharp pain in her side? "What does this have to do with anything?"

"Because you only scrapbook when something isn't right." He ignored the cars honking as they were forced to pass in the opposite lane. She barely registered them, too, because Belmont was hypnotic, his every feature imploring her, his voice resonating deep inside her mind. "Just come over here and whisper it in my ear. I'll stand between you and whatever it is. I'll make up for being so greedy with your time. I will. Nothing touches Sage while I'm around."

Don't break. Don't break yet. "There is nothing *wrong*. Except for your...reliance on me. I need to go somewhere I won't be smothered every minute of the day." She touched the door handle and he jolted, blue eyes fixating on that signal she'd be leaving. "Go to New York, Belmont. Meet your sisters and Aaron on the beach for New Year's Day, like your mother wanted. I'm not your worry. I never was."

"You can take yourself away from me, but you can't take away the worry." His tone was concrete, unbreakable.

"Don't try. I covet my right to fear for every hair on your head."

"I never asked you to," she half sobbed, half whispered.

"You *did*." He reached across the console, his fingers hovering just above her thigh, branding the skin beneath her dress. "Your heart asked mine. And mine was already begging."

"Stop," Sage pushed through clenched teeth. "Just stop. Can't you see how…how *confusing* and forward every word out of your mouth sounds?" Acid rose in the back of her throat as she laid the final nail in the coffin. The one that would keep him sitting in the Suburban while she fled and saved his soul. "Whatever you feel, Belmont, it's not the same for me. I've tried to help you because Peggy is my best friend, and she loves you. But you're not good for me. You're stopping me from living a normal, happy life."

The color drained right out of his face. "I'm sorry, Sage." Slowly, he removed his hand, stealing back the blessed warmth along with it. "Go. You have to go."

Now of course, she couldn't manage so much as a blink, fear over being parted from Belmont stabbing her in the back. "Okay. I'm going."

"Will you…" His voice had gone from robust to deadened. "Check in with Peggy, please. At least check in with Peggy. And bandage those cuts."

"Yes," Sage breathed, scrambling to get out of the car. She saw nothing, heard only the wind rushing in her ears as she staggered to the back door. Retrieving her luggage was the easy part. It was passing the front window again without glancing inside that presented the challenge. In the end, she couldn't manage it.

So the final time she saw Belmont, a war was taking place behind his eyes. And both sides were losing.

"You're doing the right thing." Her breath hitched, suitcase wheels catching on a sidewalk crack. "You're doing the right thing."

Sometimes the right thing was the most painful. Sometimes it gutted you and ruined you forever, so a single second wouldn't pass without a reminder.

Sage knew that lesson all too well.

CHAPTER TWO

Belmont was being torn in half. Those halves were not equal, however, or he would already have gone after Sage. One side was the staunch belief that she was hiding something. He'd picked up on the subtle changes in her somewhere between Hurley and Iowa, although anything subtle with Sage hit him like a tidal wave. So he'd been aware. Conscious that a packed punch was coming... but he'd still been unprepared.

The larger half of his torn being represented horror. That horror kept him rooted to the driver's seat, unable to move his paralyzed limbs, as he watched Sage's form grow smaller and smaller as it moved down the sidewalk. Jesus Christ. He'd crushed her. Wrapped himself around her, molded their bodies together, spoken gibberish into her hair one too many times. Or maybe the first time had been bad enough and her kindness, her relationship to Peggy, had forced her to try and ease his anxiety.

Anxiety. That was one way to describe the slab of asphalt pushing down on his windpipe, the waves of dizziness, the premonition that something bad would happen to his loved ones. To Sage. But she hadn't signed on to be his loved one, he'd simply...commandeered her in the name of survival. Her breath on his skin was the only thing that had ever made him feel normal.

That wasn't fair to anyone. He'd *known* it wasn't. But he'd gotten the sense Sage...benefited, too. Well, he'd been dead wrong. She was practically sprinting toward the train station to be free of his company, and God, he didn't blame her. Of course he didn't.

She was going home? Belmont didn't even know the location. Never once had she spoken about her parents, schooling, old friends. In this one sense, he'd given her space. If anyone knew about keeping the past at bay, it was Belmont. Now his silence had bought him the ultimate slide into agony. Not knowing where his Sage was going. Or how she would be welcomed. If she'd be safe, warm, happy, fed properly. Made to laugh. Made to cry.

Belmont's forehead rebounded off the steering wheel before he even registered his own movement. Lights danced in front of his eyes, accompanied by a symphony of car horns. But the action caused something else to shake loose. *You don't treat me like a woman.*

His sandbagged eyelids lifted just in time to catch Sage disappearing into the train station. Vanishing right out of his reach and making his fists clench helplessly. Explosions were detonating on the minefield inside his head, but he struggled through the smoke to focus on that remark from Sage. *I didn't treat her like a woman.*

If there had been anyone remaining in the Suburban, they would have been scared of the laugh that drifted from Belmont's mouth. It was a pitch-black sound, dense and fearsome. Not a big brotherly laugh or that of an honest, hardworking salvage boat captain. If Sage had any idea the obscene visions he entertained, she would have caught an earlier train. On Belmont's best day, he could only block the thoughts of Sage's naked body out so long, before they returned and ruled him. Sick. He was sick to think of a gentle, loving soul like Sage in such a manner. To imagine her clutching at the sheets beneath him, sweating, screaming... coming.

His head banged off the steering wheel a second time. Had she... *wanted* him to make an advance all this time? Had he been too mired in his own muck to notice? If she'd given him the slightest hint that she wanted to be touched by his hands in ways he'd only ever envisioned, stopping would have been impossible. She was so soft and taut. She fit against him like God had taken a mold of his body and created a woman who would correspond to every jut and angle of him. Belmont would have scoffed at the notion that God had nothing better to do than create him a woman. But if there was one truth in this world, it was that God had taken extra time on Sage Alexander. Her divinity was what kept Belmont's hands cherishing, instead of predatory. The possibility that she'd been waiting for him to provide pleasure and he'd missed the signals... it was insufferable. It was *unacceptable*.

His fingers dug into his eye sockets and moved in ruthless circles. Confusion swam through the middle of a vision of Sage beckoning him from a mess of sheets and pillows. *You're suffocating me.* Which was it? How could she want him to treat her like a woman, but also wish him away? Not just for a break, but for *forever*.

Oh Christ, he was going to be sick.

Belmont tilted back his head and breathed through his nose. *In, out, in, out.* Right now Sage was buying a train ticket to somewhere he might not find her. That was her choice. He had to let her make that decision, even if it hobbled his well-being. She deserved to be happy, and if that happiness lay as far away from him as possible? Well, he'd always suspected that would be the case one day. Hadn't he?

You don't treat me like a woman. His eyes opened, stillness settling over him, head to toe. She might want to divert their paths, but hell would freeze over before he let Sage walk away without knowing. Knowing all about the constant burn in his gut to taste her, to bring their mouths together and let reality fade as they kissed. She'd remember him. If she wanted to leave, she would walk away remembering that he'd spent every minute of their time together aching.

Belmont pushed open the driver's side door and stepped out into traffic. A motorist tapped his horn, but held up both hands, palms out, when Belmont glanced over. The two-way flow of cars crammed together on the road to accommodate the Suburban occupying a full lane, but as Belmont walked toward the train station—determination no doubt etched in every inch of his body—drivers eased their vehicles to the side to give him room, parting traffic as he strode down the double yellow line.

When he reached the train station, alarm slithered up his spine. Eight tracks. There were eight tracks in a town this small? Would he have time to check them all?

Urgency gripping him by the throat, Belmont surveyed the closest two tracks and found them empty, save a handful of passengers waiting with luggage at their feet. Spying an aboveground walkway, he made his way there and paused in the middle, scanning the tracks from above.

There. There was Sage. His knees almost gave out, fingers curling into the metal fence until his bones creaked. He only took enough time to catalog the way Sage stood, clutching her suitcase to her chest like a shield, before he was off. His legs felt like rubber as he descended the stairs, two at a time. Reaching the bottom, he was surprised to find a drizzle had started, pattering on the concrete walkway around him, making his footsteps sound padded. Distant. Warm rain on a cold morning created a sizzling combination where the heated moisture hit the cold tracks. The sudden humidity was cloying, but he gulped it down anyway, having no choice but to breathe if he wanted to make it to Sage.

He almost stopped when Sage's head whipped around, her suitcase crashing down at her feet. Dear God, she looked as if she might run from him. If she did, his heart would stop beating. *Don't. Don't. Don't.* Only a few yards away from Sage and he took in every detail about her in one sweep, just in case she'd changed since the last time he'd seen her. Beads of moisture hung in her hair, her freckles standing out in the paleness of her face. But it was her mouth Belmont focused on, out of pure necessity. If he tried to dissect her thoughts or what she'd said to him back in the Suburban, he would never make this *one thing* right. All he had left was correcting the error he'd made, before the world could continue spinning.

"You are a woman, Sage. You're the *only* woman,"

Belmont breathed in a rush as he reached Sage, hauling her off the ground with both arms and up against his body—

And then their lips touched for the first time.

Something parted in Belmont's mind, like clouds after a storm, and so much light shined through, it would have blinded him. Would have, if his eyes had the ability to remain open against the onslaught of euphoria. Need, too. There was *always* the need, but with his mouth finally pressing against Sage's, desire grew huge and demanding. Going against every rule he'd given himself, Belmont tilted his hips and let her feel it.

Her gasp was lost in the sizzle of moisture and steam, rain beginning to pelt the sidewalk now, but Belmont swallowed the sound, imprisoning it in his belly. Surrounding it with lust. With the cradle of Sage's thighs hugging him tight, so tight, Belmont slipped his tongue into her mouth, licked, and drew it out. Licked and drew it out. Every taste made his thoughts go fuzzy, his equilibrium wane. Breakfast tea and grape jelly. Just the faintest hint of both from Sage's mouth and he knew he would need those things to sustain him, every day, until he died.

Keeping one arm banded around her lower back, Belmont allowed his opposite hand to slide into Sage's hair, holding her steady and reveling in one final feel of her soft strands. But this time—oh, this time—he made a fist and tugged. Just enough. Could she sense now that he'd thought of mashing those strands against his stomach so many times, he'd lost count? Could she question *now* that he'd never seen her as anything but a woman?

"Belmont," she whispered, pulling away to suck in air.

"Sage," he answered, diving back in with a hard kiss. "Sage."

The train slid up alongside of where they stood on the platform, the electric hum so out of place, so wrong, so detested. But he ignored the dread, tilting her head at an angle and wrecking himself for all eternity. Because the texture of her mouth, the give, the take of it, had been the stuff of male dreams since time began. She was endless and generous, letting his tongue travel deep, greeting it with her own and whimpering, whimpering, when they parted.

His hands grew frantic in her hair. How could he stop his limbs from moving on their own, when all his concentration went into memorizing her taste? The perfect pressure of her seated on his pulsing flesh, moving on it restlessly. Could he really have been touching Sage, kissing her, *before* now? A groan rife with misery lanced through his chest and mingled into their kiss. No. *No.* He'd crowded her, made her feel used, like a freak. A freak like him. Maybe this was one final act of mercy on her part, saint that she was. And he was grateful for it. He would be grateful he'd ever been given the experience at all.

A tinny voice made an announcement to his left and reality punched him in the face. He stumbled back, still cradling Sage against his body, remaining upright just so she wouldn't fall. After she got on the train, it wouldn't matter. Nothing would.

Carefully—and under the pain of a thousand knives—he eased her down, so she could stand on her own two feet. His pulse still clamoring in his veins, Belmont stepped back. She stared at him in a way he couldn't interpret. Like maybe he was *even more* confusing than she'd imagined. Or because Sage was always thinking of others, she could have been wondering if he would be all right, once she got on the train. He didn't know. He couldn't think or reason around the impact of the kiss *and* losing her, all at the same time.

The last few weeks, he'd turned her life into a circus. His sisters had flown her to New Mexico when the cracks in his façade started to show, hoping her presence would help. Help? There were no words to describe how she'd calmed him, day in and day out, against the anxiety of constant change, the loss of his routine, the terrifying prospect of finally finding his real father. He'd taken advantage of how Sage made him feel…and now he needed to return the countless kindnesses she'd paid him, by making this moment easy. For her.

Belmont noticed a strand of sandy brown hair had gotten loose from Sage's ponytail, so he reached out and tucked it behind her ear. "Wherever you're going, Sage," he rasped, "every time you walk into a strange room, remember that you might be the smallest person in it, but you're the strongest and most beautiful. Right down to the deepest parts of your heart." Sage still hadn't moved a muscle, so he picked up her fallen suitcase and set it inside the door of the train. "But if you ever get scared or lost or lonely, know that I'm one phone call away. Whether it's tomorrow or fifty years from where we're standing, I'll come. I'll come before you know it."

A window slid open on the train. "Closing the doors, folks," a man's voice called.

"I wasn't expecting this," Sage whispered. "I wasn't prepared for this."

Belmont was already being swallowed in the whirlpool of denial and solitude, so he couldn't even begin to try and figure out what Sage hadn't been prepared for. The kiss, probably. He hadn't been prepared, either, but it had been the single greatest moment of his life.

Another warning call from the train's operator spurred Belmont into action. He couldn't make her miss her train on top of everything else, much as he wanted to. Much as he wanted to punch a hole in the side of it and render it inoperable. He grasped Sage's waist, took two steps, and set her gently inside the train, trying with all his might not to worry about the sudden fear shining in her eyes, the color streaking her cheeks.

"Good-bye, my heartbeat."

The doors closed.

CHAPTER THREE

The train moved and Sage stumbled, falling against the plastic partition, just inside the door. Her hip smarted, funny bone tingling, but she barely registered any of it. No. No, that hadn't just happened. She was still asleep in the passenger side seat of the Suburban, her feet propped up on the dusty dashboard. Right? Right?

She winced at the screeching in her head, pinching two fingers around the bridge of her nose to deaden the pressure. The pain proved one thing. This moment was real. Her lips were still wet from Belmont's kiss and he was walking away, his tall, dark form moving down the platform, steam rising off the concrete to swirl around his ankles. She refused to blink because something told her he would vanish into that mist if she did.

"Belmont," she croaked, rapping the heels of her hands against the window, slapping her palms there until the glass rattled. "Wait. *Waitwaitwait.*"

Please. Why wouldn't he turn around? He always knew when something was wrong with her. When she was sick, hungry, tired. She never even had to say a word. He wouldn't just keep walking when she was drowning on the inside. *Belmont.*

Mistake. She'd made a mistake. They weren't supposed to be apart. The train was picking up speed and already she could feel her fabric ripping at the seams. Her right hand flew to her throat, clutching at the skin, scratching it, and begging entrance for oxygen. She was losing sight of him now. He'd reached the end of the platform and was turning the corner, scaling the stairs for the aboveground walkway. If he simply turned his head, he would be able to see her beating the glass, but he didn't. *He didn't even look.*

She'd built up just enough of a reserve of courage to break away from the one person that helped drown the guilt she'd been living with. He saw her as sweet, faultless Sage and the temptation to pretend that was true, pretend the past wasn't real, was so inviting. Even though it was an illusion. Her habit's name was Belmont and it never stopped buzzing inside her like a colony of bees. That kiss had just kicked the hive.

"No," Sage heaved, turning and running for the back of the train. "No, stop the train." She whirled in a circle mid-aisle, faces and colors and cell phone screens blending together. "Can they stop it? Please, I need to get off. I have to *go* to him."

Silence. They were all looking at her like she was insane. She must be insane, right? A man more incredible and powerful than the sun had just kissed her as if his very existence depended on it...and she'd let herself get swept away by this cursed metal machine. She'd been so desperate for proof that she wasn't merely a crutch for Belmont, that he saw her as a desirable woman, but in a way, she'd also been dreading it. Fearing that confirmation. Because it would draw her back, make it excruciating to leave him. And it *was*. Time was passing. Precious seconds. Minutes? How long had she been standing in the aisle, remembering Belmont's hands, his mouth, the words he'd said in parting?

My heartbeat. He'd never called her that before. Had he always wanted to?

Turning on a heel, she sprinted farther into the back of the train, finally reaching the back window, pressing every inch of her body against it, eyes searching frantically for Belmont back at the train station. But it was too far away now. A dot. And even if she could find the train operator and convince him to go back, Belmont would be gone by the time she got there. In his Suburban and back on the road, all alone.

Sage's knees hit the cold train floor. With the shock of pain came a reminder of where she was going. Why she'd been forced to leave Belmont in the first place. This morning, she'd only had one option, but now...now she wondered if she'd made a grave mistake in underestimating Belmont's ability to cope with the situation she would face down in Louisiana. She'd given him her insecurities about not being treated like a woman and he'd barreled right through them, hadn't he? That man who'd stormed toward her on the platform and blown her every perception of love, life, and need out of the water? That man could take on anything.

She closed her eyes and thought of Belmont walking

into the sealed-off, airless darkness. A nightmare that had recurred so many times, she'd refused to let it happen in real life. No. She'd made the only decision her love allowed. She had.

Sending one final look down the endless tracks, Sage stood on lifeless legs, retrieved her suitcase, and took her seat.

* * *

Belmont stared through bloodshot eyes at the man behind the counter. The motel clerk was wearing a Santa hat and smoking a cigarette. If Belmont grabbed the lit object and applied the red, glowing end to his arm, it would allow him to feel pain somewhere other than the decaying center of his chest, but it wouldn't solve anything. It had been a long time since he'd engaged in that kind of destructive behavior. Drugs, fistfights. Long before he'd discovered the serenity of water, he'd turned to those things to distract him from the memories of being trapped inside the ground. Everything that had come with it. Betrayal. Cold that had never fully fled his bones.

The water had given him purpose. A way to resume his role as the oldest brother and make his siblings confident in him again. Working with his hands on top of a rhythm that never ended kept him centered. When he met Sage, though, "centered" took on a new meaning. One boat and a handful of salvage contracts to meet his most basic needs was no longer sufficient. No, he'd felt a new drive to earn. To make expansion plans and hire more crew members. He'd been in the middle of purchasing another vessel when the road trip put everything on pause.

But since the day they met, his motivation had been a dream that one day he could provide for Sage.

Resuming those plans *without* her? His mind couldn't make sense of it.

Gritting his teeth against the agony of not knowing her whereabouts, Belmont silently begged for the man to hurry up and find an available room. Somewhere he could stash himself while he figured out how to move forward. There was no thinking beyond that. He just needed a place where he could exist awhile.

Blinking red and green lights snagged his attention. They were wrapped around the man's computer screen. Christmas. It was almost Christmas. How would Sage spend the holiday with her family? Decorating a tree, drinking egg nog. Normal things. Good things.

Discomfort seared his throat as the clerk handed over a room key. "You're in one-oh-nine, buddy. Ice is two doors past that. Pool's closed."

He started to turn away, but the prospect of a bleak, empty room made him pause. "And if I wanted to party?"

Silence stretched. "You a cop?"

"Cops don't give a shit about places like this."

"True enough."

A drawer slid open and Belmont turned back toward the front desk, watching as the man drew out a variety of baggies, laying them on the computer keyboard. "What's your poison, big man?"

All of them. That's what he wanted to say. He wanted to hand over every green bill inside his wallet and fill his pockets with methods of dropping out, numbing himself. It would have been so easy. Too easy. Nothing would be able to reach him. That's what stopped the idea in its tracks. Hadn't he told Sage that if she needed him, he would be there before she knew it? He wouldn't be able to keep his promise if he were high or passed out. And the world would have to end before he broke his word to that woman.

"Well?" The clerk picked up a bag of pills and shook it. "What'll it be?"

Belmont was already halfway out the door before the man finished posing the question. He moved without feeling anything, a swirl of leaves slithering around his boots. The air was frigid, but he only knew that because ice patches dotted his path as he walked toward his assigned room. The pool caught his attention just up ahead. No lock. Just a sign that said, *No Swimming*. Unnecessary, he decided absently. What would anyone want with a pool in the middle of December anyway? Unless they wanted to freeze themselves to death.

His booted feet carried him closer. He stripped off his shirt and shouldered open the flimsy gate, tossing the garment onto what looked like a covered barbeque pit. With methodical movements, he lost his boots and jeans, making sure the cell phone was secure inside the pocket.

Then he dropped in and let the blistering cold suck the air out of his lungs.

Opening his mouth, he released a strangled shout unsuitable for the surface, bubbles rioting around his face and obscuring his vision. It seemed to go on forever, the cold snapping at his Adam's apple, the sound growing less and less natural. By the time he'd finished, his muscles almost ached too much from the strain to swim upward, but he managed it through sheer force of will, remembering his cell phone was above. In the real world. Not down in the depths that threatened to pull him farther and farther into their murk.

When he breached the surface and heard his cell phone ringing, Belmont almost swallowed half the pool trying to drag in lungfuls of air and swim for the edge at the same time. Rigor mortis setting in on a corpse. That's how his body felt as he propelled himself up and over the concrete lip of the pool, dragging himself on elbows toward the barbeque pit. He shook, head to toe, the cold burning like a flame, sending pain screaming through his system.

Commanding his fingers to function, it took an iron will to dig through his pocket and extricate the cell phone, answering it without looking at the screen. "Hello?" he shouted through chattering teeth into the receiver. "Sage?"

When a handful of quiet seconds passed, Belmont was horrified he might have missed the call, but a familiar voice filled his ear. A welcome one, but not the one he craved with his very soul. "Bel?" Aaron. His brother. "What's wrong?"

He fell forward onto the icy concrete, laying his cheek against it. "She's gone."

"Sage?" More silence. "Christ. Where did she go?"

"I don't know." He recalled the way he'd stormed the ticket counter after her train departed, grabbing the man by his collar and demanding information. "The train she took was headed south, but it was stopping at a hub in Charleston. From there, she could have gone anywhere. She's gone."

Aaron's voice grew louder, more forceful. "Bel, where are *you*?"

He wanted to answer. Wanted, as always, for the only family he knew to be near. Even if they weren't communicating, they were a comfort. His people. But he couldn't allow them to see him like this. It was too reminiscent of the first time. Their shocked horror as he was dragged out of the well, soaked in piss and unable to explain how he'd gotten down there.

Never. He would never tell them.

"I don't know." His words were distorted because he could barely move his lips. "My heart, Aaron. I don't think I can keep it beating without her."

A sound left his brother. It was fear. He didn't like hearing it and had no way to fix it. Not when he was letting the cold take him. "*Belmont*," Aaron shouted. "You listen to me, asshole. You listen. Get the fuck up from whatever ditch you fell into and *go find Sage*." Labored breaths. "I know how you're feeling right now. Like you have no direction or purpose. But you do. She's your purpose. Whatever happened, there's nothing that can shake that. We all know it. It seems like we've all known it forever."

"I smothered her. She told me."

"She was *lying*." In his mind's eye, he could see Aaron yanking at his tie, turning in circles. "I know you've never told a lie, so it's hard to understand, but take it from a reformed master. It's easy when you have a good reason. Or what you *think* is a good reason."

"Sage wouldn't lie. She's so good." Was he starting to fall asleep? The sky was darkening. How long had they been on the phone? "I have no way to find—"

It hit him like a bolt of electricity. Her scrapbook. She'd left her scrapbook in the foot well of the passenger seat. He could see it. The clean silver edges of it, the burgundy lettering. Classy, just like her. Maybe…maybe she'd meant to leave it for him? It was too much to hope for, but in a world where her light had been stolen away, he would grab on to any sliver of illumination he could find. Purpose. Sage. Without them, he might as well lie there forever. So he would take hold of this chance. Hold on for dear life.

"Bel?" Aaron shouted. "Tell me where you are. Me and Grace will come meet you."

Belmont slapped his free hand down on the concrete and pushed to his knees, shaking so violently, his head ached from his teeth grinding together. "I'm glad you called, Aaron. I'm always glad. I love you. I'll be fine."

Before his brother could answer, Belmont hung up the phone and stumbled for the parking lot, wearing nothing but underwear and socks. Absently he registered the motel clerk emerging from the front office and gaping at him, along with two rooms full of guests.

"Damn, bro. What did you sell him?" one of them said. "I'll take some of that."

Belmont ignored them all, prying open the Suburban's passenger door. Whatever breath remained in his body whooshed out at the proof that Sage had once sat there, beside him. Back straight, hands folded in her lap, legs crossed. God, he missed her so bad. Everything felt wrong and incomplete. How was the world still turning?

Clutching the scrapbook to his chest, Belmont passed the crowd of onlookers, let himself into his motel room, and cranked up the heat. Holding Sage's handiwork close, he collapsed on the bed, vowing to scour it cover to cover, as soon as he woke up.

CHAPTER FOUR

Sage set down her suitcase and stared across the unkempt lawn, the house from her nightmares looming at the end of the dirt path. She'd run fast and far, vowing never to set foot inside it again. Funny how she'd believed her own lies. One phone call from her mother. That was all it took for her to cave. Maybe deep down, she'd always known the new life was temporary. A fraud. That a daughter who'd taken the easy way out and left the people who depended on her didn't get a fresh start.

Oh, she'd needed time to build up the courage to return to Sibley. That's why she'd seized the chance to ride seventeen hundred miles with the Clarksons, Belmont's grounding presence at the wheel. She'd watched them take leaps of faith and push one another to their limits. Armed with those memories, now it was her turn to face her family obligation. No matter how awful that connection had treated her in the past, it refused to be ignored.

What would she find inside the house after five years? She hadn't been around to scrub the floors, beat the rugs, or kill the mice since leaving for California when she was twenty. No one would have done it in her stead, so she feared for the sight that would greet her on the other side of the door.

Her arm ached from carrying her luggage from the bus station—she'd had no choice but to walk. Her parents didn't own a car, and a cab would have cost money. She needed every penny right now. Shaking out the fatigued limb, Sage plucked up the case and put a measure of steel into her spine. Careful not to step on any of the broken glass along the path, she sailed toward the house, trying desperately not to think of Belmont. Impossible, though. It would never be a feat she could accomplish, so she might as well let the inevitable happen.

If he were walking on the path beside her, he would sense her nerves. He'd give her just a brush of his shoulder or a low hum in his throat. And she'd know there was an invisible shield around her that he wouldn't allow anything to penetrate. She'd told him he'd leaned on her too much, but it went both ways. That fact was never more obvious than right now.

I fought my own battles before and I'll do it again.

The steps creaked as Sage climbed them, the porch groaning as she moved across it. She held her fist aloft a moment, before rapping loudly on the door. "Mom?"

When the door opened, Sage held back a sound of alarm. Her mother had aged. More than five years warranted. Most of her light brown hair, once the same shade as Sage's, had turned a delicate gray. It threaded through the mousy color in an almost graceful way. Graceful. That was how people in Sibley used to describe her mother. Or so Sage had been told.

Bernadette Alexander had been a ballet dancer once upon a time, but wifehood and motherhood hadn't allowed her big-city dreams to flourish. In the earliest stages of Sage's life, Bernie had been satisfied with the path her life had taken. But being a miner's wife wasn't easy. Her husband's long hours meant solitude. Time to think about what she'd passed up. And even more hours to lament her decisions over too many glasses of Crown Royal whiskey. When Bernie was sober, however, she was an angel. A doting wife. The most hospitable of Southern hostesses, if you overlooked the mess.

Sage was relieved to see she'd caught her mother on one such afternoon.

"My girl." Bernie's hands flew to her mouth where she pressed them tight enough to turn her knuckles white. "I knew you would come. Thank God. Thank the good Lord you're home." She threw a glance over her shoulder. "Your father is sleeping just now and I'm grateful for it. We're long overdue a girl chat, just you and I, aren't we?"

"Yes, Mama," Sage murmured, her Louisiana accent flowing back like she hadn't spent years learning to hide it. Not because she was ashamed. But because she needed the past completely tucked away, where she wouldn't have to think of it every time she opened her mouth. "We're long overdue."

A pleased smile spreading across her lined face, Bernie ushered Sage inside. "Don't mind the clutter. I haven't had a chance to tidy up yet today."

Sage held her breath out of conditioning, but the smell of cat urine caught her too fast to avoid it completely.

Every few feet there were newspapers along the floor, covered in wet spots, probably weeks old. Maybe longer. Dirt caked everything. Paint peeled off the walls. It looked as if her mother had attempted to hang wallpaper at some point but stalled halfway through, leaving long strips hanging like a sad palmetto tree in the hall.

They entered the kitchen and it only got worse. Dishes stacked to overflowing in the sink, cats on the counter licking at the dirty plates. And all the while, her mother smiled as if nothing was wrong. As if they'd just walked into the pristine parlor of one of the big estates on the other side of town.

Thank God she had a place to sleep outside the house. The cottage might require some clearing out and shining up, but she couldn't abide a single night within her parents' walls.

Knowing how perceptive her mother could be, despite her seeming lack of awareness, Sage kept her features schooled and set down her suitcase near the archway. She watched as Bernie planted her hands on either side of the sink and dropped her head forward. And just stayed that way, exhaustion evident in the slope of her shoulders.

"Mama?" Sage winced at the way her voice suddenly sounded so young. "How is Daddy doing?"

"Terrible." Bernie turned and slumped against the sink, moisture coating her cheeks. As far back as Sage could remember, her mother's moods had changed with the wind, but it never failed to set off a rhythmic pounding behind her breastbone. "I told you over the phone, daughter, that man is being run into the ground. Your daddy can hardly walk up the steps by the day's end, all hunched over like he is." She sucked in a long breath through her nose. "He won't see retirement at this rate. And it's only *two months* away. I live in fear of him keeling over or killing himself with that machinery."

Guilt packed a powerful punch. Nothing in this life came without a cost and here was the proof. Sage hadn't escaped this place free and clear. Oh, no. Her father had been paying for the agreement she'd made the whole time. "I won't let that happen."

There. Now that the words had been said, Sage had to make them true. Make things right. A scream built up in her throat, but she swallowed it down and focused. She centered her attention on a spot above her mother's head and thought of Belmont. The smell of his neck. Ocean and salt and eternity. She'd stolen one of his shirts yesterday before they'd set out on the road. As soon as she was alone, she intended to wrap herself in it. How long would the smell last? A couple weeks if she was lucky.

The spot above her mother's head wavered, but she blinked and it came back into focus. She'd been raised in this squalor. No, she hadn't been raised—she'd reared *herself*, instinctively knowing from a young age that her parents weren't capable. That they were dissolvable people who turned to the bottle at the first sign of strife. She'd tried to live so small they wouldn't notice her or use her as an excuse to drink more, but they'd drowned themselves anyway. Drowned and drowned and drowned again.

So as soon as she was old enough, she'd struck a deal with the devil to get out.

For a short time, she'd enjoyed the illusion of being free, cultivating a career that she loved. Wedding planning. Who knew she'd have such a knack? It had even led Sage to a friendship with Peggy, her best friend whose spunk she already missed. Yes, she'd had it good for a short time. Better than good.

Perfect. *Too* perfect.

The devil never really left a person in peace, once hands had been shaken, though. In her heart of hearts, she'd known the fallout would eventually rain down. She'd been waiting for the call home to face the desperate decision she'd made, so she'd spent the last five years playacting. Pretending to be someone other than *that poor Alexander girl*. But that's who she was. Not some fashionable wedding planner with a perpetually sunny disposition. No, sometimes Sage was selfish, too. And now she would pay for the last five years of freedom with her future.

Sibley was where she was needed. She wouldn't abandon her parents again. Even if she survived what was to come, they would never stop needing her. And she couldn't leave it to chance that the devil wouldn't find another way to hurt them.

"I'll go to see him," Sage whispered.

"Today?" her mother asked too fast, so fast, clasping her hands beneath her chin. "Today, Sage?"

She nodded. "Okay, Mama."

* * *

The town of Sibley was divided into two halves. Rich and poor.

Augustine "Augie" Scott lived smack in the middle.

Once, while picking up cigarettes for her father at the tobacconist, Sage had overheard two stock boys debating Augie's reasons for building his massive, four-story house smack on the dividing line. *It's so he can keep an eye on both sides. See which one is coming for him next.* Sage had logged those words away, not really grasping their meaning at the time. But as she'd got older, they'd begun making sense.

Augie was the private owner of a large salt mine. One of the biggest in the state. If he didn't employ a person's father, he found a way to own them some other way. Sage's daddy was a miner, and he'd been one a few years before Augie opened the doors on the company. The rumors regarding how exactly Augie had pooled enough resources to start Scott Explorations had led to seemingly endless speculation, until one of the most vocal critics had ended up slumped over the wheel of his pickup truck, a bullet hole clean through his head. No one had talked about Augie's rise to the top much after that. They'd simply accepted.

If Sage had learned one thing while navigating Sibley life as a teenager and young woman, it was that life was full of necessary evils. When she was fourteen, she'd let the school bus driver look beneath her skirt once a week so he would change his route, meeting her at the end of her street, so the students wouldn't laugh as they drove past her house. More often than not, her father would be passed out on the lawn, her mother weeping and wringing her hands on the porch. She'd wanted to slug that bus driver right between the eyes, but she'd decided the laughter was worse than the man leering at her worn panties.

Necessary evil. And Augie was the worst one.

Her parents had a past with Augie. One that Sage had latched on to, like a rope from a rescue ship. Seeing the loophole and, in turn, her ticket out of Sibley so clearly,

Sage hadn't taken the time to wonder what grabbing that shiny ring meant about her character. How using that lifeline had made her an opportunist. A deserter of her own family.

As she stood in the very same spot she'd stood five years earlier, evening darkening the sky, those weaknesses in herself were *all* she thought about. She was on the sidewalk outside Augie's estate, staring up at the giant, sweeping American flag he flew from the roof. A few yards away lay a wrought iron gate and a Call button. Already, she could feel electronic eyes on her. Someone watching from inside, maybe even laughing. He'd very likely known the moment she'd got to town, because the man didn't like surprises.

Allowing herself some time to stall before meeting Augie, she'd cleared out the tiny, abandoned cottage on her parents' property. The small structure had served as staff quarters, once upon a time, when moneyed people had owned the house. She'd stumbled on it at age nine, and over the years, it had gone from playhouse to...home. Sage had stacked crates and dragged her thin, ratty mattress across the backyard and started sleeping there. Away from the stench of liquor and the screaming fights. Her cottage still needed some cobwebs cleared away, but she would get to that later.

Right after she met with the devil and struck a *second* deal.

Pasting a serene expression onto her face—the one she usually reserved for nervous brides or prickly mothers-in-law—Sage marched to the buzzer and pressed it. She refused to show alarm when the gate clicked open immediately, instead holding her chin up as she closed it

behind her and glided toward the front door. It opened before she even reached it, Augie leaning against the frame,
a coffee mug in his hand.

"Would you look at that?" His eyes were hard, but
somehow they still twinkled with amusement. "Sage
Alexander. West Coast life has done you good."

"Thank you." She stopped at the foot of the steps, guilt
licking her insides. "Me being away hasn't done my father
good, though."

No reaction. "Why don't you come inside and we'll
talk about it."

"I'd rather stay out here…"

He was already gone, his unhurried footsteps echoing
inside the foyer, growing fainter as she stood there trying
to calm the disquiet in her blood. *I could do it again. I
could walk right out of this yard, get back on the bus,
and forget everything in this town.* She knew what would
happen, though. Knew her parents would suffer for those
actions again, and Sage wouldn't shirk her responsibilities
this time. As a daughter. As a good person.

Reminding herself that Belmont's shirt was waiting for
her back in the cottage, Sage nodded and followed Augie
inside, leaving the door open on purpose. She'd only been
in the house once before, but nothing had changed, as
far as she could tell. Only the barest muted light came in
through the windows. Gleaming dark wood, antiques, stat-
ues, paintings, furniture that looked totally uncomfortable.
Expensive without a hint of practicality. But it was clean.
So clean. She remembered envying that about the house
during her first visit.

Augie's office was located in the back and he'd left
the door ajar, a greenish light glowing from the Tiffany

lamp she knew sat on the right corner of his desk. Sage walked inside and took a seat in a leather wingback, shaking her head when Augie held up a bottle of bourbon. It was clear he got a kick out of asking if she wanted alcohol and that smugness gave Sage the desire to throw him off-kilter. She might never shake the identity of that poor Alexander girl, but she'd developed a backbone while living in California. While driving with the Clarksons. "My mother called me crying, begging me to come home."

The bourbon bottle froze on its descent to the mini bar, before being plonked down hard. "Your mother made her bed. If she finds it lumpy now, that's none of my concern."

"You've made it your concern. You always have." Sage heard the note of distress in her voice and reined it in, knowing Augie would pounce on any sign of weakness. "It's a little clichéd, don't you think?"

He lifted the tumbler of liquor to his lips with a flourish. "Do explain."

"Making a man suffer thirty years later, just because the girl chose him." She didn't take any satisfaction from his flinch. There was none to be had in the room. "Time should have made you more accepting. But you've ground him down under your thumb instead. Are you really willing to kill him? Working him to death when it would be so easy just to let him be?"

Augie licked his lips of excess bourbon and smacked them together. "The short answer is yes. And that's all I'm required to give." He dropped into his chair. "But you didn't come all the way back to Sibley to criticize me, did you, little Sage Alexander?"

She cursed the flush of indignation rising in her cheeks.

Augie hated her. It was there in his hard gaze now, just as it always had been. She was the representation of her parents' marriage. The proof that they'd chosen to start a life together and leave him—the third member of their young trio—in the dust. Sage had allowed Augie to use her as a pawn, taking his money and going to California. A move that had hurt her parents in more ways than one. They'd lost a daughter *and* a caretaker. Her father had suffered the indignation of another man funding his daughter's freedom and he'd hit the bottle twice as hard.

Taking advantage of a necessary evil had left her fragile parents vulnerable. This slow, brazen murder of her father would be on her head, unless she could stop it.

"I came here to take his place," Sage said, clear as a bell.

Augie lost a fair amount of his smug smile. "You've come to take your father's place in the mines." Not a question. She thought he might go on staring at her forever, but a rumble began in his chest, turning into a full-fledged laugh. "You won't last a *day*."

"I guess we'll find out." Until that moment, she hadn't allowed fear to enter the equation. Leaving Belmont had been enough to contend with. But now, with her fate resting in the devil's hands, a cold shiver snaked up her spine. "He has two months until retirement. If...*when*...I make it to that day, you sign the paperwork for his pension and leave my family be."

"So they can drink themselves to death?" Augie spat, surging to his feet.

"If that's their choice."

His disgust was palpable, like she'd splashed him with holy water. The inner joke made her think of Peggy.

Peggy would have said something like that. *Don't lose your cool now.*

"Do we have a deal or not?" Sage asked.

Augie's superior air returned in a blink. "You know, your father has one of the hardest jobs, little Sage."

Her stomach lining turned to lead. "He has the hardest job because you gave it to him after I left. You put him in a younger man's position, when he should be doing the light lifting until retirement rolls around. Like the rest of the men his age."

He didn't bother denying it. "You're prepared to operate a drilling rig?" He lifted a gray eyebrow. "Underground."

"As long as I get the proper training." She stood and extended her hand. "Yes."

When they shook hands, Augie squeezed tight enough for Sage to feel her bones grind together, but she refused to flinch. She knew what it meant. He wasn't going to take it any easier on her because she was a woman.

The hint of excitement in his eyes said he might even go harder.

A vision of Belmont caught her unaware. He walked into the mine's darkness, looking back at her over his broad shoulder. Reassuringly, like always. But in the dreaded, moving image that had recurred over the last couple weeks, he emerged more withdrawn and haunted than ever, having faced his greatest fear: dark, enclosed spaces. Or worse, he never came back out at all.

Sage had never felt more alone than in that moment, but she'd never felt more justified in facing the upcoming test by herself.

"I'll report for work in the morning."

She turned and left the office on shaky legs.

CHAPTER FIVE

Belmont woke up in a cold sweat.

He was immediately inundated by the roar of Sage's train pulling away, so it took him a moment to remember where he'd fallen asleep. It wasn't the first time in his life that had happened. The end of high school had brought inescapable change. There was nothing he loathed more than having his routine taken away, which was why the road trip had been so hard at the outset. Before Sage.

An ache spearing into his throat, Belmont sat up, swiping the perspiration from his upper lip. He'd seen the inside of many strange motel rooms while trying to adjust at eighteen. *What now? Where do I belong? Where have I ever belonged?* Questions that had been easy to drown out by hiding behind a screen of chemicals. The people who partook of the same medication hadn't seemed to belong anywhere, either. They were spooks that only came out at night, prowling along the street with one purpose. Forgetting. Stopping the flight of doubt from taxiing down the runways of their brains.

Yes, a lot of mornings had started with piecing together the night before in those days. Until one morning, when he'd woken to the world pitching and rocking beneath him. Not in a bad way. It had been the ocean waves beneath the boat where he'd passed out. Something about the constant rhythm had appealed to him. It was the never-ending routine he was lacking. Sure, the tide might change, but it always resumed, and the waves *never* stopped. There was nothing more constant than the moon, and it compelled the water to dance at certain times of the day. That surety made him feel less adrift.

Forgoing college—a move that surprised no one—Belmont had gotten a job on a local fishing charter in San Diego, but was quickly lured away by marine salvage. Retrieving long-forgotten valuables from the ocean floor had given him a sense of purpose. Finding things that were lost, the way he'd been lost in the ground.

That boat waited for him now, moored to a harbor dock in San Diego, which he'd paid for through the beginning of January. His crew was taking on side jobs until he returned. They depended on *him*, though. He'd been on the verge of turning Clarkson Salvage into a universally respected name, but...that life seemed so far removed from the present. From now. When he stood on the deck, it was Sage he thought about. It was Sage's happiness he wanted to provide.

Sage.

Belmont shook off the blackness that winked in front of his eyes and dove on Sage's scrapbook, finally remembering why he'd woken with a sense of urgency. A hum was building in the back of his mind, getting louder and louder, compelling him to open the book. So he did.

And his heart tried to rip straight out of his chest. Everything Sage touched turned to magic, didn't it? Such detail. Her fingers had been *right there*, smoothing lace swatches and gluing sleek feathers. Even the way she cut pictures out of magazines was unique, with little zigzag patterns in the corners or fringe trimmed into the bottom. Every page had a different theme, all designed around a church, although the church wasn't pictured, merely written in her artistic hand. He could imagine her searching church interiors on the Internet and planning a wedding to bring them to life. Some of the locations were in Cincinnati, Iowa, and New Mexico, places they'd stopped during the road trip.

Belmont forced himself to continue turning the pages, even though he simply wanted to bury his face in the scrapbook and hunt for her scent. Anything to feel closer to her. But he kept going, some intuition spurring him on.

When he came to the final page, he knew why. Knew why her leaving behind the scrapbook had seemed odd, when she'd clearly planned every detail of her escape from him down to the T. The way she'd found the perfect train station, ten miles from a major hub, so he couldn't track her. The way she'd waited until the last minute to drop the ax. It was entirely possible he was grasping at straws, but maybe leaving the scrapbook in the Suburban was her signal to him that she was in trouble. His fingers traced the small string of pearls she'd used to outline the magazine cutout of a wedding dress. Such attention was paid to every aspect of the page, reiterating how out of Sage's character it was to be forgetful.

That was enough for Belmont to keep going, to keep scrutinizing.

Belmont started to go back to the beginning for a closer look, but the final page felt thicker than the others. It was stuck to another one. A prickle went up his neck as he carefully pried the pages apart, very conscious that his blunt, work-worn fingers could wreck the delicate handiwork. He finally got them separated and released a pent-up breath...but he quickly sucked the oxygen back in when the page was laid flat.

There was no mistaking the difference between this design and the others. It was...dark. Everything on the page was black and brown. Harsh. Even the handwriting where she'd written the name of the church was blunt and uneven, as if she'd written it in the pitch black. Had she? Had his Sage worked on this part of her book while they were sleeping?

A torn-up sound left Belmont, his fingertip shaking as he outlined the crude brown strip of muslin, a dead, pressed flower, the scrapes of a coal pencil that depicted the steeple of a church. First Baptist Church of Sibley. *Sibley.* Where was that? He thought of that hint of the South that occasionally slipped into Sage's speech and gained his feet, going out to the Suburban long enough to retrieve his luggage, along with the laptop.

Damn, he'd spent so much time resenting the electronic device with its never-ending need for updates and charging, but he was grateful as hell to have it now. He'd watched Sage and Peggy and Aaron's fingers fly around the keyboard often enough that he could use it effectively and he thanked God for that, too.

As soon as he got the laptop booted, he opened a search engine and typed in the name of the church. When the search returned not only a Louisiana address, but a picture of First Baptist, relief hit him like a two by four. It was an exact outline of the one Sage had drawn in the scrapbook.

Belmont didn't bother checking out. He showered, dressed, and went to find Sage.

* * *

Oh boy. It would really stink to die on Christmas Day.

Not that there were any presents to open or cards to receive anyway. No popcorn to string or hot chocolate to stir over the stove. What was she really missing? If she were back in California, she would most likely be sleeping late, snuggling into her pillow. She never actually *slept* when sleeping late. The pleasure was derived from knowing she *could*. That she would wake up to a clean apartment and be able to pick that day's attire from her dress collection. Not a huge collection, just about twelve. Her favorite had always been the light beige one with the pattern of bluebirds.

The memory of the soft material billowing around her in the San Diego breeze made the stiff, heavy coveralls she wore even more unbearable. There was no California sunshine down in the mine, only black, stagnant air and the cloying scent of gasoline and dust. She could feel it settling on her skin and caking, could feel the granules of dirt slipping beneath her safety mask and making themselves at home while they scraped her flesh raw.

Beneath her, the huge machine juddered and coughed,

the buzz so loud, she wore earplugs to protect her hearing. Instead she listened to her back teeth jar against one another, heard the sweat beads forming in her hair, the coughs build in her throat. She was being forced to live inside her head when she wanted the exact opposite.

She'd trained yesterday from morning until nightfall and signed liability forms that were almost enough to make her throw up, but she'd done it all with the knowledge she'd have Christmas off. At the very least, she would have a small reprieve. A chance to wrap her mind around the risks she'd acknowledged and would be taking for two months.

But there had been no break. Augie hadn't met his production quota during the week, which meant everyone had been brought in for a full nine to five, including Sage. Now she stared into the darkness, the shaking machine illuminated only by the light attached to her helmet and the rapidly dimming industrial one hanging from the overhead crossbar. Her arms burned. The muscles ached so badly, she wondered how she managed to operate the controls, to keep the giant, churning piece of metal steady as it broke through the earth.

During her childhood, her father had been less frail, but never robust. She couldn't even imagine him attempting this job with his current health. And no wonder he was ailing. If the physical effort didn't burn someone out, the atmosphere alone would do it. The longer she stayed down there, the harder it was to fill her lungs with anything but sulfur-tinged air.

When the rumbling started above Sage's head, her hands almost slipped off the controls, but she managed to turn them off, close her eyes, and listen. A crash sent her heart slamming up against her rib cage. *Oh God. What was that?* And wasn't it ridiculous that the relief on her muscles took precedent over her fear of the mine caving in? She attacked them with her thumbs, massaging in circles, and waited for the radio at her hip to crackle with life. The foreman checked on her once an hour to get a progress report, and while she'd lost track of time, she was about due—

"Alexander."

She pressed the Talk button with a wince. "Yes," she answered. "What was that noise?"

A dead line of static. "Had a small cave-in up here. We're working on getting it clear." Voices in the background. Urgent but not panicked. "Might take a couple hours, so hang tight."

Hours.

Her hysterical laughter bounced off the interior of the cave, which only served to highlight how eerily still and quiet it was. How damp and biting the air became once the machine was at rest. God, it was so *dark* outside the immediate light. She wouldn't cry. She would *not* cry. She'd walked into this mission without blinders on, knowing it was dangerous. The alternative was her father hurting himself or worse, and she couldn't allow that to happen. No, this two months of hell, followed by a lifetime of caring for her parents, was the price she paid for escaping to California. Allowing Augie to sink his claws in while she slept late in the sunshine. A part of her even believed those five glorious years had been worth it. But that belief was already starting to waver in the stark, black silence of the cave.

She unzipped her coveralls and dug into the neckline

for Belmont's shirt, which she'd worn like a cloak of armor, the Clarkson Salvage logo directly over her heart. Pressing the fragrant material to her nose, she curled up on the seat of the great metal beast and dreamed of strong arms and ocean waves lapping the shore.

* * *

Once Belmont had reached Sibley, it had been easy enough to track down Sage's house. But he hadn't liked the reaction he'd gotten when he'd asked for the Alexander residence. Hadn't liked it one bit. He'd stopped a woman as she came out of the grocery store, a cake propped on her hip. At first, she'd given him that look he'd always found confusing from women. As if he'd done something to please them before he'd even opened his mouth. There was...expectation there. Moreover, he didn't like the feeling that gratified expression gave him. As if he were being unfaithful to Sage simply by being in the midst of it.

When Sage looked at him in the same way, though? He *loved* it. The first time they met at Peggy's rehearsal dinner, she'd helped him cinch his tie. For just a brief second, she'd laid her hands on his lapels and his heart had gone wild, rebounding off his ribs and spine, lighting up parts of his brain that had always been dim. And when she'd stepped back and smiled the most beautiful, honest smile Belmont had ever seen...he'd simply had no choice but to live for her. To protect her with his every single breath. His heart had made the decision, his mind and body had approved, and her happiness had become a necessity. There was nothing simple about what Sage made him feel. But the importance of her took no effort to describe. And it never wavered. She was *the most* important.

So when the woman outside the grocery store appeared to find something distasteful about Sage's very name, he'd gotten tense. He'd remained that way on the drive over, and now, as he pulled up outside the poor excuse for a home, his eye started to tick. His esophagus burned and his gut joined in. No. He couldn't have the right address.

There was trash everywhere, strewn about the dead grass like a parade had passed through. The single tree in the front yard was dead and gnarled, hanging down over the house like a skeleton, waiting to pluck out the residents. Windows were broken, the paint was discolored. It was the farthest thing from worthy of Sage he could have gotten.

"Dear God, let me be in the wrong place," he murmured.

Belmont climbed out of the car and strode up the walkway, cats doing figure eights around his heels, yowling up at him like they hadn't eaten in a long time. Absently, he reached into his pocket and withdrew the blueberry muffin he'd grabbed at a gas station, the one time he'd stopped out of necessity for fuel. He let it drop from numb fingers to the ground, the cats setting upon it right away...but suddenly he could only picture a hungry Sage and the world flickered around him.

He knocked on the door, and before it even opened, he wanted to reach up, grip the door frame, and rip the entire place to the ground. Sage wasn't inside. It was just something he could sense in his bones. A man and woman answered instead. One of the man's arms was draped across the woman's shoulders, the other using a crutch for support. There was no question in his mind the woman had given birth to Sage, but the quality of her life had been chiseled into the lines of her face, erasing her daughter's best qualities. Life, optimism, magic.

They both reeked of alcohol and a new perspective moved in front of his vision like a pair of reading glasses. Sage never drank anything but juice, coffee, or tea. She never appeared judgmental over his siblings choosing to drown their boredom or kill time by tossing back beer or whiskey; she simply sat by with her hands folded in her lap, smiling with bright, interested eyes as if nothing was wrong.

Everything about the scene in front of him was wrong.

"There something you need, son?"

Pride hit him at being called son, so fast, before he could stop it. No man had ever called him that. He pushed aside the unwanted feeling with determination. "Where is Sage?"

The two exchanged a glance, both of them listing to the right a touch. "Haven't seen you around here before," the mother said. "Do you mind telling us who you are? How do you know our little girl?"

That description stung him like a mosquito, because Sage was a woman. He'd tasted her and held her, so he knew. He started to give his name, but broke off when he looked over their shoulders into the house. Red fireworks bloomed in his vision at the complete disaster of it, denial thickening his voice. "My name is Belmont. I'm your daughter's..." Sweat began to bead on his brow under their close attention. "I'm your daughter's."

A long silence passed.

"Oh, I see," said the woman softly, pressing a hand to her chest. "Well, I'm Bernadette—Bernie for short—and this here is Thomas."

Belmont managed a nod. "Was she here? Is she all right?"

"Yes," Thomas said, speaking up for the first time. Out of nowhere, misery twisted the man's expression, his body going slack against Bernadette. "No. She's not really all right."

The porch seemed to buckle under Belmont's legs so fast, he had to grab the doorjamb for support, but the wood broke off into his hand, leaving him nothing. All he could do was stare at the splintered remains jabbing into the center of his palm.

He looked up in astonishment as the woman comforted her husband, crooning to him in his ear as the couple swayed back and forth. Somewhere their daughter was *not really all right*, and they were too wrapped up in each other and their haze of drunkenness to care.

Not really all right. Not really all right.

Belmont stepped into the house, his eyes tearing up at the smell, at the total denial that Sage had ever walked through this door at all. "It's going to be fine. I'm here now." He waited for their full attention. "I will make her all right. In this life, I don't want anything more than to do that. Do you understand?"

He held on to his patience as Bernadette started to cry, followed by more mutual comfort between the two of them. And then he remembered what Sage had told him in the car, right before they'd reached the train station.

It's too much, the way you rely on me. My father...he

does the same thing to my mother. And vice versa. Depending on one another for support until they have no energy left to worry about themselves. Or desire to accomplish anything. There's no encouragement, only excuses for what is.

On the heels of that memory came visions of himself crushing Sage in his arms, yanking her down into his lap, cornering her, and demanding to know why she didn't feel well. How many times had he invaded her personal space, commandeering it for himself? Had she ever consented? No, no, she hadn't. He'd taken her arms around his neck as a sign of approval, when it was just her nature to be kind. He'd forced her to be his...crutch.

"She's down at the mine working," Thomas said, the words muffled by his wife's shoulder. "I couldn't handle the machinery anymore, so she took my place down deep in the belly. I've caused her nothing but problems, my poor daughter, but I couldn't do it another day. I couldn't."

Bernadette grabbed Thomas's head, pushing his face into her chest. "Of course you couldn't. No one blames you. No one."

Belmont turned and dry heaved over the porch, the lack of contents in his stomach the only saving grace in that moment. That didn't stop his body from trying to expel anything it could find, worry raking up his gut and twisting. He tried to brace his hands on his knees, but they slipped right off, sending him pitching forward.

His Sage was down in the darkness of the earth somewhere. There was no way to wrap his mind around the implications or reasons behind that fact. Not yet. Just then, there was nothing but cloying claustrophobia and total denial. They clashed together, battling for ground. Because he'd thought the idea of a closed space down in the ground was his worst nightmare, but having Sage down there was far, far worse.

"*Where?*" Belmont shouted.

CHAPTER SIX

Waiting at the mine entrance for the final barrier to be bulldozed away, Sage zipped her jumpsuit back up and straightened her spine. *Deep breaths. Don't let them see your anxiety.*

Her coworkers had been visibly horrified yesterday when she'd shown up to train. Some of them had even offered to trade jobs with her, explaining they had daughters the same age and wouldn't want them within fifty feet of the mine. But she'd declined, knowing full well Augie would never allow it. Those requests would have been denied with great pleasure and she couldn't—*wouldn't*—give him that.

Nor would she walk out of the darkness with tearstained cheeks and fear in her eyes. Lord knew it was there. Three hours spent trapped, fresh oxygen in short supply, had Sage wishing she'd devoted more time to praying. All those hours logged inside churches and she was usually focused on the seating arrangements. It all seemed so silly when her life could be in the balance if another collapse happened. Or the air ran out.

Yet those fairy tales she'd created had kept her strong in the darkness, her tears soaking Belmont's shirt. For a few hours, she'd stopped judging herself for escaping Sibley and let herself remember the joy of breaking free. Happiness *was* attainable through hard work. Mining was harder work, but it didn't diminish the joy of giving someone a happily ever after. She would sustain herself on the memories of those weddings for a long time to come.

The radio at her hip crackled. "Have you out in five minutes, Alexander."

She took a deep inhale and pressed the Talk button. "Okay. Take your time."

The casual rejoinder emerged without a thought, as if she'd just agreed to meet Peggy at the beach. Peggy. Sage closed her eyes and thought of her best friend. Would she marry Elliott the football coach someday? In some alternate universe, would they call her to plan the wedding?

Pretending she would have that freedom, Sage began to wiggle her fingers, the way she did when ideas started to percolate. Peggy would wear light pink, some kind of sparkly embellishment at her hip. Maybe a nineteen-forties film star hairstyle with a tasteful feather curved behind her ear. Her best friend would want it simple this time, unlike the prior four failed attempts to walk down the aisle. Small and tasteful out of consideration for her fiancé, who wouldn't be into a huge ceremony and reception.

But small didn't mean they couldn't have flash. That

was Peggy's style. Fuchsia and clean, crisp white. Calla lilies. Everywhere. Candle centerpieces, set on top of mirrors so the soft light would be reflected around the space. A jazz band, but an edgy one. Trombones and piano and soft vocals. They would need to incorporate Elliott into the aesthetic, too. Maybe she could tap some of his football player guests to do a choreographed dance. The napkin rings could be little gold crowns to recognize Elliott's nickname, the Kingmaker.

They could—

Daylight.

Sage's hands flew up to banish the brightness, her eyelids fluttering in an attempt to adjust. And she breathed. Heavily, deeply, sucking in greedy lungfuls of the piercing cold, winter air that snaked in through the mine's mouth. As soon as she could feel her blood pumping again with the new dose of oxygen, Sage squared her shoulders and slipped through the slight opening they'd created on the left side. It was just big enough for her to climb out, although it was clear the bulldozer would be working steadily into the night to remove the remaining debris. Someone slapped an oxygen mask over her face and told her to breathe.

She gave a thumbs-up, doing as she was told, and squinted into the late afternoon light. Silhouettes of men in hard hats were all she could make out at first, but the concerned faces of her fellow miners eventually came into focus. They patted her awkwardly on the shoulders, muttering words she didn't allow to penetrate. *You shouldn't be down there. He's gone too far.*

A car door slammed.

And then…silence.

There was no other way to describe the ten-thousand-pound hush that fell over the men. Her eyesight was still adjusting, so she tried to put a hand up to block the sunlight. Her arm wouldn't lift, though, the relief having stolen her adrenaline and left her muscles knotted, stiff. Ducking into one of the men's shadows, she traced the crew's attention until she landed on the Suburban.

Belmont.

"No. Oh, no." The words scraped out of her mouth, scooping her heart up, up along with them, leaving the organ lodged in her neck. Joy tried to blanket everything. Pure, blinding joy. Tiny humming sounds started in her ears, her nerve endings stretching in his direction. *Mine, mine, mine.* Her feet wanted to move, the legs she'd thought depleted of energy wanted to spring into action, launching herself into Belmont's arms. Everything would click and be right and good and clean if he was holding her. He'd tell her she was too good for the mine, this town, and she would believe him.

It wouldn't be true, though. The security he provided wouldn't be permanent, either. For one, her secret was out. The battle to protect him had just gotten real, maybe impossible. And two? It was imperative she remember her other reason for splitting with Belmont. After getting a refresher of her parents' relationship, there would be no ignoring the similarities to the one she'd been cultivating with Belmont. If she gave in and clung to him now, in a weak moment, she could very well drown in him.

Sage still wasn't positive Belmont wasn't a mirage. He was dusted in dancing, refracted light. Something out of a happy summer flashback, the kind she'd seen in movies. But this wasn't a happy moment, was it? No, that euphoria clamoring and clanging like cymbals beneath her skin wasn't allowed.

He's here. He's here. I can collapse now.

No. You can't. That would be too easy.

If she'd been split down the middle by an ax, she couldn't have been more firmly divided. His arms around her would be life changing at that moment. She'd been so scared in the dark and he would understand. Of anyone on the *planet*, he would understand. And she'd missed him so much. His total conviction of what was right and wrong. His dependability and the way he stuck to a decision, no matter what it cost him.

And Sage couldn't allow coming after her to cost him.

Had she known he would come? Somewhere deep down, the possibility had never stopped singing, but she'd ignored it. Because acknowledging the chance would have meant she couldn't remain in denial about needing him. By her side. Steady and constant.

A cloud moved in front of the sun, allowing Sage her first glimpse of his incredible face. *Oh Lord.* An invisible fist punched her square in the stomach. Belmont was a complex man, but she'd never seen him carrying this…amalgamation of rage and denial. Winter wind whipped around him, throwing his thick hair out in eighty directions, slapping his coat against his legs. So silent and full of motion at once.

It wasn't only Sage that he captivated, either. After only two days of work, she knew the men around her never stopped talking. Ribbing each other, speculating on the weather, trading crawfish recipes. But you could have heard a pin drop in the quiet as Belmont started moving toward her. Her belly and thigh muscles contracted with each of his footfalls, the memory of his kiss and the hard, male body rushing to the surface, flushing her cheeks.

Resisting the pull of his comfort would be the hardest test of her life. Harder than breaking free of this town or working in the mine. But she wouldn't allow herself to swirl down into the eddy, right into a codependent relationship. She wouldn't. They'd already come so close after mere weeks of traveling together and she knew from watching her parents, the pull only grew more intense over time. Swallowed people whole. Blocked out the world.

She loved the world. Maybe she'd only discovered it a handful of years ago, but she adored so many of the things it had to offer. Belmont was one of them. But she couldn't allow them to abuse each other's comfort anymore.

And there was something more important she couldn't allow. She could not let him step foot in that mine on her behalf. The very possibility was what had given her the strength to leave him in the first place, and moving backward would not only be unacceptable, it would be torture for both of them. Different kinds, but agonizing nonetheless. This was *her* debt to pay.

"Sage," Belmont whispered. "Come away from there, please."

Her insides shook in sync with his voice. "I'll come away if you do. If you stay away."

His footsteps faltered.

"From the mine," she clarified quickly. "Stay away from the mine."

Color returned to his face. "You know I can't do that."

"Well, would you look at that?" Augie's voice—coming from her right—was like a cold blast, straight from a fire hose. "Little Sage here has herself a boyfriend. A big one."

Don't you dare look at him, she wanted to scream. *Don't you dare think about him.*

But she remained still as death, eyes trained on Belmont, no way of stopping what happened next. She already knew, because she'd envisioned it in sleep so many times, usually waking in a cold sweat afterward.

Belmont was only a few yards away now, the group of miners parting to let him through, no questions asked. But he stopped and turned narrowed eyes on Augie, no sound to be heard but the cackling wind as they took each other's measure. "Are you the one who sent her down there?"

Sage caught the fleeting awareness slip across Augie's expression. A look that said, *Here's one I won't walk through so easily.* And he would have been right one hundred percent of the time if the mouth to Belmont's hell weren't yawning wide open at her back. "I am, indeed. This is my mine."

Belmont's jaw bunched, his attention landing back on Sage. "Come away from there, please, or I won't be able to stop myself from carrying you."

And I know you don't want that.

Those words remained unspoken in the wind, but Sage caught them right in the breastbone like a spear. Not wanting to trade any more words with Belmont in front of Augie, because he would use any information to his advantage, Sage went and stood by Belmont's side. The desire to tilt back her head and absorb his eye contact was so fierce, she didn't bother denying the impulse. "How did you find me?"

"The scrapbook." His eyes raced over her face. "You left me a map. I just followed it."

Still unsure if she'd left the book on purpose, or if her subconscious had guided her, she swallowed. "Did you go to my house?"

His answer came through in the silence, loud and clear. And he wasn't the kind of man who could contain his sympathy, even if the recipient didn't want it. He embodied truth. Total honesty was one of her favorite things about Belmont, but the shame was too sharp this time to appreciate it.

"Dammit, Belmont. You had no *right*."

Surprise snapped his chin up. She never cursed at him. Ever. Well, maybe he didn't know everything about her, now did he? Maybe *no one* did, because she'd kept her faults locked up inside, along with her guilt. With her back up against the wall and a desolate future stretched out in front of her, maybe she'd become the kind of woman who curses a blue streak. As soon as the shock faded from his eyes, confidence replaced it. *I am going to make it right*, they said. And he could. He could make everything in her world right, if she let him. "I need to talk to your former boss, Sage."

"Not former," she breathed. "And no. You don't."

"I understand now." His heat reached her through the jumpsuit as he shifted, putting his back to the men and shielding her from the sun. "I understand why you hid this problem from me. You know I have a weakness." He nodded at the mine without taking his gaze off her, the intensity of it stealing her breath, her reason. "You forgot something important, though, Sage. I have no greater weakness or strength than you."

Her entire being attempted to take flight, but with an enormous effort, she reeled it back in. "I would never—"

she blurted, then quieted in deference to the dozens of ears around them. "I would never associate the word *weak* with you, but everyone has one thing they can't face. It's nothing to be ashamed about." A pounding began in her temples. "And none of that matters anyway, Belmont. Because this is my responsibility. Not yours."

He'd stopped listening. Oh, he was hearing her and retaining, but the listening to reason aspect had gotten thrown out the window. She could see him switch off, could sense the decision inside him hardening like cement. This was Determined Belmont, and if she wanted to crack the wall he'd built, she would need explosives. But nothing would be accomplished right now, because he was already turning to face Augie, who looked nothing short of gleeful.

"I have two things to say to you," Belmont said, his voice taking on the quality of granite, his back muscles seeming to grow larger, more powerful beneath his coat. "First, if you call her Little Sage again, I'm going to reach down your throat and rip out your tongue."

It was almost comical, the way the miners' jaws fell open. Some of them even shuffled away from the scene, wise enough to know Augie's wrath would fall even on those who witnessed him being cut down to size. Even Sage couldn't believe the threat Belmont had made. Since he was usually strong and silent, it was out of character for him to speak with such controlled anger. Then again, no one had ever sent her down into a mine on his watch before.

For Augie's part, his expression never shifted from smug, the glint in his eye menacing, measuring. "Is that so?"

"It is," Belmont answered, leaving no doubt about his

sincerity. "If you want to communicate with her, you do it with respect. If you need help deciding what's respectful, run it past me first and I'll decide if it's worthy of her ears."

"Why don't you cut to the chase?" Augie cut in, red creeping up his neck. "I won't be lectured to on my own property."

Belmont turned and held Sage's eyes over his shoulder. There was an apology there, but his resolve was palpable. "I'll be taking her place starting now."

CHAPTER SEVEN

Sage's hand was covered in dirt. It sat there on her thigh, dusty and brown...and there was nothing he could do about it. Right? A week ago, he would have pulled over the Suburban, taken one of the water bottles from his cooler in the back, and cleaned her. He could even see the rings of black beneath her fingernails, and knowing she carried any part of the dark, cold earth along with her turned Belmont's stomach.

But he kept driving back toward her house, because she didn't want his touch. He'd smothered her and lost that privilege. Hell, he'd never really been granted it in the first place. After meeting her parents, he could imagine how much it had bothered her. Being crowded by him, having her words picked apart, every one of her movements scrutinized. Explaining that he couldn't stand to see her anything but happy probably wouldn't help. It might even make it worse at this point, since he'd arrived in Sibley today and picked up right where he left off.

Fulfilling Sage's needs wasn't something he could help. Just like the human body couldn't voluntarily drown itself. Eventually the brain forced that person to the surface for oxygen. That's how it was for him. Remaining underwater wasn't an option.

Sage sliding out of the mine through a crevice, holding an oxygen mask to her face.

Realizing his hands were strangling the steering wheel, Belmont commanded himself to relax, as much as possible. When he'd reached this point lately, he'd isolate Sage somewhere and hold her until his pulse beat normally again. But he couldn't do that. So his hands continued to shake. Would they ever stop? Finding out she was working underground had been terrible enough. Then he'd arrived and found out she was trapped. Trapped. In a place he couldn't reach her without a *machine*.

"Belmont," Sage murmured. "I was fine in there the whole time."

"Were you?"

No, said her silence. And he wanted to turn the Suburban around and murder the man who'd put her in harm's way. "I planned Peggy's wedding in my head."

He wanted her to go on talking forever. Talk and talk until he couldn't hear the sound of rubble being cleared away. "Big or small?"

"Small." She tried to lean into his line of vision with her smile, but he couldn't unglue his eyes from the road. It was already demanding too much concentration just to keep the wheel straight, but her smile would blow that focus out of the water. "Fifth time's a charm, right?"

"Yeah." He experienced the sensation of pages on his fingers. "There was a cake in the scrapbook. On the third page. Peggy would like that one."

He felt, rather than saw, Sage's smile slip. "The stained glass design?"

"Elliott and his religion. She'll want a way to show him she's...supportive." Sensing she wanted more, he cleared his throat. "Also, there's a lot of pink in it."

Sage's laugh released into the car like a string of bubbles, but it faded too fast. "You just made a really dangerous enemy back there. I wish you hadn't done that."

Her disapproval made his right eye start to twitch. Under most circumstances, he would go out of his way to make Sage happy, but the current situation didn't allow for it. Especially if appeasing her meant watching her go back down into the earth—and there was no way he would be able to live with the abomination of that. "He made an enemy out of me, too."

Driving through town, every house seemed to be lit up with Christmas lights. Red ribbons were tied to lampposts, fluttering in the cool wind. Wreaths hung on doors. But the closer they came to Sage's part of town, the more the festive atmosphere faded. When Belmont started down the road to her house, she laid a hand on his arm and said, "Wait," forcing him to suck in a hissing breath. Oh God, they hadn't touched in so long. His heart weighed down into his stomach, each beat heavy and loud, the temperature of his blood warming where it slid through his veins. Between his legs, the flesh that hungered for...whatever she could give it...bulged against the fly of his trousers.

A moan tried to break past his lips, but he disguised it

with a cough. "You don't want to go back there?" He sure as hell didn't want her staying in that ramshackle house, either, but he would fight one battle at a time. Already he risked smothering her again, after inserting himself back at the mine. "I was going to check into a motel for the night," he murmured, shifting when his erection started to pulse uncomfortably. Just the idea of her sleeping could do that to him. A vision of her reaching back to unhook her bra made his voice thick. "I could get you a room near mine."

"I have a place," Sage said in a soft tone, that dirt-covered hand slipping down the front of her jumpsuit. Were her palms sweating like his? "But I can't let you stay there with me. I just can't. You'll—"

"I'll what?"

"You'll steal all my focus. All my resolve. If I let you."

"It's all right, Sage." His heart bled. But somewhere among all the red was hope. There had to be hope if she was that affected by him, right? "I would never expect to stay."

Another glide of those palms down her legs, just before she rolled down the window, bringing cold air swirling into the car. "It used to be guest quarters for one of our neighbors, but it was abandoned, or they forgot about it. But there's plumbing and an old hearth." She pointed through the windshield. "Take a left up ahead. The road is narrow, but we should be fine. It's not far."

This realization that he knew nothing about how Sage used to live—how she coped, what terrible memories she harbored, if they haunted her—pushed up under his skin like a sewing needle. Part of him was almost afraid to see this abandoned place where she'd been staying, because if it wasn't safe in any way, he wouldn't be able to leave her there alone. Not good, when he was trying to give her space.

It was only a bumpy one-minute drive down the uneven dirt road—path, really—before they reached what looked like a large brick structure. There were no steps leading to the front door, just a one-foot drop-off down to the ground. One window on each side, but they'd been covered with what looked like wrapping paper. Which was what reminded Belmont of the day. Christmas. And that he'd been holding on to a present for Sage since New Mexico.

Before Sage could climb out, Belmont reached under the driver's seat and removed the small package. The decorative red paper and curly white bow had gotten somewhat tarnished on the cross-country drive, with people climbing in and out of the car with travel dust on their shoes, but he was more worried about her liking what was on the inside.

"Is that for me?" Sage asked.

Belmont handed her the present by way of answering. "Antique shop in Hurley." He went back to gripping the steering wheel, even though they were no longer moving. "You don't have to open it now."

"I want to." She rubbed the white ribbon between her fingers. The steering wheel creaked from the pressure of Belmont's hands. "Thank you."

"You haven't seen what it is yet."

"It doesn't matter." She sent him a sidelong look from beneath her lashes. "I don't have anything for you, though. I didn't expect... I just didn't expect."

"You should *always* expect from me," he rasped.

Dammit, the closeness of her was getting to be too much. Not holding her and breathing her in when she was *right there*, sitting so close, made him feel like a ticking time bomb, energy boiling underneath his surface. There were itches he couldn't scratch in places he couldn't reach. Everywhere. All the time. "Excuse me," he near shouted, throwing himself out of the driver's side.

The cold air tunneled down his throat, the pine needles crunching beneath his feet amplified in his ears. He kept his back to the Suburban and waited, listening through the open door as wrapping paper crinkled, the cardboard notches of the box disengaging. Her soft expulsion of breath made his eyes close, made him wish for that same sound against his neck. He was losing his composure, and there was nowhere to go, because he needed to see Sage inside safely and make sure she was comfortable.

Belmont's boot heel made a divot in the ground as he turned, intending to move past the Suburban and inspect the small house for security. But he drew up short. Sage stood at the front fender watching him, the gift held in both hands. As long as he lived, he would never forget the picture she painted. So small and mighty all at once, in her dirt-streaked jumpsuit, holding the sturdy blue antique heart clock up against her chest. As if she were trying to press it inside to replace her own real one.

Tick, tick, tick. It was all that could be heard in the fall of nighttime.

"It made me think of you." His own pounding organ rioted inside his rib cage. "You have to remember to wind it once in a while or it'll stop working."

She lifted the clock and tucked it beneath her chin. "I wouldn't want that."

"It wouldn't be your fault." He shook his head and strode past her. "You wouldn't do it on purpose."

At the door, Belmont closed his eyes and berated himself for not having the easy words for giving a gift. All he'd needed to say was, "You're welcome, glad you like it." That would have been fine. She didn't need to know he'd bought the clock because he wanted to see his actual heart up on her mantel, and this was the only way to accomplish it and keep breathing. Keep living in her world.

Hearing her footsteps, Belmont pushed open the door and stepped in, searching the wall for a light switch and coming up empty. "Um," Sage said behind him. "There's no electricity yet. I'm still waiting for them to come turn it on. Just give me a second to light some candles."

He took a moment to absorb the blow of her living in the dark. It had been nothing but blow after blow since he'd arrived in town. But Sage was the one who'd been enduring the darkness, not him, so he sucked it up and filed the rage away for later. When his pulse went back to normal, he turned and held out his hand, trying not to show a reaction to her touch as he eased her into the house. "Running water?"

"Yes, thankfully. Gas, too. They were both turned on yesterday." She brushed against him slowly in the doorway, forcing Belmont to tilt his hips away so she wouldn't know he was hard. "There's a shower stall and toilet in back. The water came out brown at first, but ran clear after about ten minutes." He squinted into the muted evening light and watched Sage set down the heart clock gently on top of a narrow wooden shelf. Then she crouched down—groaning as she went, from soreness, *dammit*—and removed a few items from inside a low, squat hearth.

Candles and matches. She lit six of them, all with one match, then set about placing them throughout the cabin.

Belmont closed the door behind him and took in the tiny room. Opposite the hearth was a twin bed, the covers neat and smooth. Tidy and careful, just like everything else she did. Beneath the bed, she'd stowed her suitcase. The one she'd been carrying when she'd gotten onto the train and gone speeding away from him.

"Are you warm enough at night?" he asked, watching their shadows dance on the walls.

"Yes."

"Good." He turned and checked the door for a lock, finding an old-fashioned deadbolt. Sturdy and well made. His boots clumped on the hollow ground as he made the rounds to each window, judging their security with a harsh eye. "If you don't have electricity, how have you been charging your phone? If you need me…"

"If I need you." She shifted, the floorboards creaking beneath her feet. "I won't let myself, Belmont. There's a reason I got on the train and it hasn't changed."

Belmont rubbed at the gritty feeling in his eyes, although the discomfort was lower, in the dead center of his chest. "If you have an emergency, though—"

"I'll charge it at my parents' house," she whispered.

He gave a grateful nod, before bracing himself. "How bad was it, Sage?"

Her sigh was shaky. "They didn't hit me, if that's what you're worried about. They just didn't know how to raise me, so I did it myself." She picked up a candle and set it back down. "They're just lost in a different world. One they created in the mind they share together. As long as they have one another, they can face the daylight. They left me out of the equation, but I guess a child's love for their parents...sometimes it doesn't come with conditions. Mine doesn't." She paused. "Or maybe I'm confusing love for responsibility. I don't expect it to make sense."

No, it didn't make sense to him. Not exactly. Sage and love were synonymous, so he couldn't imagine her parents not wanting to give her everything. To know her was to love her. That was a truth he understood, even if his experience with love meant something different. Restraint, sacrifice, bliss, pain, discipline. Loss.

"I wish I could go back and change everything."

Her exasperation flooded the room. "Now you want to go back in time and fix the past, too? You *can't*. The course was set before I even existed." She rubbed her nose with the back of her hand. "My parents weren't always sweethearts. They were friends from the time they were in diapers. And Augustine—the man who owns the mine—was their third wheel. They both loved my mama. My...mother." She paused. "She chose my father when they were all in high school and Augie never let it go. He's been taking it out on him ever since. My father isn't strong enough to handle that kind of pressure."

"I am, Sage." God, if he could just hold her, he would squeeze until she felt how unmovable he was. "I'll show you."

"No," she whispered. "You're not required to show me anything. Leave this town, Belmont. Please. I'm begging you. I'm telling you this is what I want."

His skull constricted at the reminder that she'd left him and chosen to face her problems alone. That during their time together, he hadn't given her enough faith. "I can't. I'm sorry. I'll leave when it's over."

God, could he even promise that? Her pale expression told Belmont she was wondering the same thing. Fearing he wouldn't be able to do it? Or fearful that he would? The uncertainty sent him pivoting for the door, but her voice halted him on a dime. "Wait."

CHAPTER EIGHT

Sage had never been sure about the existence of heaven or hell. She'd been brought up surrounded by small-town religion, although her parents never brought her to church on Sundays, like the rest of Sibley. She could still remember hearing the peal of bells from her porch, the feel of a tree branch in her hand as she traced the edge of the steps. Behind her, the house would be silent, save the snores coming from her father where he'd passed out on the couch. Those quiet mornings had served as their own kind of savior. She'd had time to contemplate things that usually seemed outside her control.

If heaven and hell were real, she'd wondered, how will I know which one I deserve? She wasn't being taught the Scripture, so she was already at a disadvantage. Being good was the only way to be sure. There was a copy of the Ten Commandments on the wall inside the local library, so she'd copied them down and done her best to follow them, starting with, "Honor thy father and mother," hard as it had been sometimes.

She'd broken that commandment by fleeing to California and leaving her parents exposed. And just now, with Belmont turning to leave her alone in the tiny slice of darkness, Sage wondered if maybe she'd been cut out to be a sinner, instead of a good girl. Because she lusted for this man's touch as much as she lusted for the way he could surround her with arms, words, breath, pulling her in. Taking her without taking her.

Since being caught in the mine for hours on end, she'd been shaky. Seeing Belmont again had done nothing to settle her. Lord no. Every cell in her body was running ragged, wondering why she was resisting his arms, when they could soothe her like aloe on a sunburn. Outside, he'd handed her his heart, in the form of a clock. Its tick matched her pulse for long moments, and then it didn't because hers started to race, the longer he stood in front of her.

She wouldn't fall back down the rabbit hole of depending on him—or allow him to do the same with her—but maybe it wouldn't set her back too much just to absorb his nearness? Surely she could allow herself that much after the hell of today. Come Monday, she would be going back into the mine, and taking a little of his power along with her might be the difference that pulled her through.

"You don't have to leave right away," Sage said when Belmont turned, watching her from beneath his eyebrows. "Can you wait here while I take a quick shower?"

Maybe that hadn't been the right thing to say. His big back heaved and the touch of his tongue in her mouth came crashing in like a behemoth wave. They had crossed an unspoken boundary on the train platform. There was no going back to before, to when they stopped at rough, crushing embraces. As if that hadn't been...*more* than sexual somehow.

"Yes, I'll wait," he said, his voice sounding like serrated metal. "I can light the fire for you."

I'll say. God, why did everything sound like an innuendo now? If her body weren't flush and sweating beneath the jumpsuit, she would have laughed about it. But there was nothing funny about having Belmont looming mere yards away, looking like one word of encouragement would snap his chain and send him barreling toward her. "That would be perfect. I'll just be...a few minutes."

Sage all but dove into the itty-bitty bathroom, pressing her back up against the door and willing her racing heart to calm down. Why had she asked him to stay? Her resolve would weaken with every passing second. Biting down on her lower lip, she began the excruciating task of lowering the zipper of her jumpsuit, which kicked up a protest in her triceps and shoulder muscles. When she finally got it down, she gripped the hem of her T-shirt and attempted to lift it over her head.

Her arms wouldn't cooperate. They flat out wouldn't rise any higher than her ribs, leaving the T-shirt suspended in midair. Her muscles burned like someone had doused them in lighter fluid and held them above a flame. Sage's agony must have escaped in the form of a whimper, because Belmont's boots scraped just outside the door. And her stomach hollowed with awareness, lightning racing all over her skin.

"Sage." His voice was deep, urgent. "Do you need help?"

No. Say no. She'd only gotten finished reminding him she *didn't* need him. But in this case, it would be a lie and she'd done so much of that lately. With Belmont. The most truthful person she knew. "I can't get my shirt off." Her nose started to ache, the tip probably turning red. "My arms hurt."

His growl was short and broken. A beat passed before the door opened and she felt Belmont filling the doorway behind her. She flicked a glance up to the ancient mirror and confirmed what she'd seen in her mind's eyes. Belmont towering over her like an avenging angel, outlined by candlelight. He'd taken off his coat, leaving him in a black long-sleeved shirt, which he'd rolled up to the elbows. Every inch of visible skin was shot through with strained cords of muscle, as if his frustration were written on him like a road map.

Sage still had the shirt halfway lifted, so her lower back was visible. Not a big deal to most people. But Belmont had never seen anything below her neck. Or above her knees. With the jumpsuit peeled halfway down, the band of her underwear might even be peeking out.

Breathing grew difficult as Belmont took one step closer and took hold of the T-shirt, his knuckles grazing the small of her back. "You're wearing"—his breath ghosted down her neck—"my shirt."

Sage only realized she'd closed her eyes when they popped open. *Oh God.* In the shock of Belmont arriving, she'd forgotten. "I am?" Her mouth was parched. "L-look at that."

"I am looking." She jumped when Belmont reached over her shoulder with his left hand and turned on the shower, the sound of spray filling the room. Then the roughness of his knuckles returned, sliding up her spine along with the shirt. "I like knowing there was a layer of me standing between you and the earth."

Her legs took on the consistency of Jell-O. His touch was a drug, making her languid, although it was different than the way he usually touched her. There was sex this time. So much of it. And it was that major difference that allowed Sage to accept the skimming of his fingers. Accept the part of herself that lusted. They were in a dark room and time had surely suspended anywhere outside this little plot of square footage. Words ached to leave her mouth, words that wouldn't be suitable in the sunlight. This man, so warm and brave and large at her back, knew things about her no one else did. What was one more secret? "I stole it out of your suitcase. I broke a commandment and everything."

"Why?" He breathed into her hair, sinking heat like an anchor in her belly. The shirt came off, her arms dropped to her sides, and she was left in nothing but a bra from the waist up. Inches from Belmont. "Why, sweetest girl?"

A light steam had begun curling in the air like beckoning fingers. *Maybe this is a dream.* It felt like one of the fevered fantasies she woke from on occasion, sweat slicking her breasts and neck. "Because I like the way you smell and it hadn't been washed."

His exhale was gravelly. "*Sage.*"

"Yes?"

She thought he might not respond, but finally he asked a question that made her nipples turn to hard points. "Can you manage"—a long, windy inhale—"the bra?"

Sage tried. She really, truly did. Her arms felt as though they might break off and hit the floor, but she reached

back until her muscles locked up, refusing to move farther. But Belmont was already there, pushing them back
down, holding them at her hips.

"*Jesus.* Please, stop. I can't watch it." His touch disappeared only for a second and then the cotton material
of the bra tightened over her breasts. She could feel him
working the back clasp with fingers she knew so well.
They'd tunneled through her hair so many times, twisted
in her clothing, but had never, ever, touched her with any
kind of…intent. Intent to seduce. And that's what he was
doing, intentional or not. The inhibitions she'd held close
forever, circled the drain, along with the shower water.
"Your back is so beautiful." A ghost of a fingertip traced
down her spine. "But I need to leave before I—"

"What?"

"Before I turn you around." They weren't touching, but
she could sense the shudder that ran through him. "Or look
in that mirror."

Right or wrong, the mine, their codependency aside,
Sage knew if she let him leave just then, she would regret
it for all time. Her body had been woken up. By one man.
He'd kept her on the razor's edge for thousands of miles,
surrounding her with his power and taking it away. Over
and over. And this fever wrapping around them in the tiny
bathroom was completely different from easing his anxiety. Finally, she felt like a woman standing in front of him,
instead of a calming device. This was mutual and alive
and she couldn't *stand* it to end. Tomorrow might be a
different story, but this moment was the culmination of a
thousand dreams and she could no more deny herself than
she could forget his face.

"Belmont, do you think of the kiss?"

"*I never stop,*" he groaned into her hair. "Never."

She took a deep breath for courage. "Will you shower with me?"

* * *

Was he hallucinating?

There was a high that every user chased. The more chemicals entered the bloodstream, the harder and more taxing it became to hit that peak. And it was fleeting. So fleeting. Standing close to Sage with their flesh almost touching, her naked back glistening with shower steam...he couldn't even describe the gravity shift taking place inside him, around him, beneath his feet. He worried he might not be able to stand it. What was on the other side of this raging high? The comedown would shatter him, wouldn't it?

He was going to find out, because hell if there was a choice.

Sage. Sage Alexander. Asking him into the shower.

You don't treat me like a woman. She'd once said those words to him, and he must have made some progress toward fixing that mistake. Yes. He must have, because she wanted...more. But how much more?

Belmont allowed his hands to settle on Sage's waist, holding her steady when she swayed. *God above*, she was soft there. He'd thought the skin of her neck was smooth, but the curve of her hips brought the perfect texture of her home. "The jumpsuit..." he managed, swallowing a moan when she nodded. After pushing the starchy material down to her ankles, he had to brace himself before looking. But nothing would have helped. Seeing her backside so close to his distended groin with nothing more than thin, black underwear covering that part of her...it amplified the ache between his legs until it was excruciating.

There was no choice but to move or he would implode, but he didn't want to startle her into changing her mind. So he walked her slowly, slowly into the shower stall, marveling at the sensation of water cascading down Sage's ribs and over his fingers.

"Aren't you going to...undress?"

"No," he rasped. "Too much."

Her head bobbed as if she didn't need any more explanation than that, only serving to increase the maddened tempo of his heart. She could probably hear it over the shower spray and their laboring breaths, it was so loud. Water soaked into his shirt and pants, filling his boots, but the only discomfort he could process was the material over his cock growing heavier and pressing down, welcome and unwelcome at the same time.

He leaned in to smell her hair, neck, and shoulders, catching the aroma of earth instead of her clean, sweet scent. A growl built in his throat. "Can I wash you, Sage?" His hands traveled without a command from his brain, smoothing sideways along her belly. "All of you?"

Belmont caught her with a forearm around the waist when she dipped. Supporting her weight meant bringing her close, though, and that was when lust broke free of its prison. The firm mounds of her bottom pressed against his pulsing flesh and there was no choice...no choice but to settle her there more firmly. He'd dreamed of it too many times and she'd asked, right? Yeah, he thought so. He could barely think past Sage's curves nestled against that hurting part of him, separated only by soaked material that could be removed so easily. If that was what she wanted.

"You want me," she breathed. "I was never sure. Is it me?"

Sweat mixed with steam on his forehead, wrought from the effort of not rocking his hips. "What do you mean, 'Is it me'?"

"I mean, is it me you're attracted to or would it be this way with..." Her voice dropped so low, he could barely discern her words. "Any woman?"

A shout climbed up his throat, but he jammed it back down. He'd failed so badly with Sage. Completely missed her need to be touched this way. Could he explain to her he'd had no way of knowing, without sounding foolish?

Desperate for a distraction, he used his free hand to grab a bar of plain, white soap. "Can you stand?" Her wet head bobbed once and he released his hold in degrees, making sure she was steady before pulling his arm away. Between his belly and Sage's lower back, he lathered the bar in his hand, then set it back on the small tile shelf.

His soaped-up palms coasted over her rib cage and down, raking over her hips and moving inward to her belly. When his fingertips grazed the waistband of her underwear, Sage gasped and pushed her bottom back up against his groin. Belmont gritted her name, his vision doubling before swooping back together. "I've never been with a woman like this, Sage." The truth was out, mixing with the shower mist, before he could stop it. "Never touched a woman beneath her underwear. Or her breasts. Never been inside." He couldn't swallow, so a choked sound broke loose. "I don't really have a way to explain how much it's you. Out of a million women, it would always have been you. My body…the part you feel between my legs…has never ached for anyone else."

"I—I've never been with anyone, either."

It was Belmont's turn to lose his equilibrium. He couldn't save himself from pitching forward and pinning Sage up against the shower wall. "It was wrong of me to hope for that. It wouldn't have changed anything." He dropped his lips to her wet neck and kissed her with an open mouth. "But I've wondered if there are men on this earth I'd want to damn to hell."

Sage's head dropped to the left, giving him room to slide his mouth up to her ear, feel her shiver against him. "What else did you wonder about?"

Honesty and starvation welled inside him. "I wondered how I'd give you pleasure. If you'd be able to tell me how. Or if I'd have to…try everything until you cried out and I knew."

She pushed up with her backside, elevating his groin, inviting him to grind forward, so he did. He did it hard. And firebursts blinked in front of his eyes, the promise of satisfaction riding low and painful in his gut. But nothing compared to the flood of need that almost sank him when she spoke again. "I've touched myself, Belmont." Even in the muted candlelight coming from the bedroom, he saw the pink flush steal up her neck and cheeks. He loved that display of Sageness so much, he licked it. He licked the increasing wealth of pink, up and down, left to right, until she started to whimper. "I know what I like."

"Show me."

CHAPTER NINE

When had she gotten so brave?

Maybe it was leaving Belmont in the first place. Or coming home to a place she feared in the deepest recesses of her soul, the close call she'd faced this afternoon. It could simply be the darkness of the bathroom and embracing her sexual nature. Whatever it was, Sage wasn't questioning it. She was all but seated on Belmont's thick bulge, her tiptoes wobbling on the wet shower floor. His tongue had left a path from her neck to her ear, and now his breath fanned the spot, sending electricity zapping downward to every feminine part of her body.

There was still a warning in the back of her mind, telling her to tread carefully. When they got close, they consumed each other. Their mutual reliance was an excuse to ignore their issues for just a little longer. A little longer. But facing away from Belmont while he touched her kept it about the physical. Kept Sage from forgetting her resolve completely.

She'd never been more intimate with another human being and he...he was still wearing his clothes. And boots. In the shower. It was so *them*, to feel their way in the literal dark. Since coming on the road trip, she'd sensed that Belmont could only take her in doses—take himself *around* her in doses—and she could relate now. If he took his pants off, Sage didn't know what she would do. Just having his palms below her belly button was enough to make her world spin. The water trickling down between them, along their sides, only highlighted their proximity and made it seem so real. So real her knees shook, her pulse pounding in her temples.

Show me.

He'd actually said that.

Oh boy. It was one thing to experiment with your own body in private, but quite another to articulate, to instruct, a man. Not just a man, though. *Belmont.* Larger than life and...and he'd just told her he would pick her out of a million women. She was having a hard time coping with the gravity of that, let alone concentrating enough to explain how to give her pleasure.

"Sage." Belmont's voice echoed off the shower walls, sounding as if it had come down from a sky full of thunderclouds. "You could recite the alphabet and I would be grateful for it. Especially the way you pronounce your *m*'s." His middle finger dipped below the waistband of her panties. "I love everything you say. So I'm not sure you have any idea what...listening to you talk about that place beneath your underwear...is going to do to me."

Whoa. "Can you tell me?" He dragged her higher on his lap and they both moaned. "What it'll do to your body. It might help me talk about m-mine."

For long moments, the only sound in the bathroom was shower spray splattering on the walls. "There was one time in Iowa. You were going out on that girls' night...and I didn't like it. I already didn't want you to go, but then you walked out in these shoes."

Sage closed her eyes and tried to picture the ones he meant. "The reddish-brown ones with the buckle?"

"*Yes.*" The way he growled the single word made Sage anxious to writhe her bottom. And she did. There was no help for it. Belmont heaved a tortured noise into her ear and lifted her off the ground, bracing her against the wall. "Yes, those shoes. They made your legs stretch. Your calf muscles...I'd never seen them that way before. And the whole night, I wondered. What would it be like to have them locked behind my back?" His erection was so stiff now, she knew he must be in pain. It was there in his voice, too. "We both slept in the cabin that night, after you came home to me, and I shouldn't have done it, Sage."

"Done what?" she breathed.

His sigh was contrite, but there was a tinge of excitement there, too. "I pulled up your covers when you were sleeping, just to the knee. No higher, I promise." His finger traveled farther into her panties, separating the lips of her sex, and Sage stopped breathing. "They slid together and apart in the sheets...and your feet were bare, too. I only watched for a few seconds, but it was longer than I should have looked without asking." His low hum of approval sent heat slithering around and around her tummy. "You can feel how hard you make me. And I've enjoyed it. Wanting you is a privilege. I earn it by not touching myself. Just looking, wanting, and...*aching.*"

If Sage had been standing, she would have fallen over

from the back-to-back shocks. Her legs had turned him on, and he'd been resisting even his own self-pleasure. "You haven't touched yourself?"

"No. That doesn't mean I haven't been tempted." His finger slipped over her clit without warning and she screamed through her teeth, bucking against Belmont. He stiffened for a moment, then reversed his touch, finding the bundle of nerves again. "Right there."

"Yes," she managed. "Yes, *right there.*" The pad of his finger slipped over her throbbing nub again, sending her feet scrambling against his shin bones, curving her arches around them and using them for support. "*Ohhh.* Belmont, yes."

"You said my *name* while I'm touching you here." Through the haze of encroaching bliss, she heard the disbelief and awe in his tone, which somehow drove her higher, closer to the sun. "Did the shower make you wet here through your underwear?" His voice was the deepest of blacks. "Or is this—"

"It's you. It's you." He started using two fingers, massaging her most sensitive spot in luscious circles, fast and slow, fast and slow, as if he were learning through her reactions.

"Put your head back on my shoulder," he ground out. "I can't see your eyes."

Danger. She shouldn't. Being face to face with Belmont brought too much gravity. It would suck her back in, turn her back into someone she couldn't be. But the gathering of release put a hole in her defenses. This was the man she'd clung to for dozens of hours, quietly begging for more. For all. So she didn't just put her head on his shoulder, she threw it, using a foot on his knee as leverage to cinch higher. "There. There," she choked out, peering up into his shadowed face. Shadowed, save his eyes, which practically glowed like blue coal as they raced over her face. "I'm right here."

"*I missed you.*" A tremor moved through his huge body. "Don't keep me banished."

"Please. Please just let me have this. Just this." Her whisper was jagged because the stroking of Belmont's fingers was bringing on a euphoric quickening in her stomach, those muscles beginning to shudder and contract. She felt her mouth move into an almost dazed smile, totally involuntary, probably because her body had been begging for this kind of release for so long. Consuming and intense and bestowed upon her by the man who'd inspired her quest for pleasure in the first place. "Don't stop. It feels so perfect."

"*You* feel perfect." His petting turned up a notch, just the right amount of hard and *quick quick quick*. Like their bodies sensed what was right for the other and provided, just as a matter of fact. "I can..." He groaned. "God, I can see your pretty breasts, Sage. Let me have them next time. My mouth on them..."

"Yes," she whimpered, lust gathering up her insides and squeezing. "Al-almost..."

"If I'd known," Belmont started, licking her neck, rolling his hips. "If I'd known I could do this to you with my two fingers, I would have used lotion to make them softer. I—"

"Don't change them. Don't change anything."

That bliss she was chasing had plateaued at the highest possible point, making her frantic to go over the edge. Her inner walls were beating with tight, little spasms, which was the point at which she usually stopped, satisfied she'd had an orgasm and the process was over. Wasn't it? There seemed to be *more*, higher pleasure begging to be taken. Something shiny and scary, all at once. But half the fear came from missing out, from not climbing to that next level.

"I need your fingers inside me," Sage got out. "Please. I need."

His strangled groan was like a thunder crack in the air, but he didn't hesitate. His middle finger felt for her entrance and tested with two shallow pushes, before sliding deep. "I give Sage what she needs," he rasped into her wet hair. "That's what I do. Feel what I do."

Sage's flesh clamped around the thick presence of Belmont's finger and she broke. She broke right down the middle, her legs jerking, the private, untested muscles low in her stomach convulsing until she screamed. It was like waking up in the bottom of a pool and marveling at the feeling of being encapsulated in cool, fresh heaven, but still scrambling for the air that waited at the top. So much relief. Almost too much to stand. "Oh my God. *Belmont.* Please don't let go of me yet."

He pressed her more securely against the shower wall, and that turned out to be everything she needed. His heated strength at her back and an anchor in front. She slowly drifted back down to earth, her body loosening and going slack. Sleep tried to claim her right then and there, but Belmont's actions kept her lucid. Still breathing like an overworked stallion, he picked up the soap once again and washed her, starting with her fingertips, her wrists. Huge, calloused hands moved over her flesh with reverence, even as his rasping inhales told of suppressed impulses. Ones they hadn't even begun to explore.

And they couldn't. Having an ongoing physical relationship with Belmont would never work. He already
treated her as if she were his to protect... that responsibility would only intensify within him if they went further.
No matter how much she craved that, she couldn't allow
it to happen.

Sage was distracted from those heavy thoughts when
Belmont, still soaked head to toe, his black, unruly hair
clinging in clumps to his face, eased her out of the shower
and wrapped her in a towel. Then he scooped her up and carried her to the twin bed, laying her on the scratchy sheets
and stepping back. Away. She caught a fast glimpse of the
large outline of flesh jutting out from behind his fly before
he turned on a heel and started tending to the hearth fire.

"Belmont," Sage whispered, something twisting in her
chest. She'd been so shocked and distracted by her own
pleasure, she hadn't stopped to consider how much pain *he*
must be in. Just as the orange fire began glowing in the iron
fireplace, Sage sat up, careful to keep the towel up around
her shoulders. "I don't know how to help you without..."

Falling back under our spell. She shouldn't have been
so selfish. Now he was hurting because of her. But as
Sage sat there, trying to work out a way to make the one-
sided situation right, it became more and more obvious
she didn't have to bother. His withdrawal was palpable
across the room, so familiar she almost laughed. Almost.

Belmont didn't turn around when he spoke to her, his
voice gruff and distant. "You'll be safe here. Please don't
open the door for anyone."

Even though she'd known what was coming, it didn't
stop an anvil from dropping on her chest. "You're
leaving."

This was his routine. If he wasn't holding her and using her to calm his anxiety, he was disappearing. He couldn't stand being in the same room with her for longer than a few minutes, unless she was stuffed up against his chest and being overwhelmed by him. What he didn't realize? It murdered her every time he turned his back and left. Every time.

This. This was part of the reason she'd had to leave him in the first place. How could she have forgotten? It was full throttle or nothing, and she couldn't live that way. It wasn't healthy and it was one of her worst fears come true. Becoming a half, instead of a whole.

"I'm sorry," Belmont muttered, his grip making the doorjamb creak. "I wish..." He cleared his throat. "Please lock this door behind me."

She flinched when the door clicked shut behind him.

* * *

I wish...

What? What would he have said?

I wish I could separate you from my darkness, because I know that's what you need. I wish I could feel normal and allow you to feel the same. I wish I knew what would happen if we were actually skin to skin.

Useless wishes, because there was no normal for Belmont. His first memory was of Miriam crying over his crib and over time he'd slowly realized they'd been abandoned. Miriam had moved on at some undefined point, but something about that feeling would never completely leave him. One father had found the very idea of him lacking. And when a new father had arrived...

Belmont stumbled on the sidewalk when he felt the press of hands on his back, but there was no one behind him. He didn't even have to turn around to confirm it. He'd felt those hands so many times in his life, the way they almost punctured his skin through sheer force. Maybe he didn't have to turn around, but out of respect for his sanity, he looked down, confirming there was no hole in the ground before him. Nothing to fall into.

And then he could only picture Sage coming out of the mine. Sage wrapped in a towel across the room, watching him. A normal man would have removed the damp clothes that still clung to his frame and lay down beside her. Gathered her body close and protected her as she slept. But he'd done her an injustice, without making a conscious decision. When he'd started relying on Sage to keep himself from imploding, he'd allowed her to get swallowed up in the deepest parts of his lake. He'd associated her with the results of his trauma and he didn't know how to break her free. How to hold her like a capable, well-meaning man and release her when the time came. Step back and be more than a drain on her resources, ample though they were. To just love Sage without...overwhelming them both. What he felt in her presence was so big and demanding, he didn't know how to stay put in the midst of it and keep himself contained.

But tonight he'd touched her. Between her legs. He was still raw and keyed up from the indescribable pleasure of feeling Sage twist and moan and shake, all because of something he was doing. Rubbing the tiny bud hidden inside the folds of her...pussy. *Christ.* Could he call it that? The very act of thinking the word made his erection throb with renewed need. Back at the cottage, he'd secretly hoped for her towel to fall. So he'd have no choice but to move closer. If he'd done so, would they have had sex?

He should be ashamed that the very possibility had brought him into town. Brought him to the sidewalk outside of a convenience store—the only establishment in town open on Christmas Day—standing in the projected artificial light. He couldn't help it, though. The compulsion to protect Sage was so firmly ingrained, he couldn't deny it, so he'd come to buy condoms. For the first time in his life.

A stiff wind caused the automatic doors to roll open and Belmont took that as a sign. He walked inside and scanned the aisles, finding a handful of locals browsing. Some looked to be buying last-minute gifts or boxes of candy, others carrying on casual conversations across the store at the pharmacy counter. They turned to watch him and his skin prickled under the attention. Briefly, he wondered how Aaron went about purchasing protection. The image of his brother's cocky stroll, the way he would probably toss the package across the counter and wink, got Belmont moving again. Nearly smiling.

But that smile faltered when the door opened behind him, signaling a new arrival into the store. Everyone went so silent, Belmont got the distinct premonition that he would turn and find Sage's boss from the mine following on his heels. Automatically, his hands balled into fists, his bones bracing for an oncoming battle, but when he glanced back toward the door, he was surprised to find a woman instead.

She was older than him, probably by a good fifteen years. And Belmont had spent enough time in dark places to recognize she was a prostitute. It seemed everyone in the store knew it, too, by the way they sneered and turned their backs. The woman laughed in response, her heels clacking on the linoleum floor, but the lines around her mouth were tight.

When she threw a challenging look at Belmont, he felt the need to nod at her in greeting, instead of avoiding her. A flicker of shock passed across her face, but he was already turning for the personal health aisle, ready to make his purchase. The motel room he'd rented two blocks down was waiting for him. He would probably pace there all night, waiting for morning, when he could go back to Sage. Without work at the mine to distract him until Monday, he would find out her plans and hope she didn't mind him accompanying her. Something about the town in general made him nervous and leaving her alone longer than it took the sun to rise wasn't an option.

Belmont stopped in front of the condom section, his mouth drying up at the abundance of choices. Natural feeling, ultra-sensitive, fire and ice. Classic, extended, pleasure pack. Which one was the correct one for Sage? The fact that she wouldn't have any idea, either, made the decision even more important. Her first time—*if* there was going to be a first time—couldn't be ruined by something like the wrong size or brand. *Jesus.* He was starting to sweat, the bright lights beating down on him. From across the store, he heard laughter and would have left if it weren't for the prospect of Sage wanting him inside her... and not being able to give her what she needed. No, he'd withstand the laughter over her disappointment any day.

"You look like a Magnum man to me," the woman crooned at his right elbow. "You need some help putting it on later?"

Her snicker cut off when Belmont glanced over. "No," he answered, his tongue feeling thick in his mouth, ears burning hot. Every eye in the place was zeroed in on him, so he kept his voice low. "But I'd be grateful if you could...which one is best for the woman?"

"Ah." The woman hugged her thin jacket tighter around her body. "Having a laugh at my expense, are you?"

"No." He held her tired gaze. "It's more likely you're having a laugh at mine."

Keeping her narrowed focus on him, she reached out and snagged a black package from the rack, tucking it into the crook of her arm. "No. And I reckon people don't laugh at you very often, either."

"Why?"

A laugh puffed out of her. "Why would you care what I think?"

He couldn't tell if she really expected an answer to that question, so he went back to staring at the selection of boxes. There was a row of packages still swaying, clueing him into which ones the woman had taken, so he started to reach for those.

"This is for...your girlfriend?" the woman asked.

"She's not my girlfriend," Belmont responded, the memory of Sage's shuddering stomach making his palms heat. "She's the one I live to protect. This is only a small part of keeping her safe, and I could already be failing."

Belmont didn't know what compelled him to talk so candidly to a stranger. Maybe it was their lack of acquaintance that made it easy, all its own. The side of her body that faced the store's other patrons was stiff, her shoulder wedged right up beneath her ear, as if to shield herself from their judgment. Perhaps it was that small tell—that proof that she didn't belong any more than he did—that made it so natural to speak his mind.

"Thanks for your help," he said when she didn't respond.

"No, wait." She stepped closer, then backed away, seeming unsure of herself. "Tell me about her. I can...I can help."

Relief blustered in his stomach. "My Sage is small. Only comes to three inches below my shoulder. She looks delicate, but she's strong." The memory of Sage's whispered confessions in the dark made him light-headed. "She hasn't done this before. Maybe she won't want to. I'm still waiting to see if she..."

"If she what?"

"Wants me in that way," he muttered. "The whole way."

This time, when the woman laughed, it sounded dazed. "I think you're safe on that front." They both turned their attention to the rows of colorful boxes. "It's been a while since my first time, but I was nervous. And when women are nervous, they need a little extra..." She tapped a finger against an orange box that proclaimed extra lubrication. "This isn't me coming on to you, all right? But I've got kind of a sixth sense when it comes to these things, so..." Between two fingers, she plucked up the XL size and handed it over. "Am I right?"

Belmont couldn't bring himself to look at her as he gave a jerky nod. Things like size had never occurred to him as important. He'd noticed in places like the locker room growing up that he was built differently than most, but it hadn't been part of his consciousness. Until now when there was a possibility Sage might see and touch him there. Weight dropped low and hot between his legs, so he started to make his exit, not wanting to be around anyone but Sage when those feelings hit him.

"I'm Libby, by the way," she said quickly as he passed.

"I'm Belmont." He put out his hand for a shake. A few moments passed when she only stared, but finally placed her hand inside his, staring as he squeezed and released. "Thank you," he said. "Merry Christmas."

"Same to you."

Any activity in the store seemed to be at a standstill as Belmont paid at the register. But it picked up again when the sound of singing intruded on the shop's fluorescent bubble. Carolers? Paper bag in hand, Belmont stepped back outside into the cold and observed from the curb as a group of people, young and old, moved through the silent two-lane main street of town. *Sage is missing this.* She hadn't gotten a real Christmas. Maybe she never had. And at that moment, she was alone in a tiny room, curled up on an ancient bed, alone where he'd left her. Listening to the tick of his heart clock in the darkness. After a curt exit. One she would never demand an explanation for, because that was Sage. Accepting and kind, even when she shouldn't be.

But she deserved better. He could do better.

An idea struck Belmont and he stepped into the street.

CHAPTER TEN

Sage was still awake, staring up at the ceiling of the cottage, when she heard the crunch of tires. Two sets?

The fact that there was more than one car sent her heart careening up into her throat. She jackknifed into a sitting position and remained frozen for long moments, watching headlights cut through the thin wrapping paper over the windows. Oh God. Who was it? Augie? Maybe some of his men? She'd been so sure no one knew about this place—even her parents—but there was every possibility they'd discovered it while she'd been gone. After the scene that day at the mine, she expected her boss to be livid, but she was safe here. Or so she'd thought.

Sage's legs trembled as she turned on the mattress and reached for her coat. Slowly, as if her movements might alert them to her presence inside—she dragged the garment around her shoulders and buttoned it to her chin. Her cell phone was off inside her suitcase, but she needed to call Belmont. Her throat constricted at how fast she'd defaulted to relying on him. Her fingers hesitated around the handle of her suitcase. Could she deal with whatever and whoever had come for her alone?

Before she could make up her mind, the singing started.

It was eerie at first. She swore it was one of the cars' stereos blasting "O Come, All Ye Faithful." Maybe to unnerve her? After she'd had the worst-case scenarios trample over her common sense, it was Belmont's voice calling her name through the door that caused Sage's pulse to slow down to a normal pace. Well. As normal as it could ever be with Belmont close.

Confusion having swapped places with fear, Sage crossed to the door and opened it. The elevated landing put her at eye level with Belmont. *There he is*, her blood seemed to whisper. The pull between them was so intense, she had to focus on staying still, instead of leaping toward Belmont where she knew he would hold her off the ground. His eyes were shadowed, his hair being torn at by the wind, coat whipping around his unmoving figure. Having him right there, so solid and vigilant in the darkness with so little warning, robbed her of speech. "What..."

"Sage."

Behind him, a choir was captured in the glow of the Suburban's headlights, the eight members singing their hearts out. The music was nothing short of beautiful. If God himself had descended with a host of angels at his side, she wouldn't have been surprised, because surely they were calling right to him with their heartfelt harmonies and smiling faces.

She didn't realize all ten of her fingers were pressed

to her mouth until Belmont's warm hands closed over her own and drew them away. "What did you do, Belmont?"

He was staring at her fingers, white puffs of his breath coasting off them, between them. "They were singing in town and I wanted you to hear them."

"So you just brought them here?" His touch was making her stomach flip, with warning, with lust. "That was pretty trusting of them to follow a stranger into the woods."

"I told them no one would appreciate their singing more than you." The corner of his mouth edged up. "They drew the line at riding with me, though."

Her laughter was mixed with an exhale. "You were right about my appreciating them. Nothing has ever sounded better."

The relief in his expression was brief. "I'm sorry about how I left earlier. I'm sorry about how I always leave."

Sage pressed her lips together, because it was too tempting to tell him that behavior was okay. To pretend that giving every ounce of herself over to him—and then watching him flee with it like a thief—didn't hurt. It did. It was painful every time, whether it was just an embrace or they were bordering on intimate. With the latter, there was more than pain; there was punctured feminine pride, self-doubt, and a bruised heart.

"Why do you do it?" she whispered, just as the carolers started in on a new song, "Away in a Manger." "If you know you'll be sorry afterwards, why leave like I'm...burning you?"

"You *stop* me from burning." He choked on the words, like they'd been stored up inside of him forever. "At first. At first you do. But after I'm calm, after you bring me back down to earth with your smell, the way you touch me and whisper to me ... I do burn. I burn so hot, I'm afraid I'll eat you alive."

Sage sucked in a gasp, fireworks going off on the backs of her eyelids. Belmont looked almost pained at having revealed so much truth. But he didn't take it back. He didn't walk away, either. Truth. He was giving her honesty and she would do the same. "And now, after what we did in the shower, you think m-maybe I wouldn't mind being eaten alive?"

His fingers flexed at his sides. "I'd die before making that assumption."

"I did," Sage said quietly. "All those times, I wanted you to eat me alive." His breath started to come so fast, it formed a dense white cloud around his face. "But it's wrapped up in how easy it is to let you numb me to everything else. Everything but you. When you held me during the trip, Belmont, you weren't the only one who needed it. Not by a damn sight. I was coming back here and I was scared. We were using each other."

He turned his vibrating body toward Sage, blocking the wind, tension rolling off him like smoke. "You don't have to be scared anymore. I'm here."

"No, I *need* to be scared. The fear is mine to own. I earned it."

"No." Outrage bathed his expression. "No, you could never—"

"*Yes*, Belmont." She searched for the words to make him understand. "You *would* have eaten me alive, if we'd gotten that far. I would have disappeared into you. Us. Maybe you would have disappeared into me, too. But I can't forget who I am on my own. I can't lose myself."

Her throat burned. "And I'm sorry, but I'm not your perfect Sage. I get angry. I make mistakes. I made one that brought me back here. Don't take my failings away from me."

"Tell me. *Everything.*"

She wanted to lay every card on the table, but couldn't risk him trying to reshuffle the deck. Couldn't risk him trying to ease her guilt, when she needed to hold on to it. "It's Christmas." Her swallow hurt on the way down. "Can we just listen to the carolers?"

Frustration lingered in his expressive eyes, but he unblocked her view of the singers, his shoulder an inch away from touching her. "If you're not my perfect Sage, let me learn you. Prove it. So I can prove to you I'm not going anywhere."

Sage couldn't answer. What would she say? No? Already she'd hurt this incredible man. Disappointing him caused her pain, too. If she said yes, though, she'd be an open book to him. *Let me learn you.* Would he still want a less than perfect version of her? "I don't know just now."

His nod was stilted.

"Merry Christmas, Belmont."

Long moments passed while they listened to the song finish. When it was over and the carolers started the next, Belmont turned toward her again. "Merry Christmas, sweetest girl." His brow knit together as he scrutinized her mouth. "After what you said, after me leaving, I know I've forfeited my right. But I have a need to kiss you. The way I should have done earlier."

Oh boy. *Ohhhh* boy. Despite the touching they'd done earlier, he hadn't kissed her. Not once. Although, to be fair, she hadn't even been facing the right direction, had

she? Their mouths hadn't actually met since the train platform. Despite a wave of trepidation over being vulnerable
to this man who could consume her so easily, she couldn't
stop the excitement from opening up like a thousand um-
brellas in her bloodstream. But, no. No. Kissing Belmont
would set her back, same way it had done when she'd
boarded the train and watched him walk away, dragging
her resolve to be independent along behind him.

"I would say yes if I thought it could just be a kiss."
Moving on its own, her traitorous tongue slipped out to
wet her lips and his eyes turned to liquid at the movement.
"But nothing is ever that simple with you and me."

"I understand," he rasped. Clearly troubled, he started
to back away. Cold air rushed between them and she panicked. Her knees started to shake and it hit her. She'd quit
Belmont cold turkey and her body was reeling at the lack
of him. Words flew out of her mouth, tumbling over one
another. "But I—I do kind of owe you, since you bought
me that lovely clock for Christmas and I didn't get you a
thing."

Based on the dramatic uptick of his gaze, it had been
the wrong thing to say. Was there a right thing to say here?
"Ah, Sage. You'll never owe me anything. Not even if I
buy you a present every day for fifty years." The furrow
of his brow deepened. "That's not a bad idea."

That did it. His seriousness about giving her a gift every day for fifty years crumbled her resolve. Just a kiss.
Just one? *It's Christmas.* She could forgive herself for be-
having like a woman who'd been surprised by carolers
and asked politely for a kiss, couldn't she? From a man
with a heart so big, he could barely operate around the
size of it? Taking a deep breath for the courage to stop af-

ter one, Sage grabbed Belmont by the lapels of his jacket, drew him close, and molded their lips together.

He made this sound—*mmmhh*—and followed it with a groan so long and deep, she got lost in the never-ending vibration of it. His salty ocean eternity scent clashed with the forest, his texture, the heat of his body, exploding her senses. She'd barely processed that her feet had left the landing before they were dangling in midair, Belmont's forearm slung beneath her bottom, the opposite arm wrapped around her back. So tight, like he'd never expected to hold her again. And it *was* holding, the hallmark of their dependency on each other. Which would have alarmed her if there weren't a million more things demanding her attention.

Unlike the morning they'd kissed on the platform, he wasn't clean-shaven. Felt like his chin and cheeks hadn't even *seen* a razor since that first time their mouths had met. Those rough whiskers rasped on her face now and she nuzzled closer, harder, wanting him to leave burn marks on her skin. Was that crazy? She didn't know. It felt right. It felt as if Belmont heartily approved of the decision because he slanted his mouth on hers all the harder, licking against her tongue, crushing her to his big chest.

Around them, the music seemed to get bigger, swallowing them whole. It rang in her ears and inside her heart, the only other audible sound her rioting pulse. Her sole problem in that moment was not being able to open her mouth wide enough to satisfy Belmont's appetite, which seemed to grow stronger with every stroke of lips and tongue.

The thick ridge forever straining behind his fly grazed her stomach—and just like that, she was standing back in the doorway, Belmont's giant hands on her hips to steady her. His cheekbones were stained with color, his nostrils flaring as he sucked in breath after breath. "I was so sick over putting you on the train last time, I didn't get enough of the way you taste."

"Oh," Sage breathed. "And?"

He had to think about it. Not the sentiment, but the right words. She could see him weighing and measuring them behind the incredible blue of his eyes. "And I'm going to do everything I can…" His hand left her waist, his thumb brushing across her lower lip. "To make sure you never make me go a day without it."

The moment cut itself out of time. Everything else was before or after. Belmont, white plumes of breath wreathing his gorgeous face, carolers belting about joy behind him, twinkles of snow beginning to fall. And there she stood in her coat, watching it all from above, like an out-of-body experience. He was making a vow—and when Belmont made a vow, it became fact, surely as if it were etched in stone and read to the masses.

She'd made her own vow, though. To herself. Her parents. The devil. The sentiment paused on her lips, though, when his fingers slipped into her hair and cradled the back of her head, his thumb massaging her scalp. "Where can I find you in the morning?"

"Uh…" She worked for a deep breath. "I'm going to clean my parents' house. Make sure they're okay for food and everything."

That thumb had stopped moving. "Then I'll be there, too."

Sage knew there was no point in arguing. Her battles would have to be chosen very carefully going forward.

They had the weekend in front of them, clear of the under-ground hell that lay at their feet like a trap, but it would loom closer soon enough. Two days. And then they would stop pretending that he hadn't vowed to face his greatest fear to keep her safe. And how she would do anything in her power to prevent it.

"Good night, Belmont."

He nodded once. "I'm going to sleep out here in the backseat." His gaze cut to the side. "I won't rest knowing you're out here alone."

You can stay in here with me.

Don't. Don't say it. He'd hurt her and swept her off her feet, all in the space of a couple hours. If she started giving in to her impulses, she would be right back at the begin-ning of the road trip, letting him overwhelm her at every turn. So instead of inviting him inside, she took the extra blanket off the nearby shelf and handed it to him.

"I'll see you in the morning."

As she closed the door, there was something new in Belmont's expression she'd only seen in glimpses, but never in a prolonged way.

Hunger. It kept her awake until the dawn light began to break.

* * *

When Belmont woke up the following morning, Sage had already gone up to her parents' house. His later than usual rise might have had something to do with the fact that he hadn't slept since passing out in the motel room, al-most three days prior. Last night, after sending Sage back into the cottage and positioning himself in the Suburban to have a perfect view of the door, blackness had claimed him so fast and hard, his head ached this morning from the impact of unconsciousness.

Lord knew Sage was an early bird, too. Every morning of the road trip, she would set out on a quest for coffee, whether it was at a motel, a hotel, or a cabin. He would follow. Most of the time, they didn't exchange words during the process of Sage ordering and doctoring her coffee. Removing the lid to blow steam off the surface through pursed, soft-looking lips. Something about that lack of pressure between them at the break of day tended to dissipate toward the end of her first cup, though, and they'd be back to... tense.

Her shoulders would creep closer to her eyes the nearer Belmont came, and she would begin sending him looks from beneath her lashes. He knew those glances like the back of his hand. *Does he need me? Will he soon? When will it happen?*

It being his inevitable need to have Sage plastered against him, anchoring him, reminding him with murmured words that change happened all the time and it wouldn't split him down the center. That he couldn't control the universe or his family or the outcome of a situation.

Apparently he'd been blind, though. Because all that time, she'd craved their contact, too.

When you held me during the trip, Belmont, you weren't the only one who needed it.

His growl shattered the silent atmosphere of the car. When she'd made the confession last night, it had taken every drop of his willpower not to pounce. Knowing she hadn't simply been tolerating him... but benefiting?

Loving his arms around her? Refraining from touching her would be a lesson in torture from this point forward. But he would not—*would not*—allow them to use each other. They were more than that. Strong and real and good. As Belmont trod through the woods behind Sage's parents' house, he recalled the first time he'd held Sage. It was a memory he hadn't pulled up in a while, because he'd stacked so many more fresh ones of her on top of it. That moment before the wedding rehearsal, after she'd straightened his tie, laid her hands on his lapels, and stepped back, he'd frozen up. Cold had started in his hands and moved higher until his jaw locked, teeth grinding. He was preparing to be the focus of a large group of people, to make a speech and dance. But it was the change, too, that got to him. The letting go of his little sister and standing aside as she went about a new life. He'd been happy for her, but the very idea of the future unfolding and being left up to chance stabbed him between the shoulder blades.

They'd stared at each other—him and Sage—for what seemed like hours, in the back room of that church. Until slowly, so slowly, she'd reached out and took his hand. And like a drowning man being thrown a life preserver, he'd hauled her forward. She'd been stiff as a board at first, but she'd gone more and more slack with each passing second, her head lolling to one side, giving Belmont a place to bury his face.

"Thank you," he'd said, astounded to find his pulse returning to normal. "Thank you, Miss Alexander."

"Please. It's Sage," she'd responded, lighter than a feather. "And...any time, Mr.—"

"Belmont."

They'd both sighed.

He could still hear it now as he stopped at the bottom of the house's stoop. *Any time.* Someone else might have heard those words and recognized them as a pleasantry. Not him. He'd taken them literally, hadn't he?

I'm not your perfect Sage. I get angry. I make mistakes.

The words she'd thrown out last night echoed in his ears like a resounding gong. He'd always known there was more to her—more she kept hidden under the surface—but as someone who hid their past like an ugly secret, he'd kept himself from pressing. Did she think he wouldn't like what was revealed? Jesus, what he wouldn't do to put that fear to rest. Now. Today. But his knee-jerk reaction was to sweep her up and make those promises into her hair. Make her *feel* his dedication by forcing their heartbeats into close quarters. Sage needed more, though. Needed different. So he'd give it to her. He always would.

Swallowing the lump in his throat, Belmont climbed the stairs, finding the door ajar by an inch. He pushed it open with a slow hand, not wanting to startle anyone inside. The scent of lemon cleaner found his nose, Sage's hum filling his ears. For a while, all he could do was lean against the doorjamb and watch her move. Urgency built in his chest, demanding he go help and ease her load, but it was fighting against the way she paralyzed him. *So beautiful.*

Her hair was on the very top of her head in a ponytail. He'd never seen it like that before. It sprouted in all different directions, like a fistful of flowers picked from the garden. She was wearing his shirt again, the one with *Clarkson Salvage* over the pocket.

Pride filled his lungs. If she only knew what it did to him, seeing that logo on her chest. How many hours had he spent becoming an expert at his trade, the drive to be her provider flowing in his bloodstream? Thousands? It was worth every minute of work just to see her in the shirt. The neck was so wide on Sage's petite figure, her shifting collarbone was on full display as she scrubbed the kitchen island. Which inevitably drew his eye lower to the sway of her breasts.

A week ago, he would have turned faster than a finger snap and descended the stairs in one giant lunge, needing to get away before the lust had a chance to take hold. But everything was...changing now. And like *all* change, it made him nervous, because there was a chance he could ruin the tenuous bond between them and not be able to revert back, if things went wrong. If *he* did things wrong. His body, however, his heart and hands and eyes, were eager. So eager. They had kissed twice now. His fingers had rubbed the slick female flesh he'd never expected to touch. What would happen now? What came next?

Belmont wished he hadn't worn the black sweatpants now. He'd thought them appropriate for cleaning, but there was nothing appropriate about the way they...clung. To him. And his predicament wouldn't get any better with Sage around. Experience told him that.

"*Oh.*" Sage jumped backward, dropping the sponge in her hand. "I didn't see you there."

"Good morning," he said under his breath, striding into the kitchen and gauging Sage's progress, judging she'd been working alone for about half an hour. "Sorry to startle you. I couldn't think of a way to get your attention without..." He nodded at the discarded sponge.

She plucked at the edge of her yellow elbow-high gloves. "Maybe a bird call next time?"

The corner of Belmont's mouth lifted. "What would that sound like?"

Pink bled into her cheeks, but she puckered her lips as if to whistle, then executed a light, trilling chirp. "There. Just like that."

Compelled by something heavy down deep in his stomach, Belmont started moving to the left, one slow step at a time, around the kitchen island in Sage's direction. "I didn't know you could make sounds like that."

"There was a bird that used to nest on my bedroom window. Growing up." He watched her start to fidget the closer he came, knew he should stop and give her some space, but they were inside this house. This house in which she'd grown up and been unhappy. It was there in the stiffness of her back how difficult it was to stand inside the four crumbling walls, and he could no more stop himself from easing her than he could pause time. "They don't have the same species in San Diego, as far as I know," she said in a rush. "Or if it's there, I've never heard it singing."

"Do you miss it?"

"The bird?"

Belmont shook his head. "San Diego."

Sage didn't answer. The sudden stubborn set of her chin told him she wouldn't be, either. As the lower half of her body came into view, he dug his nails into his palms, hard enough to leave marks. She was wearing shorts. Ones that stopped just south of her bottom. The feel of her pressed against his lap while he pushed her, *thrust* her, into the shower wall stirred and thickened his cock. The shorts highlighted more than just her backside, though. They revealed Sage's legs. Legs that made him a little...insane.

They weren't as pale as they should be. As far as he knew, she didn't spend a lot of time at the beach. He'd made enough subtle inquiries to Sage and Peggy to know Sage worked indoors, and most of her time was spent in an office or catering halls or churches. If she'd been spending a lot of time near the ocean, he wouldn't have been able to relax, wondering if she was wearing enough sunscreen or if she was a strong swimmer. So without the outdoors, why were her legs so tan? It was a question that had burned in his belly for months, ever since he'd caught a glimpse of her thighs as she climbed into the passenger side of Peggy's Volkswagen Bug. Long before the road trip. And he'd only grown more curious when she'd worn those shoes with the buckle, back in Iowa. Lord, that sleek flex of her calves...

His abdomen knit tighter than a drum, Belmont paused a foot away and planted one hand on the counter, making sure she saw it. "Tell me what you miss about San Diego."

Sage picked up the sponge and started scrubbing again. "The people."

"Why?"

"None of them knew who I'd been before."

There was a whole wealth of Louisiana packed into those words, and Belmont could see it had been deliberate. He'd caught touches of the South in her phrasing and cadence before, but never so much or all at once. Knowing she'd been holding such a vital part of herself back was like a fishing pole reeling his heart out through his mouth.

TESSA BAILEY

"I want to know who you were before. It's still a part of who you are now."

Her nod was jerky. "Maybe. People seldom change so much they're unrecognizable." She rolled her lips inward. "I miss my apartment."

"I was never inside of it," he said, kicking himself for stating the obvious. "What did it look like?"

A fond expression lit up her features. "The bathroom was a robin's egg blue. The tiles, the sink, everything. The real estate agent apologized for it being ugly, but I used to love taking baths in there." They traded a look that punched Belmont in the gut. Sage in the bathtub, covered in bubbles. *God have mercy.* "It was mine. I didn't care if it was old."

"You'll go back there someday soon. I'll make sure you get the same apartment."

"*No*, Belmont." He watched as she gulped in breaths, clearly attempting to keep her cool. He wished she wouldn't. How many times had he done the opposite around her? "The jig is up. I'm not a wedding planner. I was just a fraud pretending to be one. Pretending this place doesn't exist. But it does. I thought maybe I was capable of forgetting how much my parents need me, leaving it all behind, but I'm not." Her accent was honey-thick, denser than he'd ever heard it. "My leaving made things worse for my parents. Harder. And they're never going to get better." She paused in her scrubbing, then went at it again. "I can't go wear pretty dresses in the sunshine and act like everything is dandy. I took that man's money so I could afford to leave and it hurt them. I let myself down by forgetting my responsibilities. So this is where I'm staying. Until they don't need me anymore."

In other words, *forever*. Acid singed his windpipe, the ground seeming to rise up, up to knee level. This is where he didn't do well. Sensing change on the horizon. But this was so much more than change. This was the loss of Sage. This was potential Armageddon. And that meant he needed to pull his shit together and blow the winds of change in another direction. Some unfamiliar insight told him pushing Sage right now wasn't the wisest course of action, though. She didn't need to be cornered or reasoned with. She needed a friend. The new knowledge that his touch made *her* feel healed made the pull in her direction even more intense. Almost unbearable to deny. But he would. He would.

"I understand feeling responsible for family, even when the bond seems like it's fading. Or was never there to begin with. One day you wake up and realize...you were just ignoring the bond. That *you* let it weaken."

"Are you talking about your brother?"

"Yes." Aaron's smirk appeared in his head, just for a second, before dimming. "We were best friends when we were younger, but I locked him out after." *After*. He didn't have to explain. The sympathy that danced across her features meant she knew he was referring to him being trapped in the well. "When I tried to...make progress with him in Iowa, I felt like a fraud, too. Maybe we all do sometimes. For different reasons. But I've seen the weddings you planned, Sage. You're the furthest damn thing from a fraud I know."

Her smile was tight, telling him she wasn't ready to accept what he knew to be true. "How have you seen the weddings? None of your sister's ever took place."

The back of his neck turned hot. "When Peggy asked

me to walk her down the aisle, she came with me to get fitted for a tuxedo. You know how she talks and gets excited." He couldn't help a small smile, thinking about his youngest sister. "I hadn't even met you yet, but when she showed me the pictures of what you'd done, I could see you cared. All those details. Not a single thing overlooked or rushed. All real. *You're* real."

Belmont took a step closer to Sage and her entire body locked up on a gasp, her eyes closing, hands ceasing their scrubbing. Belmont froze, too. She wanted to be held, but he couldn't give in. Not if it meant they'd be using each other. They had to find sturdier ground first. So he went with his intended goal of retrieving one of the sponges stacked on the other side of the island, bringing it back toward himself without so much as grazing her body. Her breasts.

Under *his* shirt.

They both slipped back into motion slowly at first, cleaning side by side, and picking up speed. Sage seemed deep in thought, but Belmont couldn't settle his mind on anything but her. Having her close. When he finally spoke again, his voice was far deeper than when he'd walked into the kitchen. "What do you miss about this place?"

The smile she sent him was mild, but brave. "Nothing, really. I didn't do a lot of…experiencing when I lived here." She shrugged one shoulder. "I mostly stayed at home or down in the cottage, if I wasn't at school."

Belmont took an empty bucket out from beneath the sink and began to fill it with warm water. "School activities weren't my thing, either." He couldn't help but feel silly making small talk with Sage, this woman who was the center of his galaxy, when he wanted to be across the kitchen absorbing eye contact from her, whispering non-sense against her neck. But this was normal. She needed normal. And no one else would be giving it to her, save him. "I used to drive Peggy to cheerleading practice and pick Rita up from detention, but I don't think that counts." Sage looked sad at the mention of Peggy, so he pushed on. "What about school dances? Did you—"

His own frown cut him off. Why was he asking her that? He didn't want to know if she'd spent any amount of time with some kid's sweaty hands on her. So when Sage answered in the negative, he was simultaneously relieved and upset on her behalf. But it gave him an idea.

"Will you show me the school later?" He braced himself for her to say no. "I want to see where you grew up. I want to see all the places you spent time."

She didn't look up, but a line formed between her brows. "Why, Belmont?"

"Because every minute of your life has been impor-tant," he said simply, hoping she understood. *I want to learn you.* "Every minute was important to me, even though I wasn't there. I'm here now and I want to see."

Finally, hazel eyes turned on him, so deep and inviting, he would have drowned in them if she gave him the slight-est encouragement. He swore she was getting ready to tell him she didn't want to share her past with him. He was braced and ready for it. So his lungs almost exploded with fresh oxygen when she said, "You want to see my room?" instead.

CHAPTER ELEVEN

Sage's stomach was a bustling butterfly sanctuary as she moved down the uneven hall, toward her childhood bedroom. Upstairs, she could hear the sleep sounds coming from her parents, familiar in a déjà vu kind of way. In her youth, those sounds had signaled peace. The chance to move around her home without having to witness the sickness surrounding her parents like sticky gray clouds. Without being the focus of an irritable hungover crying jag or tirade.

She'd never felt anything but alone inside the house, but with Belmont's steady footsteps *thunking* behind her on the floorboards, she was...surrounded. That's how large his energy was. It filled every available space and slipped in between the strands of her hair and beneath her clothes. It bombarded her, replacing her dejection with awareness. He draped her in static, lifting her skin in goose bumps and sensitizing every inch of her body.

Before they'd kissed, Belmont had been capable of doing that to her, but those reactions were now multiplied by a thousand. A *million*.

And just because they were in silent opposition about him going into the mine didn't mean he deserved to have so much of her resentment. Right that moment, however, she had nowhere else to place it. She could cast the unwanted emotion out like a fly-fishing line, and his presence was so big, it would probably land on him anyway. She didn't want to revisit the places that had shaped her. Didn't want to peel back layers and let people in on her secret: She was nothing but a big old faker. Her wedding planning skills had been a stroke of luck that she'd bolstered by poring over magazines and scouring the Internet. Nothing about her was polished or put together—it was all an act. She would always be that poor Alexander girl.

Where did the old Sage start and the new one begin? She no longer had the energy to maintain the illusion of glass-half-full wedding planner. Belmont would see the real her if she lowered her guard completely. He saw *everything*. And while she was darn proud of what she'd accomplished without proper schooling or encouragement, having him acknowledge that she was a fraud would knock her right off the pedestal he'd placed her on.

So what had she done? Offered to show him her room—the lowest possible pit of despair—just to get her fall from grace out of the way. His presence usually reassured her, but just then, she wanted to turn around and beat his chest with her fists. How dare he come to Sibley and force her to reveal herself? How dare he take away the one thing that could have kept her warm at night? The fact that once upon a time, she'd won the devotion of this extraordinary man.

How long would it last once he saw her worst?

Sage knew the exact moment Belmont realized what she was doing, too. His hand landed on her shoulder just outside the door, slowing her to a stop. "Sage," he said, so close to the back of her head, his breath bathed her neck. "Let's make a trade."

She didn't want a different plan. Didn't want more sweetness from him. She just wanted to rip off the Band-Aid, but she answered anyway, in a dull voice. "What do you mean?"

"A place for a place." His frustration over having to knit words and explanations together was clear. "You show me something that's important to you, a place or a thing or a story. And I'll give you the same." He paused. "If you want...the same from me."

The offer was too tempting to turn down. A chance to get inside Belmont's head? It was a place long denied to everyone. Maybe once he realized Sage wasn't perfect, he would change his mind about wanting to know her more, but...she loved this man. Seemed like she'd loved him for a million years. If there was the slightest possibility she could repair what was damaged inside him—with words, with actions—she had to seize it. "I show you my room, you tell me something no one else knows?"

His swallow was audible. "Yes."

Not wanting to give him time to change his mind, Sage turned the rusted brass knob and pushed the door open.

Since arriving back in Sibley, she hadn't ventured into

the room. There was no reason to. No fond memories remained inside the ten-foot-by-ten-foot space. No pennants from the local sports team or graduation pictures taped to the wall. There was nothing. The black mold that she'd desperately tried to scrub away and hide behind paint had taken over, crawling up the edges toward the ceiling, framing the windows like some macabre outline. Obviously there had been a leak directly upstairs, because a huge chunk of the ceiling had caved in, the torn bulge hanging suspended in the center of the room. Above it, the ceiling beams were visible along with a hole that peeked into the second-floor bathroom.

Sage straightened her spine and edged into the room, staying close to the wall just in case the rest of the room decided to cave in. When her foot nudged an empty bottle of whiskey, she pulled her leg back and kicked it across the room, not so much as flinching when it shattered against the dingy skirting board. God, it felt *good*. The resentment she'd been harboring broke free and ran amok inside of her.

Her gaze shot toward Belmont, and as expected, the man looked like he'd just seen the ghost of Napoleon. The second he fully entered the room, it was entirely new. He had that effect on everything. Instead of a scene from a nightmare, it now looked like a movie set, the hero arriving to save the day.

But she didn't want to be saved. She wanted to be her own hero. Even if she failed, at least it would be at her own expense. Not at the expense of others, like her parents. Like Belmont. The room was the epicenter of everything she'd run away from. The worst parts of her upbringing that slipped into her nightmares regularly.

Recognizing the self-pity didn't make it any easier to avoid. It rose up and swallowed her whole.

"I'm so angry. I don't want to be, but I am," Sage heaved out. "Did you know I could get mad? Did you know I'm not serene and understanding all the time?"

Belmont was still. So still. But dead focused on her. "Tell me why you're angry."

She crunched a piece of broken glass beneath her heel, grinding down. "Because I hate feeling responsible. I *hate* it. Why should I feel responsible when this is what they gave me?" She lifted her hands and dropped them help-lessly. "I should have laughed when my mother called and told me Augie was trying to kill my father. This place al-most killed me. Everything inside of me. I left here a shell. And I decorated myself, same as I decorated churches. I'm a lie."

He was silent for long beats, thoughts whizzing through the blue of his eyes. "I won't deny you're the kind of beautiful that makes me hungry, Sage, but you're no shell. God, no." His tread creaked across the floor in her direction. "Call yourself a lie? You proved yourself wrong by coming back here. You can't turn off your sense of re-sponsibility, your love. Your beauty runs so deep, maybe even you can't understand it."

Her anger tried to nosedive, but she held on for dear life. "You can't *do* this," she cried out. "You can't say and do the right thing every time. Just let me be pissed off. Let me feel guilty and shitty and robbed. Okay?"

"Okay." She reeled a little at the loss of his stare, the weight of it falling to the floor. Before she could ask what he was looking for, he produced an uneven metal rod. Or a pipe. At some stage, it had probably been part of the deteriorating plumbing, but she stopped speculating when he pressed the cold length of it into her hand. "Be mad. I'm right here with you."

Her laugh was more a brittle exhale than anything else. "You don't want to see me break things. You want me to pretty them up. You want me to make *you* better. Pretty *you* up." Air razed the inside of her windpipe. "We're just like them."

"No. We're going to fight until we're not." He nodded at the pipe. "Right now is about you, though. Get as ugly as you want and I'm going to stand right here, having your back."

A huge, horrendous sob broke from her throat, freedom finding its mark in the center of her chest. She walked toward the closest piece of furniture—a bureau. Surprisingly, it had held up pretty well, the little pink rosebuds she'd painted on the surface still visible beneath the dust and grime. She pulled out the top drawer, wincing at the sound of scraping, splintered wood. And then she bashed it with the pipe, again and again, until spikes and nails were all that remained. Chunks of lumber flew in every direction, so she closed her eyes during the downward swings to protect herself. Every drawer received the same treatment, the muscles aching in her arms in a satisfying way. *So satisfying.* Her teeth hurt from being clenched, her throat sore from gritting out unintelligible words. By the time she'd finished, her heart was going wild inside her rib cage. A good wild. The kind that made a person feel like they could jump ten feet high.

When she dropped the metal onto the ground, she drooped, only to find her back pressed to Belmont's chest. He didn't touch her, he simply stood there and propped her up while she caught her breath, his heartbeat eternal against her.

"Impressive," he rumbled.

And she laughed for the first time ever inside her childhood bedroom.

CHAPTER TWELVE

Sage's laugh made Belmont close his eyes. He couldn't stand there too long absorbing it, because he didn't want to risk her withdrawing. Putting the line back in the sand between them. But for a few seconds, he let it soothe his ears and reverberate down to his feet.

Had he placed Sage on a pedestal and refused to acknowledge she might have any faults? Yes. He'd done that. And to be frank with himself, Belmont wasn't sure he'd stop easily. The fact that she was so troubled over coming back to Sibley only highlighted how selfless her decision had been. It made her even more incredible in his eyes. He sensed, though, if he explained that to her, she'd turn the metal pipe in his direction. So he looked for a way to cheer her up instead, his gaze landing on something brightly colored in the bureau's rubble.

He gave Sage's head a nudge with his chin, then stepped around her, stooping down to pick up the stapled-together sheaf of papers, which appeared to have glued cutouts of a...boy. On every available inch.

"Oh my God. Don't look at that."

Too late. He was already leafing through page after page of collages. The same smirk greeted him over and over again, an advertisement for teeth whitening if he ever saw one. What was Sage doing with a veritable shrine to this person in her room? There was a terrible discomfort in his chest. His hands wanted to rip the item down the middle. He might have done it if his goal wasn't to cheer up Sage.

"Who is this?" Belmont asked, still flipping through the sea of obnoxious, smiling faces. *So much denim.* "He looks familiar."

Sage hurried into the spot beside him. "He's no one. Can I have that back, please?"

Belmont handed it over, but he couldn't stop his frown. In all the time he'd spent around Sage, she'd never shown interest in a man. Once, he'd allowed himself to imagine her on a date, holding someone's hand. He didn't sleep afterward for two days. There wasn't a man alive that would work harder to fill her needs than Belmont. His jealousy—which, in his estimation, was a weak word for what he felt—was shot through with outrage. Sage getting less than she deserved? Not in this lifetime.

"He's obviously someone, Sage, if you took the time to catalog every expression he's ever made." He eyed the makeshift book with distaste. "Is that...are those the kind of men you like?"

"What do you mean, what *kind* of men?"

The floorboards creaked beneath his boots as he shifted. "Blond."

"It's Justin Timberlake, okay?" Sage made this giggle-snort sound that was so sweet, his jealousy almost ebbed. Almost. "I can't believe this. We're standing inside my nightmare and it should be awful. But we're arguing about 'N Sync's former front man, like we're back in the Suburban with everyone...and it doesn't seem so scary." She swiped at an eye with the back of her wrist and sighed. "I think his hair is nice."

"It's very..." His mouth twisted. "Curly."

"Yes, it is." A laugh tinkled out of her, easing his frown. She seemed to almost be *enjoying* his discomfort. Teasing him about it. "When I was a teenager, he was my type. Didn't you have a type when you were in high school?"

Intuition told Belmont this was where he was supposed to tease her in return. Was this...flirting? Did she like this sort of thing? "No one in real life. But I guess I thought Storm from the *X-Men* movies was pretty." Her face started to fall and he panicked. He really needed to practice this whole flirting thing. "I have a different type now." He turned his body toward her, just an inch or so, and electric heat fired through him at her response. Was it wishful thinking, or did her eyes continue to drop to his stomach...and lower? The more she looked, the more indecent he felt in the thin sweatpants. They hid nothing, especially when her interest made him harden behind the seam.

"What should I do..." Belmont asked. "If a woman is my type. But she has a different type?"

"Types change over time," she said in a breathy way. "Maybe some people develop a thing for redheads after meeting one they liked. You see?"

His jealousy curled its lip. "Sounds like you know a lot about this."

"Well, I have you fooled then. I don't know anything about it." He held his breath when Sage reached out to cup his cheek. *Don't move. Don't ruin it.* "Things are complicated between us. We spent a long time buried in each other and now we're trying to come up for air. I don't know if we can breathe separately and still be—"

"Together?" Hope unfurled inside him like a banner. More than he'd had in a long time. "Are you telling me that's possible?"

"I don't know." She shook her head. "But you brought Christmas carolers to my door last night, Belmont. If you weren't a woman's type after that, she wouldn't deserve you."

Incapable of checking himself, he turned his head and kissed the inside of her wrist. "Yes, you would."

At the jump of her pulse against his mouth, Belmont sensed the crossroads between them. A physical one. They had two options. Break apart or give in and cling. Sage knew it, too, because she dropped her hand and took the booklet from beneath her arm, examining the cover despite Belmont's grumbling. "It was just my way of escaping. Pretending to walk down a red carpet or riding in a limousine. Wearing pretty dresses and getting compliments. Little things that girls dream about."

"What do you dream about now?"

Her expression seemed troubled for a passing second. "It's my turn to question you now, isn't it?" she said, a little too brightly. "Or are you cheating, trying to combine two turns in one?"

She was back to flirting with him now. Did women

flirt because they eventually wanted more? The possibility roughened his voice, like fine sand granules. "If you want me to remember the rules, you have to stop glowing like some kind of angel." He moved a step closer. "You said you want compliments. Like that?"

"That was lovely," she breathed, clearly surprised.

Belmont nodded, his gaze skating over her pink cheeks. "I've got about a million of them. For you." Honesty crawled up his throat. "I was thinking I should save them up so I never run out, but just about every second, I think of a new one. So I think we're good."

"Yes. Good." Again, her attention slipped down to his belly. His lap. Then zipped back up like she'd burned her eyes. "I like your sweatpants." Color spread down her cheeks and neck. "I mean, I like that you're comfortable. In them."

"I'm not comfortable in anything, Sage." His blunt fingertips skated down his abdomen, but dropped away before he could make contact with that part of himself that pulsed nonstop for her. "Everything is heavy. All the time."

"Oh." Belmont didn't realize he was growling at the Justin Whatshisname tribute until Sage dropped it to the ground, nudging it aside with her toe. "Bye bye bye," she murmured. "If you knew who Justin Timberlake was, you would have laughed at that joke."

"Sorry, Sage. I'm never going to laugh at anything that involves him."

They stared at each other. "No, I'll probably never enjoy *X-Men* again, either." He was still reeling at the idea of Sage being jealous of *him*, when she rushed to continue. "It's my turn to ask a question, right? Tell me about a typical day for Belmont." She wet her lips. "Before the road trip. Tell me how you spent the hours between morning and night."

The sounds of boat wake, boots on the deck, a shower running, voices in his ear. Those things came to him in flashes. "You want to know about my day."

"Yes."

He leaned back against the wall and crossed his arms, a relaxed pose that was totally at odds with the discomfort he experienced when talking about himself. "My apartment is near the marina, so I can hear the water when I wake up. I...like that. Like knowing it's right outside, the tide moving in and out." He tried to clear the hesitancy from his voice. "I shower and eat something—usually boiled eggs and toast. And then..." He shrugged, letting the truth come out. "I check in on everyone. I call the store for Peggy and the restaurant for Rita, to make sure they made it to work all right. Aaron...I couldn't call anyone to check on him, so I bought that laptop. He's always posting something on the Twitter, so..."

Sage made a small sound. "You bought a laptop just to follow Aaron? Why didn't you just call him directly? All of them?"

"I'm not good at conversation."

"Is that really what it's about?" The sudden emotion packed into her gaze was so much, he could barely maintain eye contact. "They would have loved to hear your voice."

He was slowly starting to believe that, and Sage's confidence nudged him that much closer. For as long as he could remember, he'd tried to limit his interference in his siblings' lives. They'd never treated him like less than a full brother, but their different fathers had always made him feel like an intruder. Especially after what happened at the well. "After that, I go down to the boat, make sure the equipment is functioning the way it's supposed to. The men start to arrive midmorning and we head out to one of the sites."

Belmont watched Sage carefully to gauge her interest in his job, his blood rushing to see the curiosity on her face. What would she think if she knew he'd saved up enough for a house? That he'd pictured her inside of it every day since they met, walking the halls, laying in a backyard full of green grass?

That would never be a reality if she stayed in Sibley. If both of them stayed.

"When I come home, I check on everyone again. I memorize the following day's tide schedule, confirm appointments, and I listen to the water." He captured her eyes with his own, held them with all his might. All his truth. "And in between all of it, starting when I wake up through when I finally fall sleep, I think of you." His throat started to hurt. "I check in on you, too."

Sage seemed to be recalling something, her back straightening. "All those hang-ups first thing in the morning. That was you?"

He nodded slowly, his focus unwavering. "I know you're going to try and stop me from going into that cave, Sage."

There it was. The elephant in the room had just become the gauntlet between them. The division was excruciating for him, but he wouldn't hide his intentions from her. Apparently she wouldn't disguise hers, either. "I *am* going to stop you. I know what it'll do to you."

Belmont hardened his jaw, grinding his teeth at the very idea of watching her go back into the ground. "I've known for weeks something was coming and I know we have more than just a disagreement ahead. I wish there was some way I could stand aside and let you jump this obstacle on your own. I can see you want to so bad, but I'm not physically able to let you. I *can't*. Please understand." His throat worked. "I love the tide because it's constant. No matter how often it gets low or rises high, it'll keep coming back. Know the same about me, Sage."

"I do," she whispered.

He pushed off the wall, stopping in front of her long enough to lay a lingering kiss on her cheek. And then he left the room to go clean.

CHAPTER THIRTEEN

Belmont sat down on the porch outside Sage's parents' house and tugged the folded, faded documents from his pocket. In the mad rush to reach Sibley, he hadn't had time to look at them recently. The long list of men who might be his father.

Miriam had never told him his father's name. And he'd never asked.

She'd been so sad in his early memories and he'd never wanted to see her like that again. Those times when he'd stood outside her bedroom and listened as she wept. Huge, heart-wrenching sobs that made him worry she had fallen down and hurt herself. But through the crack in the door, he could see she was unharmed, so he would just bed down and wait, wait until she stopped.

Belmont had read the entire journal his mother had left behind, cover to cover. There was no mention of his father's name. He'd never been capable of frustration with Miriam, though. If anyone understood his need to do things in his own time, it had been her, so he wouldn't begrudge her leaving out the information he needed. If anything, he'd been surprised by how much Miriam had understood his siblings. Understood *him*. He'd caught himself wishing she'd said the words in her journal out loud, only to realize he did the same thing. Kept his thoughts trapped inside, never sharing. After reading Miriam's final thoughts, he'd started trying to be more open with his family. Rita, Aaron, Peggy. Sage. Had they noticed?

Belmont stared out over the weed-ridden front yard. After having no luck on his own, he'd hired a private investigator back in San Diego to find his father, a move that had been way outside of his comfort zone, but proved somewhat fruitful. Since his mother had been a public figure, her life was well documented online, and by building a timeline and speaking to people she'd worked with, the investigator had given him a list. Unfortunately, it was a long one.

Why did he want to find his father?

Belmont didn't really have a straightforward answer to that. No, he'd been plagued with uncertainties, instead, since he could remember. As the oldest, he'd never questioned his desire to protect those he loved, but he'd often wondered if he was doing it right. After all, his methods weren't conventional. There was no one to ask, though. No example to learn from.

Now that he was a man, his motivation had become less about needing a role model and more about learning his history. Getting the closure for Miriam that he sensed she'd never really gotten. And maybe in the process, he'd find some for the fatherless child he'd once been. The child who'd faded as far as possible into the background while his siblings spent time with a different father.

Like everything, however, Sage's appearance in his life had factored into the decision to search for the man who'd helped conceive him, bringing everything full circle. Back to the beginning, where he wished for an example to follow. Only this time it was spurred by his own desire to be a father one day. A husband. Was it in his blood to be those things, if it wasn't in his father's?

He'd decided to start from the very beginning. With the man who'd decided he wasn't worth sticking around for. For all Belmont knew, it could be as simple as his father being too young when he'd gotten Miriam pregnant and couldn't live up to the responsibility. Or it could have very well been Miriam who'd decided she wanted to pursue her career and not settle down. That would have been her personality. But Belmont wouldn't know until he came face to face with him.

Belmont stared down at the names until they started to blur.

With precise movements, he folded the list back up and tucked it into his pocket. There was no time to be indecisive right now. Whatever was inside him, Sage would have every ounce of it at her disposal. Keeping her safe was his purpose. He'd resume looking for his father when he could afford to put his concentration into the search.

* * *

As soon as the door closed behind Belmont, Sage had immediately felt the house expand. Filling all the cracks his huge presence had occupied. They'd been cleaning for hours in silence, but a little while ago, they'd accidentally brushed together in the hallway and he'd excused himself. She could see him outside, sitting on the porch, his shoulders hunched forward, and yearned to go to him, massage the tension from those bunched muscles, but intuition told her she'd end up on his lap, being rocked, having the breath squeezed out of her.

She wanted that treatment *way* too much. And that was the problem.

She'd made the decision to separate herself from a relationship so reminiscent of her parents. But the way she and Belmont were communicating now, the way they were refusing to give in to the need for unhealthy comfort...that felt nothing like the marriage she'd grown up watching. Was it possible they could get somewhere? Somewhere in the sun?

They were going out tonight. There'd been an unspoken agreement that it was a friendly outing, not a romantic one. Sage almost laughed at that. With barely an effort, Belmont could make roadkill romantic. What chance did *she* have in the line of his fire?

If they could stay this course they were on, would she be willing to try for *more* than this newfound friendship with Belmont? So much of her frustration stemmed from him not recognizing her as a woman. Sure, that was only a small portion of their issues, but knowing he desired her? It made a difference. It meant she wasn't his crutch. As long as they remained that way...maybe they weren't doomed.

The sound of footsteps coming down the stairs cut short the bloom of excitement in her breast. Her father had finally woken up. She was simultaneously relieved and nervous. Relieved because he'd gotten a full morning of rest and wouldn't be in a foul, shouting mood. One of his hangover tempers would bring Belmont roaring back inside like a gale force wind, ready to sweep her away. Thomas, however, would be full of self-pity—his default when he was sober—and in some ways, that mood was even worse than the shouting, destructive one.

Sage moved to the kitchen, swiping at the kitchen counter with a lemon-scented rag, even though it had already been cleaned to a shine.

Her father stopped halfway between her and the living room, scanning the rooms through bloodshot eyes. "Did some fixing up, did you?"

"Yes. Some." Her hand stopped moving on the counter. "Can I make you breakfast?"

"No," he said, waving her off. "Your mother likes to fuss. Let her do it."

Sage had forgotten that part. First thing in the morning—or afternoon, rather—her mother was at the top of her game. Her hair would be in a careful updo and her dress would be clean and pressed. They were going to have a *fresh start*, Bernadette would say. They were going to have a *healthy* day. She would set down a plate of eggs in front of her father with a flourish and stand to Thomas's right while he took each and every bite, winking at Sage, who sat across the table eating a bowl of Cocoa Puffs she'd poured herself.

When she was a child, the mornings had been a cross between hopeful and confusing. Why couldn't her parents be like that all the time? What was stopping them? Maybe this time. Maybe.

By the time her father returned home from work, Bernie would be on her third drink, the loneliness having crept in and captured her. Sage would watch from the floor of the living room as Thomas was greeted by his weeping wife. Some nights her mother would be aimless in her misery with no specific target. Other times she would accuse Thomas of meeting another woman or not loving her anymore. As Sage got older, she started recognizing the devices her mother would use to get sympathy from Thomas. And Thomas was more than happy to comply, because he craved the attention from Bernie. Craved the excuse to drink. It was a cycle, the two of them feeding off each other and the alcohol while Sage sat alone in the corner or slipped out into the woods alone.

Around the time she'd entered middle school, she'd stopped hoping they would magically change and started making herself scarce in the evening times, since sunset seemed to be the signal for everything in the house to go to pot.

Sage watched as Thomas took a seat at the kitchen table, stretching his fingers on the surface like he hadn't seen the top uncluttered in a while. A cat jumped up onto the surface and began to yowl.

"Do you still take your eggs over medium?" Sage asked, desperate to fill the heavy silence. "Funny, I take them the same way—"

"I'm awful sorry you had to come here, Sage." He stroked the cat's head. "We've always depended on you more than we should."

Pleasure rose up swiftly inside her, cutting through the anger she'd shared with Belmont earlier, splashing like a fountain. Her resentment hadn't killed the part of her that wanted approval from her parents, it seemed. "I had to come," she said. "Mama called me worried about you and

I—I worried I might not make it before something bad happened."

"You don't know what a relief it is to know I don't have to go into the mine again." Finally, he turned and met her gaze. "Your mother would have a hard time without me, Sage. It pains me just thinking about it."

The surge of pride she'd felt at her father's gratefulness took a nosedive. This wasn't about her. It was about them. The same way it had always been. She turned around and braced herself on the counter. "I don't want to think about it, either." She felt the need to impress on him that selflessness existed. It was a real, beautiful thing, and it was sitting right outside on the porch. "Belmont came here to take my place, but I won't let him." She swallowed. "I won't let him, but I think him offering deserves a thank-you."

"I will thank him," Thomas said, right behind her. Sage turned to find her father had stood and made his way into the kitchen, wringing his hands at his waist. "But it's you I'm thanking right now, Sage. I was angry when you left here, because it was on that *man's* dime. I didn't get a chance to explain that I—"

"*Daddy.*" The guilt was so fierce, she was forced to cut him off. Was her father aware of her guilt for taking Augie's money and leaving? Was he using it? The head games seemed too much like the ones her parents played together; she couldn't help but be suspicious. But no. No, she'd already agreed to take his place in the mine. She was being ridiculous. On top of the guilt, now she felt shame for judging him. "You don't have to say anything."

"Yes, I do." He shifted on the broken-up linoleum. "We don't deserve this kind of dedication from you. We weren't good parents. Still aren't. But believe me when I say..." He glanced over toward the hallway, where the sounds of Bernadette rousing could be heard. She got the impression he was about to say more, but he stopped, unable to meet her eyes. "We appreciate what you're doing for us. More than words can say."

Sage prayed her voice would sound natural when she spoke. "You're welcome. I love you both. No matter what." When her response seemed to pain him, instead of reassure him, she asked, "Is there something you want to tell me?"

He didn't answer for a moment. "No." His mouth turned down at the corners. "I don't know why we can't just...pull together. It seems possible and then, when one of us caves, the other caves like they were just waiting. Just waiting."

Sage heard a creak out on the porch, felt Belmont's pull like a magnet. "I think I know what you mean."

CHAPTER FOURTEEN

Belmont braced both of his hands on the wobbly motel desk and breathed. He'd cleaned side by side with Sage for three hours and the proximity had taken its toll. The need for contact with her was piercing. Watching her across the living room as she'd vacuumed the curtains, her leg muscles straining, her teeth sank into her lower lip in concentration...Lord, his hands had started shaking.

What would she do if I yanked the vacuum out of her hands and tunneled her fingers through my hair instead? Dragged them under my shirt, over my face, crammed them against my mouth? His imagination had run rampant for hours on end. He'd battled the need to hold her down and demand more thoughts and memories out of her, to bathe her neck in his breath. Things he would have done, to a point, a matter of days ago. And she would have let him. She would have soothed him. He'd never used enough heroin to become an addict, but he imagined that not holding Sage in his arms whenever his anxiety deemed it necessary was a lot like detoxing from the drug itself.

For all his lust, though, there was a change taking place between them. A good one. They were communicating in a different way. Hell, they'd flirted. Every time he commanded himself to leave her untouched, to shoulder his own burden, it got easier. Mostly because he could see how being independent of him was helping Sage. She'd let out her anger, she'd laughed inside a place she called a nightmare. Would she have done those things if clinging to him had been an option? No. He didn't think so. That had to mean they were headed in the right direction.

Belmont opened his eyes, his attention landing on his cell phone. All the missed calls on the screen. Not from Sage—he'd made sure. They were from his brother and sisters.

He could only recall his last conversation with Aaron in bits and pieces, but he was pretty sure his brother deserved a phone call to let him know he'd found Sage and everything would be fine. But he couldn't bring himself to pick up the phone and dial. The relationship with his brother was different now. So different from how it had been in California. If he called Aaron...Aaron would really come. Perhaps even Peggy and Rita, too. And he couldn't have that. The situation was too unsettled and he already had his mind occupied with keeping Sage safe. He couldn't be in five places at once.

Nor could he be in New York on New Year's Day. This entire trip had been planned because of Miriam's final wish, but Belmont would rather saw off his own arm than abandon Sage. God knew his siblings wouldn't expect him to leave her, either. Having met Sage, his mother would understand, too. He had to believe that.

Biting down on the guilt, he tore his gaze off the cell phone and went back to preparing. It was now late in the afternoon and he was due to pick up Sage in thirty-six minutes. More time spent around her, holding himself back until she gave some sign of…encouragement. Until then, he was in an invisible straitjacket. The strain was like a belt cinching tighter around his stomach, loosening a degree, then yanking tighter than ever.

A knock on the door.

Belmont's head came up slowly, his knuckles turning white on the desk. It wasn't Sage, the motel manager, or one of his fellow down-and-out guests. No, he'd been expecting a certain man to come find him. He went to the window and drew back the heavy beige curtains to confirm, and indeed, Augustine Scott stared back at him through the water spots on the glass.

"One minute," Belmont said, letting the curtain drop back into place. He loosened the towel still hung around his waist from the shower and draped it on the back of a chair. Then he dressed slowly, perversely enjoying making the other man wait. Belmont wasn't a vindictive person by nature, but the usual rules didn't apply when someone sent his Sage down into a dangerous mine. All bets were off after that.

When he finally opened the door and stepped out to join Augustine in the cold December air, the older man's eyes didn't quite hide his temper. "I'm not a man accustomed to cooling my heels."

"I know what kind of man you are."

Gray eyebrows shot up, the mine owner's amusement clear. "Well, don't keep me in suspense, young man. Enlighten me."

Belmont scanned the parking lot and saw two occupied cars, telling him that Augustine hadn't come alone. Probably wise, considering the threat Belmont had made earlier. "I'd rather you get to the reason you came here," he said. "I have more important things to do."

For some reason, Augustine found that funny, his deep laugh sending frosted air curling in front of his face. "You are some kind of mystery, aren't you? I usually have someone pegged with a couple words out of their mouth, but you..." He shook his head. "I can't decide if you're delusional or if you're the real deal."

Belmont had no idea what that meant, and frankly, he didn't care. "Maybe if the reason for your visit isn't that important, you can wait until I come to work Monday morning."

"So impatient," Augustine laughed. "This is Louisiana, young man. We get to the meat when we're good and ready." He was getting a lot of pleasure from calling him *young man*, which was precisely why Belmont refused to take the bait. "Came to tell you work begins tomorrow, instead of Monday. You didn't think I'd let you start without the proper training, did you?"

"Hadn't thought of it," Belmont lied. He'd thought of the training, but only in terms of how long they'd shown Sage the ropes, before letting her do a job meant for a man twice her size. "Tomorrow it is."

A glint appeared in the older man's eyes. "You know I bet you can use this to your advantage with that stubborn girl of yours." The syrupy hum in Augustine's throat made Belmont's stomach turn. "Yes, *sir*. The night before you go down into the big, bad mine in her stead, something tells me she'll be feeling mighty grateful."

Fury laced through Belmont's veins and solidified, like asphalt drying under the summer sun. "Do you want to die?"

Augustine's face lost its color, but retained its bravado. "Come again?"

"I said..." Belmont stepped closer, until the older man was forced to tilt back his chin. "Do you. Want. To *die*? Because if you speak of her again with any disrespect, I'll spend my life in a cell, just so she can live in a world free of you. You want to know if I'm the real deal? Say another ugly word about her and find out."

The sounds of car doors slamming infiltrated the red haze surrounding Belmont and he braced himself for a fight, but Augustine held up a hand, keeping whoever approached at bay. Not for one second did he take his eyes off Belmont. "Don't look now," the other man murmured, "but I do believe things just got interesting."

Twenty-four minutes until I pick up Sage. And that was the only thing keeping Belmont cemented in place as Augustine turned and sauntered toward the parking lot. But he'd only taken about six steps when he turned back around, holding up a finger in the air.

"Now, wait just a minute," Augustine said. "There was something I forgot to mention." He tapped a finger against his temple. "Getting a little slow in my old age, don't you know."

Belmont crossed his arms and waited, which only served to amuse the other man.

Although when he spoke again, his expression turned serious as a heart attack. "Maybe I should allow you to work the first two months without letting you in on this fun little secret, but I find myself impatient to put you in your place, you see." He licked his lips. "Sage's daddy is the town loser and always has been. Nothing about that changed when his daughter went away."

Belmont was stuck on what Augustine had said about *the first two months*. The *first* two. His eye started to twitch over the possibilities. What was coming?

"All that drinking and missing work sure put old Thomas and Bernadette in the hole. And you know where people in Sibley come when they're in debt to the bank?" Augustine spread his arms wide and turned in a circle. "They come to *my* bank."

"How much do they owe?" Belmont bit out, his heart trying to squeeze out through his ribs. Sage. She would be devastated by this. "Tell me and go."

"Oh, my bank charges a high interest." The mine owner winked. "Enough to keep you down in that mine for a few years to come. If you want to keep a roof over their heads, that is. I wouldn't blame you one damn bit if you packed Sage up and got on the next train, leaving old Thomas to reap what he done sown."

Sage would mind, though. She would never do it. He'd seen the determination in her that morning in the kitchen. *I thought maybe I was capable of forgetting how much my parents need me, leaving it all behind, but I'm not. I let myself down by forgetting my responsibilities. So this is where I'm staying. Until they don't need me anymore.*

Which meant he was staying, too.

"Like I said..." Belmont inclined his head. "I'll see you in the morning."

Augustine laughed his way to the parking lot, calling back over his shoulder, "Oh, you're the real deal, all right. I won't question it again."

"See that you don't."

CHAPTER FIFTEEN

Having Belmont's stride hitch when she walked out onto the porch was one of the finest moments in Sage's life. Being picked up for a date—whether or not they were labeling it as such—sent her back in time to glitzy daydreams of Justin Timberlake picking her up for the prom, pulling up with that thousand-watt grin, his upper body sticking up out of the moon roof.

Those had been the imaginings of a lonely teenager. Even now she couldn't think of the pop star without imagining him in a mock turtleneck and too much hair gel, because that's how he'd been immortalized in her mind. He'd never been a man to her, while Belmont...

Sweet heaven.

He'd showered and shaved, dressed himself in dark, loose jeans and a slate-colored button-down shirt. His unbuttoned coat flared out behind him as he closed the distance between her and the Suburban. And yes, there it was, that falter in his rangy-hipped stride. He stopped at the edge of the steps and raked a hand down over the bottom of his face, sending thrill after thrill down her legs, curling the toes in her shoes.

Yes, those shoes. The reddish-brown ones with the buckle.

She'd packed one daring outfit for the road trip. One. And she'd never expected to actually wear it. The midnight blue dress and black stockings wouldn't have been considered provocative to most women. Peggy would even call it conservative. But the neckline plunged lower than anything in Sage's closet—or suitcase, as it were— and the bodice clung. Tight. It was a thin sweater material with a tight herringbone pattern that you couldn't really see unless you were up close.

Did she plan to let Belmont get up close?

She didn't know yet. There was an almost imperceptible line between what was right between them and what her sixth sense classified as too much. Something harmful disguised as the greatest feeling in the world. So she would wait and see. And pray he didn't overwhelm her into falling back into old habits. God knew resisting the man who'd burrowed himself down deep in her heart was getting harder by the minute.

"You wore the shoes," he rumbled.

Especially when he noticed everything. *Everything.*

"Yes."

A muscle shifted in his cheek. "You wore *that* with them."

Don't tug on the hem. It can't go any lower. "I did."

Feeling a little like they were performing the balcony scene from *Romeo and Juliet*, Sage started to descend the stairs, but Belmont held up a hand. "Wait." He moved up to her level, leaned down to take a long whiff of her hair...then he breezed past, knocking on her door.

Sage spun around so fast she almost planted on her backside. "W-what are you doing?"

Her father answered the knock, an eyebrow lifted in inquiry. Rightly so. It wasn't very often someone knocked on her parents' door. She doubted that fact had changed since she'd been in California. When she'd said her good-byes and walked outside to wait for Belmont on the porch, she could tell her father had been waiting for her to leave so he could pour his first drink of the night. He'd had the shakes and his right hand still trembled, all the way to connecting with Belmont's offered hand.

No words were exchanged, just an understanding passing between two men. Maybe she wasn't meant to fully grasp the meaning there. As far as how it affected her, watching the show of respect Belmont paid her father...she would never be able to adequately describe it. Pressure pushed out from all sides in her chest, and whether or not it was warranted, there was no denying the twinkle of pride she experienced. In herself. She was back in this town where she'd never been looked on with anything but pity or disdain, and with that one hand-shake, a tiny part of what had always been withheld was restored.

The same happened again when Belmont opened the passenger side door for her a moment later and helped her up, nodding through the windshield at her shell-shocked father as they reversed down toward the road.

"Thank you for that," Sage said around the golf ball in her throat, laying a hand on top of his on the steering wheel. "I've decided we have to call this an official date now that you've shaken my daddy's hand. I don't know if there's a dating rule book, but if there is, that's probably on the first page."

Before he turned out onto the main road, Belmont leaned down and rubbed his smooth cheek over the backs of her knuckles. "What else is in this book?"

"Hmmm." She took her hand back and tucked it into her lap, praying his warmth would linger. "I've made something of a study of this with my couples. When they come in for their consultation, I like to ask them where they went on their first date." She could feel how anxious he was for her to keep going, which helped assure Sage she wasn't rambling, thanks to her nerves. Or maybe she *was* and he simply didn't mind. "The most common answer is they met online and planned a coffee date in a controlled environment. Both of them always have friends on speed dial, just in case it goes south. There's no…risk involved." She gave in and tugged on the hem of her dress. "None of the women ever took a man to their old high school on the first date. But for some reason…it seems perfectly typical for us."

"Maybe we have our own typical." His attention swung in her direction. "The high school. Is that where you're taking me?"

She slid him a smile. "You're the one driving."

"That may be, but you're in control." His gaze dipped to her feet and climbed up to her knees, before cutting away. "I go on your word tonight, Sage."

The flesh he'd stroked last night tingled between her legs. Without thinking, she crossed them and almost

moaned at the rasp of nylon. Holding himself back physically from her was difficult for him—the lines around
his mouth and eyes spoke volumes—but there was no
denying the bliss of having a man so powerful in check.
Knowing he was waiting, hoping, for a green light. "Drive
straight through town. It's about half a mile past it on the
right."

Belmont gave a nod and they drove the remaining distance in silence, Sage watching familiar storefronts and
faces pass by outside the window. In her youth, she'd
loathed coming to the shops, especially alone. Three times
a week, she would be sent to the deli to buy cigarettes for
her father and the sympathy that would pour off everyone
as she crossed the road, little black plastic bag in hand,
would crawl over her skin like snails.

When they reached the high school, the parking lot
was empty, except for patches of ice and garbage dancing
in the wind. Twilight had fallen, outlining the two-story
limestone building in a blue that reminded her of Belmont's eyes. She thought they were just going to sit in
the car, giving her a chance to ask him for another secret,
but he surprised her by exiting the car and rounding to the
passenger side. He opened the door and held out a hand,
which she simply took, warmth spearing straight up to her
shoulder.

"Show me around," he murmured, stepping back so
their bodies wouldn't brush as she climbed out of the
Suburban. "Show me where you ate lunch. Show me
anything."

The sound of her heels clunking on the asphalt made
the moment surreal. It seemed like yesterday when she
walked the same route, her knockoff Vans squeaking with

every step. Keeping hold of Belmont's hand, she brought him around back of the main building, spying the corrugated metal overhead that shaded the outdoor lunch tables in the afternoon. She led him over and dipped her chin to indicate the far left table. "There. I sat there most of the time. The cafeteria was too...crowded."

He squeezed her hand. "I know what you mean."

Sage scanned the grounds, her gaze snagging on the gymnasium. "There would be a pep rally in there every Friday before the football game." If she listened closely, Sage thought she could hear the stomping of the feet, the shrill whistles coming from the bleachers. "I used to love them, even though I wouldn't attend any of the games."

"Why did you love them?"

"Because everyone was looking at the team and the cheerleaders. No one bothered with the people in the stands, so I could just hide inside the noise and watch." Belmont started leading her toward the gymnasium and she followed. "And I loved the promise of the rallies. No one had won or lost yet. There was only optimism. Just like weddings. It's all the good and none of the bad." She peered through the cool nighttime at Belmont. "Does that make sense?"

"Yes." They stopped at the gymnasium door, each of them leaning in to look through the vertical rectangle of glass. "I wish I could see you. Smiling in the stands."

In San Diego, she wouldn't have even tried the door to see if it was open, but they were in small-town Louisiana, so reaching out and trying the handle was a no-brainer. The teeth of the lock clicked and the rusty metal door groaned open several inches. But it rattled to a halt, revealing the chains keeping the gym off limits from the inside. "Bummer," she muttered. "Kids were probably sneaking in at night to make out."

"Wait here."

Before she could ask his intention, Belmont stalked off the way they'd come, back toward the car. She heard the Suburban door slam a minute later and his tall form was returning...holding a pair of bolt cutters down by his side. "Belmont, you can't just..."

Despite her protest, there was a long squeeze of excitement in her belly when Belmont casually inserted the bolt cutter through the opening and snapped the chains in half. Using his big booted foot, he kicked the door open, sending the chains skittering across the wood floor...

Then he turned and winked at her.

And suddenly, it was clear as glass she was giving herself to Belmont that night. She would find a way to make it good and right. If she didn't seize this magical moment with this phenomenal man, she would regret it until the day she died.

He swept a hand toward the door and bowed, that touch of uncharacteristic smugness still in place, indicating she should precede him inside. "Arrested for trespassing." Pursing her lips, she stepped inside and over the pile of chains. "That's another story I haven't heard for a first date."

"Does coffee and speed dial appeal to you more?" he asked, following her into the gym, dark except for the glowing red exit signs.

"It sounds awful, actually. I'm always waiting for someone to tell me they were kidnapped by pirates," Sage answered, stopping at the edge of the basketball court. "Or maybe they got locked in the public library together overnight and fell in love over their mutual appreciation of encyclopedias."

Belmont picked up her hand and sighed right into the sensitive palm. "Don't hold your breath on that one, Sage."

A laugh tickled up her throat. "Isn't it silly? There's no one here to stop me and I still feel like I need permission to walk out into the middle of the court—"

Sage yipped as Belmont lifted her into his arms and strode forward, stopping when they reached the half court line, right over the Sibley High School logo. She threw back her head, resting it on his bicep as he turned in a slow circle, giving her a 180-degree view of the room. Just as fast as he'd scooped her up, though, Belmont sighed and set her down. "I'm sorry, I wasn't thinking." He stepped back, rubbing his thumb over the crease of his chin. Back and forth, back and forth. "It hasn't been easy to break the habit of picking you up."

"It's okay," Sage managed through her closing throat. "Belmont." She reached out for his hands and pulled him back closer, laying his palms on her cheeks and saying the first things that came to mind. "Don't apologize for doing something you thought was good and helpful. I'm glad we're here together. Doing this."

His voice was murky. "Are you?"

"Yes."

It took them five minutes to get back to the semi-easy place where they'd been existing. But easy was different this time. It took Sage breathing against his thumbs where they framed her face. It took Belmont syncing his own inhales and exhales with hers. The routine was familiar, this place they would go where silence reigned and they just swayed, swayed together, trying to hear each other's heartbeats. Trying to forget there was an outside world with pressures and problems. But the routine had shifted out of necessity since she'd left him standing on the train station platform. It was less about absorbing the weight of each other and more about...learning to exist inside their own weight...together.

The buzz of the exit signs, the melting snow dripping from outside trees onto the gymnasium roof, joined with their steady breaths. And somewhere along the line, they began dancing, although Sage couldn't pinpoint when the slow circles started. Only knew she was facing the door one minute, bleachers the next. Belmont's hands were still curved around her cheeks, so she took his left one and slowly laid it on her hip, twining their fingers together with the other.

CHAPTER SIXTEEN

There were too many things to concentrate on at once and all of them were incredible. He had to keep his feet moving at the right tempo, because he was *dancing with Sage*. His hand itched to squeeze her hip. Same with his other one where she'd captured him with graceful fingers. But he kept his breathing even, swayed her and prayed for a sign that she wanted...just wanted. Like he did.

Belmont's eye muscles started to twinge from closing his eyes so tight, so he forced himself to let go of the tension, his lids remaining hooded. He could only see the curling flyaway hairs over her right ear this way, but he wouldn't be greedy. Their bodies were still a good few inches apart, and Lord knew, the effort it cost him to remain composed had started a blinding ache down in the center of his abdomen.

Her sweet scent had slipped into his bloodstream like

a drug, setting off a potent chemical reaction that didn't know *how* to be satisfied. It knew what appeasement felt like. That careful balance he found when Sage gave it to him. The ability to exist inside his own skin. Relief was something else entirely. It was disrespectful to think of Sage the way his brain threatened to do. Pumping bodies, open mouths, bare legs. Was he beyond resisting those images now? Christ, it seemed he might be.

So he focused on their gripped hands, the cadence of her breath. "When we walked in here, I wanted..." He ground his back teeth when she moved closer, the tips of her breasts pressing into his stomach. "I wanted to give you a dance. Since you'd never been to one."

"Not here, no. Thank you." Sage's voice was thready, but he resisted the urge to pull back and study her face, in case he couldn't stop himself from kissing her. "There is an instructor I hire to teach my brides and grooms how to dance, though. She taught me a little."

His mouth curved. If Sage was being taught something, her forehead would wrinkle, her tongue poking out to the left. He imagined that's how she looked while learning dance steps. "I can tell you've been taught," he murmured. "You're doing great."

"Liar," she breathed. "This...this is nothing like dancing with another woman."

"Good." His hand tightened on her hip and he gave a mental curse. "This is nothing like anything else. For me."

Then he had no choice but to look Sage in the eye, because that was what she wanted. She tilted her head and gave him a dose of hazel. "I've shown you this place," she whispered. "Can I ask *you* something now?"

A crank turned in his middle. He wanted to give her an

unequivocal yes, but in the state of arousal she'd put him in, he didn't know if there was room for him to concentrate on anything else. Apart from maintaining a careful distance, giving her the dance, breathing. "I think so," he said in a rush. "Ask me."

Her eyes traveled over Belmont's face, making him wonder what she saw. "Why haven't you been with a woman, Belmont?"

No. Lord, no. *This* he couldn't handle. He couldn't talk candidly about sex with the woman who'd inspired his starvation and given it a name. "Sage, can you ask me something else?" His cock tented the leg of his pants, hard and thick, so he tilted his lower body away. "Anything else."

"No." She released their joined hands and settled her palm on Belmont's chest, tracing it down, down over his heaving stomach, where it paused. "It's something I need to know right now. If we're going to lie with each other—"

Lie with each other. Belmont surged forward, his rope fraying so dramatically that one single string remained. That string was what kept his arms down at his sides, even while he locked the curves of their necks together. Even while he stopped attempting to hide his erection. "I don't like being vulnerable," he started, his mouth dry. "I've seen…things. Videos. And I know they're acting, but to let yourself be that way in front of another person…that means trusting them." He opened his mouth on her skin, his tongue aching to lick the cords of her neck. "I've never trusted anyone the way I trust you. Not while *wanting* at the same time. And want…*want* isn't the right word for this feeling inside me, Sage."

"What is the right word?"

"Famine," he ground out. "I've been in a famine."

It wasn't right to hand over his pain to Sage again. Again. It was like he couldn't stop, though. She was the only one who understood. And when her right hand traveled down over his belt buckle, her featherlight touch grazing his bulge, Belmont froze, his pulse turning up several octaves in his ears, his blood catching fire. The reassurances he wanted to give her remained trapped in his mouth, even as his mind demanded he issue them. *You don't have to. I'll be fine.* The words wouldn't come out.

"You've waited until you could trust someone. Me." Sage whispered into his hair, the pressure of her hand increasing, her grip shifting until her palm conformed to his straining flesh. "Do you trust me to touch you here?"

"*Anywhere,*" Belmont rasped.

Filling his lungs through a straw, Belmont drove his fingers into Sage's hair and stared down between their bodies, watching as she fondled him through his pants. "My own hand would have been second best. I wanted to wait for yours."

"I'm glad."

Despite the cold of the gymnasium, sweat beaded on his upper lip and he ached to be free of his clothes, exposed to anything and everything, as long as Sage's hand was warming that thick, heavy part of him. His grunts were agonized and harsh, but he couldn't stem their flow, at least not until she started to unfasten his pants. Then he went silent, save his roughened breath. He was very aware that Sage was seeing a man's cock for the first time, so he focused on her face, scrutinizing the play of reactions there. The concentration, the shyness, the lack of confidence—

"You can't hurt me, Sage. You're amazing. Everything you're doing is right." His fingers tightened around the strands of her hair. "And you can stop if you want to."

"No." She lowered his zipper and Belmont bit down on his lower lip until it bled. "I've wanted to touch you this way forever."

He was still in awe over that revelation when Sage reached inside his underwear and took hold of his erection. Euphoria singed his nerve endings. He made a choked noise as his ball sack tightened with such speed, he thought he might spend himself in her hand, just from that one single touch. Paired with her gorgeous mouth falling open, her hazel eyes clouding, holding back was nearly impossible. It had been so long since he'd stroked his own flesh, the very connection of skin on skin caused moisture to crown on the head.

"Belmont," Sage murmured, giving him a firm jack of her fist. "You have to tell me what you like. What feels good."

He was still seeing bursts of light from the first stroke. Having her ask for instruction in that sweet voice almost overwhelmed him. "I haven't... in a while. But I've always gone fast." Holding her gaze so he could spot any signs of doubt, Belmont slipped a hand into his pants and covered Sage's grip with his own. He pushed their joined hands to his base. "Oh, Jesus..." He sucked in a labored breath. "Press down hard when you get to the bottom. I like the way it feels when there's... force there. On my..."

My balls. He couldn't say a word like that to Sage, could he?

"You can say anything in front of me." Their mutual grip glided up, up to his tip, ripping an animal groan from

Belmont's throat. "I like hearing you say these things. It makes me—"

"What?"

His eyes fell and remained riveted on her neckline, where her small breasts shuddered up and down, while their hands increased the pace of their strokes. "I think it makes me want sex."

"Yeah?" The atmosphere started to grow woolen and slow around him, heat building behind his ears, in his throat, at the base of his spine, between his legs. An intense twist spun faster and faster in his stomach like a top. "Are you wet just like last night?"

Her nod was vigorous, along with the pumps of her fist.

"I might die knowing that." *Lord.* She was perfect now, moving in the exact way he needed to get rid of the pain. Where would it land? On her dress? Was he an evil man for liking the idea of her being painted in his lust? His abdominal muscles started to quicken, but he bore down on the oncoming blast of sensation, wanting to prolong the anticipation as long as possible. Who knew when she'd touch him again? It could be hours or days or years.

Words clamored inside his throat, looking for a way out. *I like hearing you say these things*, she'd said. "I think about licking that place where you're wet. Constantly. I think about how much you'll like it, if I do it right."

"You would," she wheezed. "You would do it so right."

A vision robbed him of reason. Sage letting her knees fall open, those shoes with the buckle resting on his shoulders. He'd have to take her panties off. That would be *his* job. The responsibility of making Sage naked from the waist down was what pushed Belmont into the point of no return. Knowing the end was near, he finally stopped avoiding the sight of Sage's pumping hand on his flesh. His head fell forward, his chin burying itself in his chest. And he would never forget it, the slick movements of her white hand climbing and sliding, climbing and sliding down his swollen cock. "I can't hold it in anymore."

"Don't."

Belmont dropped his mouth down to snare hers, wanting to swallow that single word of permission, to show her how grateful it made him, but the kiss turned into more right away. Their lips were coated in steam from hot, rapid breaths and their tongues met without delay. Eager, willing, desperate. She moaned, causing more moisture to seep from his tip...and there was no more waiting. The combination of her incredible mouth, moving in time with her stroking fist, was a heaven he'd never dared dream of.

But he couldn't ruin her dress. She'd put it on for *him*. He could still see her on the top of the porch, pride straightening her back.

Her teeth grazed his tongue and that shock sent searing pressure climbing up his cock. With a strangled shout, he twisted a hand in the hem of Sage's dress and held it high, at the notch of her throat, watching in awe and disbelief as white ropes tugged from his body, striping Sage's smooth, slight curves.

"Jesus, Jesus...*Sage*...I'm all over your belly." He pushed the words out through clenched teeth. "Look how gorgeous you are."

His climax seemed to go on forever and Sage's reaction only made it more potent, more unbelievable. Watching him go over the edge seemed to elevate her to another plane, as well. She was sobbing by the time he finished,

her hazel eyes glassy and unfocused. Her thighs flexed
and chafed against each other, that triangle of sunny yellow cotton at their apex leaving nothing to his fevered
imagination. They were damp with his come, molding
them to her...pussy. He still wasn't sure if he should call
it that, but he knew—he *knew*—that she wanted the same
kind of pleasure she'd just given him. It was there in the
red of her cheekbones, the shuddering of her stomach.

Belmont was never more thankful that he carried a
handkerchief out of habit in his back pocket—usually to
wipe away sweat while working on the boat—because he
needed to help Sage feel good and he couldn't do that until he cleaned her up. Maintaining his hold on her dress
with one hand, he whipped the material free of his back
pocket and wiped away what he'd done. What she'd done
to him. "I didn't want to get your dress." Was this his
voice, so ragged and deep? It belonged inside a nightmare,
but she didn't seem to mind. "Sage, I won't ever let anyone else touch me there. Never. Even if you don't ever
do that again. It was so good...so perfect...and then you
kissed me and I'm yours forever. I just need you to know
that."

"I know, Belmont," she whispered choppily. "I know."
She knows. She knows. Thank God she knows.

* * *

Sage was going to explode.

There had been times on the road trip where she'd been
aroused by Belmont. So many times. Those rare moments
he smiled from the driver's seat, just for her. That morning when she'd spilled hot coffee down her knuckles and

he'd blown on the raw skin, his expression pained. And once when his lips had accidentally brushed her earlobe. Oh yeah, she'd been hot with serious frequency, with no real satisfaction to be had, because the only true way to relief was Belmont. She'd learned that last night.

Maybe last night was the reason her hormones were going wild now. She knew what was possible. Coupled with her front-row seat to Belmont's groaning, shaking orgasm, and having the evidence of it soaking her panties, she was in dire need of touching. Of…mastering.

Belmont finished cleaning her off and they stared at each other, time seeming to pass too fast and too slow, all at once. "I'm keeping this," he rasped, turning the handkerchief inside out and tucking it into his front pocket. Then he fastened himself back into his pants, the movement shifting the veins in his hands. "I don't know if that's something people do. But it's something I'm doing. I'll keep anything that reminds me of you."

"I don't care what other people do." Sage eased the hem of her dress from his fist and let it drop. "Maybe you should cut it down the center and give me the other half."

"I will." His nostrils flared, eyes glazing. "After I use the dry side to wipe my chin of you."

"Belmont."

Her shock was short lived when he swept her up into his arms, marching toward the bleachers. Sage had a feeling there wouldn't be an apology for manhandling her this time. No, there was boldness to him that hadn't been there before. Her doing? Sage's head spun at the possibility her touch had changed him in some way for the better. As she watched his profile, her breath caught at his intensity. His determination. It hardened him even more than usual,

turning his jaw to granite, his arms to unbreakable steel.
"Tell me you trust me to take care of you," Belmont demanded, settling Sage onto the edge of the bleachers, four
tiers off the ground and level with his huge, heaving chest.
"Tell me you know I'll move my tongue around until I
find the right spot. Until I learn."

"I trust you," Sage breathed with zero hesitation. Because it was the truth.

Briefly, his eyes closed. Muttering her name again and
again, Belmont whipped off his coat and laid it down
behind Sage, using their pressed-together foreheads to re-
cline her. Once he'd laid her flat, he seemed to...expand,
his presence growing larger, looming above her. "I've
needed you like this." He trailed his open mouth through
her cleavage, all the way down to her belly. And those
hands—those giant, calloused hands—climbed up her
stockings, pausing at the knees, before traveling higher.
"I've needed you laid out on your back. Needed to hear
your breath and have you watch me, wondering what I'm
going to do. To you." He lifted her dress, gathering the
material around her waist, his gaze riveted on the yellow
fabric between her legs. "Is it still wet?"

"Yes," she managed.

"Not just from what I did..." He kissed the spot where
her belly met the panties. "But from you wanting me,
too?"

"*Yes*, Belmont."

The heel of his palm pressed down on Sage's mound
and every muscle in her body jerked, a half moan, half
gasp flying from her mouth. So he did it again. And again.
Until her hips were lifting off the wooden platform in a
rhythmic dance to meet him. "Can I call it your pussy,

Sage?" His breath fanned the insides of her thighs. "I need to know before I do my job and take off your underwear. Before it tempts me."

His tone, those forbidden words coming from Belmont, caused her stomach and thigh muscles to contract. Hard. "You can call it w-whatever you want."

Those blue eyes locked on hers, from all the way down her body. "I want you to call it satisfied afterwards. That's what I want more than anything."

A groan built in her throat, the urge to speed him along fierce, but she knew better than to rush Belmont. Knew he always delivered, whether he made a person wait for words...or kisses. She stabbed her teeth into her lower lip as Belmont began sliding the panties down her legs with the utmost care, his breath hissing when they reached mid-thigh. He paused for several heavy beats, before ripping them down the remaining distance. "Lord above," he breathed, a split second before he lunged forward and fixed his open mouth over as much of Sage's private flesh as he could manage, his lips stretching wider and rubbing, moving in a circle, opening her folds and spreading her dampness with every hungry movement. "It's sweet," he groaned. "It's so sweet."

"Oh...please..." A tremor moved through Sage's knees and Belmont grasped them without delay, filling her needs like they were his own. His mouth continued to slip through her wetness, exploring, kissing her with stiff lips, as his hands glided down to her ankles, lifting them to rest on his too-broad shoulders. "T-too much. So open."

His lips were shiny when his head came up, his eyelids at half-mast. "Be vulnerable for me, Sage. Sweetest girl. Beautiful, so beautiful down here." He pressed long, lingering kisses on her core, wreaking havoc on her senses. "I'll slow down. Go slower and lick until you want to open your legs even wider. I'm begging you to let me keep you spread. Please. It's hard not to be greedy when you're the best thing I've ever tasted."

By the time his speech ended, her back was arched in lust for his mouth. Had she really meant to close her knees? "Yes, I will. I *will*. Just kiss me there again."

She'd barely finished speaking when Belmont resumed those writhing circles with his lips, reminding her of the way they'd kissed during his orgasm. All-out wet and shameless and starved. Through the haze, she watched his arms flex as they gripped her hips, the muscles shifting in his cheek as his mouth opened and closed, his eyelashes dark on swarthy cheeks. And then his stiff lips closed around her clit and she screamed. Was instantly a mess, yanking his head closer with desperate fingers.

"*Theretheretherethere*," she chanted, bucking on the bleachers. "Don't stop."

His growl into her flesh was one of dark interest. His thumbs dug into her hipbones once, before both hands slid between her bottom and the bleachers, cupping and lifting. He ground her into his enthusiastic mouth, giving her no place to turn but pleasure. Mind-blowing, shaking, moaning pleasure. His sensual attack on her clit went on and on, the entirety of his lower face entering the mix, pushing and sliding and nipping until oblivion rolled through Sage.

"Belmont!"

"Again."

"Bel—"

"*Again. Please.*" His shoulders pressed down, bringing

her ankles up near her ears...and Belmont's tongue sank into her heat, dragging back out with a savoring lick. "*Again*."

He made love to her with his tongue, thrusting it in and twisting his face right and left, before withdrawing it slowly, moaning deep in his throat as he went. The very act of watching Belmont performing an act so sexual would have been enough to push her into a second climax, but she'd lost control of her body at that point, so she didn't have a say. Wave after wave of brutal warmth undulated in her stomach, bringing her hips off the bleachers without a mental command. The image of Belmont winked in and out as her eyes went blind, her screams sounding as if someone else were issuing them far off in the distance.

His long middle finger shoved into her contracting center right when she required the sensation of being filled and pleasure wrung her dry. Her body twisted on the bleachers, feet scrambling on Belmont's back as he grunted and growled against her flesh, that finger pushing deep, deep as it would go until she swore to God, her life began and ended with that single, thick digit. "Good, so *good*...Belmont, I'm..."

He licked her right inner thigh, from the knee to her core. "You're what?"

"I'm satisfied," she murmured, her head lolling on the wood. "You satisfied me."

"Mmmm." Something primal snapped in his eyes, the glow they cast so beautiful she couldn't get a decent breath. It appeared Belmont couldn't, either. He dragged his lower lip through his teeth and removed the handkerchief from his pocket, his gaze never leaving her. She watched through a fevered fog as he wiped the sheen from his mouth, side to side, then ripped the material down the middle with the use of his teeth. "We're two halves of a whole, you and I, Sage. I know there are things we need to work on. Me, mostly. I need work. But I know your heart, sweetest girl. You wouldn't have given yourself over to me like that if you didn't believe. In me. In us." He tucked one half of the handkerchief into her panties, then dragged them up her leg, gently arranging them back in place. "So no more trading places for secrets. Anything you want to know about me, you ask and I'll tell you. I'll tear myself down the middle and let you see it all."

CHAPTER SEVENTEEN

Sage didn't want to sit down in a restaurant, so Belmont went into a Dairy Queen and ordered chicken sandwiches to go. He was simultaneously anxious leaving Sage in the parked car and grateful for ten minutes alone. He needed to retreat into his head and wouldn't have Sage feeling self-conscious over his silence. She seemed to understand. Of course she did, his Sage. *His Sage.* There was no debate on the topic now. He'd come here knowing he'd made mistakes and she was graciously letting him correct them.

God, he loved her. He loved her so much, his bones felt like they were made of liquid as he walked back to the Suburban. His heart hadn't quit jackhammering since they'd left the gymnasium, hand in hand. Relief and fear and elation and determination had made permanent homes in his stomach, taking turns sending signals to his mind. *I love her. There's a chance she'll love me back and make my life worth living. It could actually happen.*

But he was lying by omission to her.

Belmont blew out a shaky breath. He'd never been anything but truthful with Sage. Sure, he continued to reveal his feelings for her in increments, out of worry that the entire thousand-ton magnitude of his obsession could scare her away. Not telling her that come tomorrow morning, he would be leaving for the mine and working off her father's debts for far longer than the two months she'd expected? That was a betrayal of her trust. And it was making him ill.

There was nothing he could do about it, though. He knew enough about Sage's backbone to sense she would dig her heels in. She wouldn't understand that he would face any hell during the day, as long as he had the privilege of holding her at night. And it *would* be hell. Day in and day out. Belmont hadn't allowed himself to consider descending into the darkness tomorrow morning, but with the moment looming close, his nerves were pulling taut. The only thing that would get him through the inundation of memories would be the knowledge that Sage waited on the other side.

God willing, she would still be waiting, once she knew he'd withheld information about her father and Augustine. Just until tomorrow.

His only option was to show Sage he was capable of overcoming the past, so they could have a future. Part of him even looked forward to that intangible point in time when she would smile over her pride in him. Unfortunately, he didn't see a way around just *going in*. Not giving her an opportunity to stop him. Because God knew, if a pleading, tearstained Sage tried to stop him from doing anything and he was forced to deny her, it would rend him in two.

When he opened the driver's side door, Sage smiled over at him shyly and Belmont almost blurted out everything, right then and there. He handed her a chicken sandwich instead.

"Thank you." She started to unwrap the meal and stopped. "I know what you said about no more places and secrets, but I thought we could go see the church. If you wanted to."

"Of course I do." He avoided her gaze, even though he wanted to drink it in, and started the Suburban. "I only meant...that one wasn't required for the other."

"I know." She reached out and touched his shoulder, not nearly as long or as hard as he needed. "I know what you meant and I'm glad. Maybe we just needed some help getting started."

Her soft voice, nightfall, the low of the engine and that teasing fleeting touch of her hand, all worked to seduce Belmont. Already he needed Sage. *Had* needed her before the underwear had been peeled from her body. Her taste was at home on his lips, his tongue swiping at it for a fix every other second. It was as though some kind of Band-Aid had been ripped off his need, revealing how deep the cut she'd made really ran. All the way to his heart. But hell if it didn't detour elsewhere first. Somewhere...insatiable. Somewhere only Sage had ever touched and tempted. Perhaps that was why his lust was so highly concentrated—it had only ever belonged to one woman.

"Is everything all right?" Sage asked, her fingers picking at the foil wrapper of her sandwich. "You haven't said much since we left the school."

He started to hedge, but the words halted in their

inception. There would be no unnecessary lying to Sage. Ever. The necessary one was bad enough. "I'm thinking of having you again," he said, his voice scraping out. "I'll probably be thinking about it constantly now that I know how much you love to come." His face was hot and Sage's chin had dropped, but he forced himself to keep going. "That shouldn't surprise you. I live to make you happy and I've never seen you as happy as when my tongue was between your legs. I want to see you that way as often as possible."

"I like making you happy, too." Her nipples had turned to points, making Belmont's palms itch. "It's harder to tell when you're happy, though. Maybe you could say it out loud?"

"I will," he vowed. "Every time from now on." He reached out and raked his fingers through her hair, tracing her cheekbone with his thumb. "I've satisfied you, Sage. Provided you with food. You're still here. I get more time with you tonight. And you've got a piece of me tucked into your underwear. I doubt I could get much happier than I am right now."

Her wide smile let a flock of birds loose in his chest, but she seemed to catch herself and it dimmed. "You would make me happy if you let me continue working at the mine, the way I planned. I'm stronger than I look, Belmont. I can handle it."

"I can't." He knew she was strong. Not *years'* worth of strong, though. But if he told her about Augie upping the ante, she would try even harder to keep him out of it. So he'd take a different tactic by telling her an alternate truth. One he'd held inside for a long time. "Before we left San Diego, I was getting ready to sign a contract on a second boat. Been working on expanding for a while now."

Her nod was hesitant, as if she didn't understand the abrupt subject change. "I didn't know. That's great, Belmont."

"The business was built for us." He held her gaze, memorizing the sight of her absorbing that. "Maybe if I'd told you sooner that I already spend my days working and planning to make you mine, you wouldn't doubt I can handle what's ahead. It would be a given."

"Belmont," she breathed.

"When I found out you were down there, I almost lost my mind. At least if I take your place, there's a chance I'll stay sane."

Her eyes went glassy. "Thank you for always thinking of me. For caring. But a chance you'll stay sane isn't good enough."

He slid their palms together and squeezed her fingers. It took her a few beats, but she gave him a brave smile. One that made him a bastard for not being truthful. It also told him the argument was far from over.

"Go back through town toward the house," she said quietly. "But turn right on the service road. The church is about a mile down."

Belmont nodded and took his hand back. He ate with one hand as they drove, watching Sage out of the corner of his eye to make sure she finished her meal. The night had gone pitch black by the time they reached the church, and only one flickering streetlight lit the adjacent parking lot. Belmont retrieved a flashlight from the back of the Suburban and helped Sage from the passenger side, pride curling in his middle when she held his hand, so he could lead her up the steps.

Unlike the high school gymnasium, there was nothing

to stop them from gaining entry into the church. The front door eased right open with a tired groan and they walked in, their footfalls sounding hollow as they walked down the aisle together. The impact of leading Sage toward the altar was like a shoehorn trying to wedge between his ribs, but he forced himself to retain the outward appearance of calm.

I'll marry you one day. I'll marry you, Sage Alexander.

Sage released his hand when they reached the end of the aisle. He let her go with a lump in his throat, watching through the thin beam of his flashlight as she slid open a drawer in back of the altar and removed candles, lighting them one by one. The mirrored glass and glossy idols glowed with reflection, illuminating the front of the church.

"You knew those were there," Belmont said, taking Sage's hand to help her back down the stairs. "Did you spend a lot of time here?"

"Not during the day." She sat down in the front pew and he followed suit, watching the flickering flames dance in her eyes. "At night. Like this. When everyone was sleeping, I would come here and decorate. In my mind."

Thinking of her there alone in the darkness made his arms burn with the need to lash out, but he wrapped himself in her voice and relaxed, little by little. "Do it for me now. Tell me how you would make it look for a wedding."

Her lips tripped up. "Who's getting married?"

"Us."

Sage's mouth popped open, her hands twisting in her skirt. Maybe it was too much, maybe he shouldn't have said it, but he wouldn't take it back even if the world were burning. They were the only two people alive in that moment, in this dark, empty church in Sibley, and he would have Sage for his woman, even if it were make believe. "Belmont..." He brought her hand to his mouth, laying a kiss on the inside of her wrist where her pulse beat wildly. "I would, um... I wouldn't marry you here. I would want you near the ocean, where you would be relaxed."

"The ocean." His entire body felt as if it were expanding, his skin warming under an imaginary sun. Time squealed to a halt. Sage was actually talking about marrying him. "Sage, as long as you were with me, I could marry you at the bottom of a well."

She made a harsh sound, turning luminous eyes on him. "You've never mentioned the well."

Look at how she responds when I'm honest. Guilt sank its teeth into his gut once more over what would happen come the morning. "Will you finish telling me about the wedding?"

Sage nodded, her voice going softer than usual, burrowing right into his chest. "It would just be the five of us. The original five that started the road trip. But... Jasper, Elliott, and Grace would be there, too." Mischief twinkled in her eyes. "I would have Rita become certified as a minister so she could perform the ceremony. You're most comfortable with her, so, yes, I think that would be best. And then you would take us out on your boat. No parties or drinking or music... we could just drift. Just drift."

Belmont had to turn his face away so she wouldn't see how affected he was by her words. The vision she'd created. "If we were the kind of people that could turn our backs on this place and leave without looking back, I would give you that tomorrow, Sage. I would give it to you over and over again until the world stopped turning."

"I know," she whispered. "That's why you have to leave, Belmont. This place could very well swallow me back up. The thought of it happening to us both is my greatest fear. You need to go back to the ocean and live for both of us."

She might as well have stabbed him with a dagger. "Do you see and hear and feel me, Sage, but continue to think my leaving is a possibility?"

"No, but I can't seem to stop trying." She blew out a breath. "We might as well say everything out loud, right? You and me, Belmont...there's been a connection since the beginning. It's gotten so strong, I don't know how we would manage apart. We know one another's faults and strengths. We can predict and soothe each other and...we know what might cause the other to self-destruct." Her grip on his hand squeezed tight. "I've been down there and I know what it's like. I can *feel* what it'll do to you."

Lord, how was he supposed to communicate when she was saying the kind of things that would send him to the grave happy? "Sage," he said, trying to keep his voice level. "I've been down there, too. Into the earth. Some of me is still there."

A long silence passed. "Will you tell me about it?"

* * *

Will you tell me about it?

Belmont had known this question was coming. Sage eventually asking about his four days in the defunct well in California had been a small part of the reason he'd begun trading her places for secrets. There had been a pressure building inside him since the first time they met.

There. There was a person he could unburden himself to without being told what needed to come next. Or having his decisions questioned.

Now, though. Now that they were standing at this yawning doorway, he hesitated.

Sage's hand shifted inside his. "If you need more time to talk about it—"

"No." He softened his tone. "No, it's just that I don't like the idea of upsetting you."

A pause. "I'm upset already knowing what happened." He could feel her studying his face, reading him. The connection. "It's worse than I thought?"

Belmont's nod was stiff, his rib cage made of spikes. He took several deep breaths through his nose and battled the urge to drag Sage onto his lap. To band his arms around her so she couldn't move and soak up all her clean, pure energy. "It was a field trip. Aaron's class was going to a farm in Ramona for the day. I asked Miriam if I could call in sick to school and go with him. It was far away and... I just wanted to make sure my brother was all right." His swallow was thick. "I didn't realize until we got on the bus that Lawrence—Aaron's father—had volunteered as a chaperone for the day."

Sage's confusion was tangible. The Clarksons didn't speak of their estranged dad very often. Or maybe they only abstained around Belmont, since he had a different father than the other three. Whatever the reason, Sage clearly hadn't been expecting the man's name to enter the conversation.

The center of Belmont's back heated, knots forming beneath his spine. He couldn't dive straight into the deep end yet. Not yet. "I could tell Aaron wanted to be alone with his father. It was important for him to have that time. So I went off on my own." Sage slid closer and pressed their legs together, hip to knee, giving Belmont some added strength. "I knocked myself out with the fall, so I didn't wake up until it was dark. They were used to me wandering off, same way I do now. They were used to me showing up when I was good and ready. So they weren't looking yet when I started to...call out."

His vocal cords throbbed with the memory of waking up in the pitch black and shouting himself hoarse, the memory of how he'd gotten down there making him question the decision to call out at all. *Maybe I should stay silent?* he could remember thinking.

"There was a baby goat down there. It was still alive, but I think maybe it had been down there for a while. It must have wandered off from the farm." His shrug was tight. Everything was tight. "That's when I really started trying to get someone's attention. But I should have waited until morning, because I lost my voice."

Sage turned and knelt beside him on the pew, throwing her arms as far as they would go around him and holding tight. "I know this part and I hate thinking about it."

"I don't want to upset you."

"Belmont," she burst out into his neck. "This is about you. Not me."

Everything is about you, he wanted to explain, but knew it wasn't the right moment. And Lord, getting out these words that had been sitting on his sternum, making it difficult to breathe for over two decades, was getting easier as he went along. It would be over soon. He just wanted to get it over with so he could get on with comforting Sage. She would need it.

"I could hear them in the distance, but I couldn't get my voice loud enough to get their attention," Belmont continued. "And when the goat died, I didn't try again for a while."

Sage sagged against him and he released her hand, in favor of putting an arm around her waist. "I'm sorry. I'm so sorry."

This was it. There was nothing else lying between the goat dying and rescue, except for a lot of losing consciousness and being thirsty. They'd found him when the farm owner pulled out an older property map that depicted the well, which hadn't been added to the newer set. He'd told her everything, except the main thing.

"There's more, isn't there?" she whispered, kissing his shoulder. "You're so stiff."

"Lawrence pushed me," Belmont shoved through numb lips. "Aaron's father. He followed me while the class was eating lunch." Sage froze like a statue and he ached to hold her, rub warmth into her arms, but the end was so close. No more keeping it inside. "I tried to walk faster, because I knew he didn't like me. I reminded him of Miriam being with someone else. And I think, maybe even still loving that man. My father." He strummed her waist with his thumb. "Every time we were in the same room alone, he would stop smiling and just...stare at me. So I walked faster and eventually I started to run."

Moisture dripped onto his shoulders and rolled into the neckline of his shirt. His Sage was crying, so he rushed through the rest, already searching his pockets for a second handkerchief so he could dry her eyes.

"I can still feel his hands punching into the middle of my back." The right side of his forehead started to throb at the memory of being bashed off hard stone. "I've always wondered if the well actually saved my life, because if I hadn't fallen into it, I think he might've found another way."

By the time he finished, Sage was doing her best to crush him with her small arms. And he just let her, rubbing comforting circles onto every part of her he could reach.

"But Belmont..." Sage's voice was muddled in his hair. "Didn't Lawrence stay in their lives after that happened?"

He nodded. "Only for a while. I tried to be gone whenever he came to pick up the others and...I think Miriam sensed something was off."

"You were only ten." Sage's body shook with a sob. "They would have rallied around you. They would have protected you. Oh *God*—"

"One day, he stopped coming," Belmont said. "And I never wanted that, either. I know what it's like to wonder why your father isn't around. To wonder if you weren't good enough or if you did something wrong. If you were just...*wrong*." His siblings' faces filtered through his mind. "I didn't want that for them. I didn't tell anyone what happened because they deserved that chance I never got with their father. He was decent to them, even if he wasn't to me."

Sage released him and sat back on her folded legs. The candlelight made her tears look like two golden rivers, cascading down her cheeks. Her expression was one of incredulity, which he'd expected, but he hadn't counted on the *love*. She was full to brimming with it, and there was no mistaking the emotion on the person he knew best in the world.

He could almost hear some of the tiny rifts inside him closing up. Sealing tight. He'd never told anyone about Lawrence for a reason. In his mind, he knew his mother and siblings would have been upset by what happened, but maybe his heart hadn't believed it. Not completely. What if he'd been friendlier to Lawrence? What if he hadn't hidden his envy over them having a father well enough and it made the man angry? He knew they would never ask him those questions, but he'd been asking them of himself for years. So much that he'd started to doubt their reactions.

That doubt faded now as Sage's tenderness caged him in. "You're not in danger from him anymore or I don't know what I would do. The unfairness of it will never be all right."

"I don't want them to know, Sage. I never want them to know."

"You didn't even have to tell me that," she whispered. "I already knew. Because you're a man who values everyone's happiness above himself. And that's what makes you the greatest man any of us will ever know. There's never been anyone like you, Belmont. There never will be again. How lucky am I that I get to love you?"

Belmont's heart stopped beating...then it started again in a new rhythm.

CHAPTER EIGHTEEN

For a short measure of time, everything right and wrong with the world collided in one place. Right there, in the first pew, between Sage and Belmont. Right, because she'd just allowed her heart to sing out loud and his expression was breathtaking and fierce and beautifully Belmont. Wrong, because he'd been suffering in silence all by himself.

The scrap of time hovering between them was fragile. So fragile. Because she wanted to cling and croon and cower against the world with him, but it couldn't be that way. Support was a good thing. A *great* thing. But their individual strengths had been lessened by relying too heavily on each other. She'd been there with him, and while it was divine, they were capable of more. Standing on their own foundations and loving each other separately, as well as together. So words were needed first. Understanding. Before they could give in to the pull between them.

"You love me, Sage."

"Yes. *Yes.*"

He turned away with a rough sound and came back. "I've been doing better. I haven't been crowding you as much. Is that why?"

She wanted to dive forward and lay her head in his lap, but she forced herself to remain still. "Love like mine for you doesn't hinge on anything to be true. It just is." His hands were shaking and flexing with the need to reach for her. She could see them and she ached, but clarification was needed first. "I want us to touch and make love, Belmont. I need that."

His chest expanded, dipped, grew larger than before. "Come over here to me. Just come a little closer and I'll hand you everything inside of me."

"I will," she fairly wheezed under the effect of him. "But I need you to know it's not because I feel sorry about the story you just told me. I do. I'll be sad about it forever, straight through until the next life." She searched for the right words. "But I want you to feel my comfort through words. I—I want my hands on you to be about something else, though. Does that make sense?"

"Yes." His voice left no room for doubt. "Need. Not neediness. We'll learn together, Sage."

The confidence in his deep tone bolstered her own. "Look how far we've already come since you came to Sibley. Someday I'll just wrap myself around you whenever I feel like it, without having to worry or explain, like we're doing now. And it'll be okay. Won't it?"

"We'll make it okay." His throat muscles worked. "Thank God there's a way for me to be good for you. Thank God for that."

Gratitude flooded Sage, but it was eclipsed almost immediately by desire so powerful, she fell forward onto her hands and knees, requiring her to crawl to Belmont. There was a heavy moment where they hovered, hovered, right on the brink of touching, before she was in his arms, heat swamping her belly like boiled syrup.

This time was different. In the gymnasium, their touches had been hesitant. That was not the case now. Belmont settled her onto his lap, straddling him. His hands were everywhere at once, sliding over the curves of her bottom, burrowing into her hair. She could barely keep up with the demands of his tongue; he stroked it against hers without ceasing for breath, their lips struggling to be wide enough. But the wicked fervor inside Sage built until she matched Belmont's desperation, scooting close enough on his lap to meet his insistent bulge and riding it, sliding the still-damp cotton of her panties up and down his rigid fly.

"Belmont," she moaned, her head falling back. "I need you now."

"Sage." He clasped Sage's cheeks, his eyes so deep she almost fell into them. "I love you, too. You already knew, right? Tell me you knew every single time I looked at you."

"I knew," she whispered, laying a hard kiss on his sculpted mouth. "But I really don't mind you saying it."

Their laughter was exhilarated, like fizz inside a champagne bottle. "I'm the happiest I've ever been in my life right now. I thought you should know."

"I'm so happy, too." Beneath her, Belmont rocked his hips and they both groaned, teeth gritted. "It's so silly," Sage said, conforming her palms to his muscular chest. "But I w-wish we were somewhere warm so I could…"

"So we could see each other without clothes on." His big hands coasted up her rib cage and covered her breasts, massaging them with reverence. At the juncture of her thighs, his erection swelled, pushing up against her panties. "I want that, too. Your breasts... I haven't seen them yet and I already want them for my last meal. But I wouldn't be able to think straight if you were cold." Leaning forward, he closed his mouth around one of her nipples and sucked hard through the dress, his growl breaking every inch of her out in goose bumps. "Me, on the other hand..."

Belmont sat back in the pew, shrugging off his coat and stripping free of his shirt, buttons popping off and clinking all over the church floor. And then he was bare-chested in front of her for the very first time. If Sage had been thinking lustful thoughts before, they *rioted* through her mind now, overturning buses and setting structure fires. "You can't—" She broke off and started again. "I don't want your shirt off around anyone but me."

He fell back against the pew, a frown marring his features, but there was a quirk on his lips that told Sage he was a touch amused. "I work on a boat, sweetest girl. It comes off now and again."

Oh, she could see that. He was... golden baked and one hundred percent brawn, with moles in strategic places. Like the angels themselves hadn't been able to stop kissing him when he wasn't looking. "I know." Even as she slammed her eyes shut, she reached out and traced the lines of his meaty pectorals with greedy fingertips. "That wasn't even realistic of me—"

His hand locked around her wrist. "The shirt stays on going forward." Keeping her attention, he licked her middle finger from base to tip. "Such a small thing to make the center of my universe happy. You think I wouldn't jump at that chance?"

So they could drown in each other, no matter what, it seemed. "Is there a small thing I could do that would make you happy, Belmont?"

"Happier?"

She ducked her head.

He brought her attention back up. "You could let me button you into those dresses of yours every morning. The ones you wear...especially the bird one. That's my favorite."

"It's my favorite, too," she managed. "You just want to button them up?"

"Yes." He moved in and traced her neckline with his tongue. "At the foot of my bed."

"Okay."

"That's not a small thing, though, Sage." Another drag of that tongue. "It's a huge thing."

Her thighs were beginning to tremble on either side of his hips. "I'll let you do it anyway."

"Because you love me."

"Yes," she whispered, a split second before they dove back toward each other's mouths and consumed, because there was no other description for how they worshiped each other's lips. Their bodies moved so close, they couldn't have been pried apart if God himself had walked down off the altar. Sage felt not an ounce of shame as she pushed Belmont back against the creaking wood of the pew, undulating the softest part of herself over the hardest part of him. Making him shudder and groan into her mouth was the greatest triumph she could imagine, even though she knew Belmont *allowed* her assault. Loved it. Was man enough to let his strength be pinned by a girl half his size.

And she wanted more reaction, more awe, more lust. As much as he could give and as much as she could stand. So with barely a coherent thought, she yanked down the neckline of her dress, the bra beneath. She ended the kiss, leaning back so Belmont could see her topless for the first time, but she only caught a hazy peek of male starvation, before he jackknifed and bent down all in one move, burying his face between her breasts with a choked recitation of her name. "Beauty. You little *beauty*." He turned a matter of inches, rasping his rough cheek over her right nipple...and then he sucked. Sucked her breasts in turn, as though they contained the elixir for eternal life. "You don't know what it did to me, knowing you were one room over. Or one seat behind me in the Suburban. So classy with your legs crossed and your back straight. And all I could think about was the color of your nipples. If they would get redder when I sucked them. I should have been ashamed of myself. By the amount of times I pictured you showering or getting ready for bed. Just one room over. *One room*."

Amazing. Amazing when she'd been so uncertain if he saw her as a woman at all. Turned out, he'd been holding back out of respect. Of course he had, her Belmont. "They're yours now," she murmured, in between gasps for air. *His mouth.* "You can lift up my shirt whenever you want to see."

Sage opened her eyes to find his expression was one of pain, even though his low grunts spoke only of satisfaction. His mouth on her breasts had distracted her mind from his distended flesh, but certainly not her body, since she continued to grind down on him without cease. "Sage..." He groaned, his head pitching to one side. "I don't want to rush you. You feel so perfect on top of me, but that part of me you're moving on, sweetest girl...it hurts. I thought you were making it ache before, but now...watching you moan and hump me—"

"I'm sorry, honey, I'm sorry."

His pain cleared like clouds parting. "Honey?"

"Yeah."

She scooched closer to kiss him and boom—the agony flew back into his expression, the cords in his neck standing out like a road map. "Fuck. Oh, fuck."

Belmont rarely cursed and she loved that about him, but that loss of his composure turned Sage on now. Big time. "Do we need..." Heat bloomed in her cheeks and neck. "I think we n-need protection. Even though it's our first time and all, and—"

His eyes were overflowing with affection when he pressed a finger to her lips. Then his hand dropped to his pocket, taking out a black, square packet with gold writing. "Kiss me while I put it on?" He wet his lower lip like the swing of a hypnotist's watch. Sage planted one hand on Belmont's rock-mountain chest, using her other to help him unzip. The kiss was different this time, more provocative. More baiting. It seemed only right that he close his teeth around her lower lip and hold, while they helped each other roll the latex down to his pulsing root.

"I want you to take your pretty yellow underwear off, but I don't want you to stand up." His voice coasted over her like warm oil. "Tomorrow I'll make sure to buy you more, but right now I'm going to rip them, okay? Because I don't want you anywhere but against me."

"Okay," she managed on a choppy breath. "I don't want to be away, either."

The rip echoed in the silent church. It turned him on. She could see it. His eyes flared, a low sound coming from deep in his throat as he dropped the torn material onto the pew, never taking his attention off her once. "I'm just going to...to tuck the top of it inside you, Sage." Saying the words seemed to undo him, his eyes squeezing shut. "After that, it'll be up to you how much to take. And how much time you need. I won't rush you. Even if it looks like I'm hurting or frustrated, you don't rush. Okay?"

"Yes, Belmont." Both of them held their breath as the thick head of Belmont's erection slid inside her entrance, making a wet, slippery sound between them. As soon as those first couple inches were inside Sage, Belmont's hands flew out to the sides, gripping the pew behind him, stretching and flexing the muscles of his powerful chest. Having him inside her, watching the display of male beauty up close, made Sage start panting, triggered her heart into a gallop. "It feels so good." She reached down and circled his hardness, rolling her hips forward to take another length of flesh inside her. "You...do you have any idea how much I want you?" She breathed. "I don't even think I knew what that meant until right now."

A bead of sweat rolled down the side of his face, his teeth were cinched together, that massive chest was *heaving*. "Explain it to m-me."

The feminine thrill quivered in Sage's belly, sparking out to her limbs. She was on top. She was in control.

Tonight wasn't about her, it was about both of them, but her words, her movements were bringing him pleasure. The encouragement in his eyes to free the secrets she'd been keeping, both mental and physical…it broke an undiscovered part of her loose.

Sage dug her fingernails into the meat of Belmont's shoulders, loving his satisfied grunt. "You're so hot," she murmured against his mouth. "You're so huge and hot and you don't even realize it. Some mornings, when you follow me to get coffee and you've got the car keys in your hand…you look like the master of the world. And I've wanted you to…"

"*What?*" he prompted hoarsely. "*Tell me.*"

She pressed herself down, taking another two inches of his erection, stopping just at the point of pain, his strangled groan splitting the air. "I've wanted you…to want to…fuck me."

"Sage," Belmont ground out, surging forward. He wrapped a forearm around her back and those muscles strained, as if he wanted to yank her the final distance onto his arousal, but just managed to restrain himself. "I've wanted that, too, but I can't do that—"

"Will you say it?"

"I can't fuck you—" His body shuddered hard. "Not like I want to. Not the first time."

"I know," she said, rubbing their lips together. "But you want to."

"Yes. *Yes.*" The forearm around the small of her back dragged lower, his palm closing around the left cheek of her bottom. "But, no. No extra pain for my Sage. I'll die first."

"Just a little?" she whispered, barely aware of what she

was going to ask, until the question was out. "Just a little. I want to remember you taking it." *My virginity.* "I want to remember exactly how it felt when—"

"When I push all the way in, Sage?" His hand turned to a fist on her backside, the opposite one making the pew groan within its grip. "I'm only halfway in right now and you're already trying to close your thighs on me." His gaze danced over every bit of her face. "Do you really know what you're asking for?"

"Yes." Her fingertips skated up his chest and neck, tangling in his hair. "Belmont, *please.*"

Sage was on her back within seconds, the wood creaking beneath her. Belmont's size was too substantial for the pew, so looming above her, he braced a knee on the wood and one foot on the floor, both of Sage's legs still spread around his waist. "I love you. God help me. I love you. *God*—" With a bitten off growl, he thrust the remainder of his thick flesh into Sage, resting their foreheads together and keeping their gazes fastened. "I love you. I love you. How can you feel this good? I love you."

She was so mesmerized by Belmont's intensity, she almost forgot about the shock of discomfort. Somehow in the low candlelight, the blue of his eyes blazed, every emotion known to mankind taking turns swimming in their depths. His hair fell all around his face, obscuring some of the beauty, and Sage frantically attempted to push it back, not wanting any part of him hidden. "I love you, too," she whimpered. "It doesn't hurt when you're looking at me."

"Then I won't stop."

"Don't." Sage shifted her hips and their moans crashed together. "Don't stop."

What came next was what Sage had been dreaming about in heated snippets for as long as she'd known the man so intimately connected with her body. Belmont's hold on his control weakened just a touch, the animal eclipsing the man, and her body became the object of his lust. Flesh that he couldn't stop himself from possessing in a base, fundamental way.

His face found the crook of her neck, a place to groan her name as he pumped, pumped, sliding her a short distance up the pew, before dragging her back and entering her harder, faster. He held her down the way a man clings to his final day on earth and Sage gloried in it. She opened her thighs as far as the bench would allow, dug her nails into his backside and urged him on, memorizing his harried words of gratitude and praise and rapture.

"Am I hurting you, Sage?" He near shouted, even as he pushed her knee higher, giving himself an angle that made his jaw go slack. "*Jesus*. It's just that you're so small inside here. I've never...there's nothing else this tight. I can't believe how you feel."

That's when she finally managed to stop marveling at the man moving inside her and focused on how it felt. Good. The answer was good...at first. He was all smooth and sleek, reaching places that were untouched only moments before. Absently, she decided to watch Belmont operate his boat at the first opportunity, to witness the way he moved, because she'd had no idea. No clue he could roll so fluidly, his hips slowing and angling and maintaining such a wicked cant. And then he found the right place to rub and all coherent thought turned to mist.

"Oh. Oh, there. Right there." Her back arched all on its own. "The way you're sliding on me."

His sudden focus zapped like an electrical surge, his scrutiny fell over her like a blanket. "I'm not moving. I'll stay right here."

"Please."

"You don't have to say *please* to me, sweetest girl." Belmont's hair was draping down on either side of his face again, so she could only see the way he bore down on that bottom lip with white teeth, only catch the occasional glimpses of hot blue eyes, but her hands were too busy clinging to his thrusting bottom to tuck the strands behind his ears. "You have no idea, Sage. No idea what it's doing to me...knowing I can make you feel good this way. Look at you. Do you want me to fuck you harder now?"

"Y-yes. Keep going." *Ohh.* Oh, the part of him just beneath the latex was grinding on her clit. So good. So *amazing.* She was still so sensitive there from his mouth, and every slick ride of his hips was building that firestorm again. Watching Belmont's tongue lick at her had pushed her past the breaking point last time, but now his clenching abdomen muscles, his rough-cut, straining arms, and that connection—that connection that *boomed* between them—were the light show she couldn't stop staring at. And this was her man, forever, till death, and no one had ever touched the flesh he drove into her. Harder and harder, while his breath grew shorter, her name on his lips getting more biting and desperate. As he twisted his hips and cursed, dragging his steel erection sideways over that bud—

Sage shot through the atmosphere to a place that didn't allow for breathing or thinking. She hung there as the most immense pleasure she'd ever experienced pierced the lower half of her body, contracting every available muscle and wringing, wringing her out like a sponge as she screamed.

"Belmont."

"I'm here," he rumbled, his voice like a revolution of a tornado. It was right in her ear, his breath funneling right into her mind, where she needed it.

His body was poised to snap and she responded automatically, frantic to ease her mate, undulating her hips and encouraging him to break with her. Which he did... in the most beautiful, monstrous way. She could only cling and accept as Belmont bore down, her back squeaking on the pew as he pumped, pinning her to the creaking wood one final time and shouting her name into the dark church.

"Sage."

His giant frame quaked, his face screwed up in the same blissful agony she'd just experienced. It seemed to go on for hours and she wished it would. Could have lain beneath this man and watched the orgasm gut him forever, knowing she'd been the one to share it with him. But when he fell forward and gathered her close, she amended that wish. There was nothing better in the entire world than being held by Belmont.

"Sweetest girl," he said into her hair, his voice made of gravel. "I need you. I need you."

"You have me." She kissed his cheek, his chin. "I'm right here."

"Forever, though." He pushed up on one elbow and found her eyes with his own. "You asked what a day is like for me. I never want a day like that again. When I call you, I need you to know it's me on the other end, because you know my breath so well. I need to share the tide with you in the morning and the night. I think maybe I have been, even when you weren't there. Let's not face days alone when we can face them together, Sage. Promise me that's possible."

Sage couldn't predict the future. Monday morning—the coming months—were so uncertain. Would Belmont force his way past her resolve and into the mine? Or would she find a way to block him? There were no answers tonight, though, except the one in her heart. Her life was intertwined with this man's. Looking down at her, he *was* past, present, future. So she couldn't deny his request to face their days together. Wouldn't they always share the tide together, whether they were beside each other or apart? In the moment, nothing was more certain. "I promise."

His answering smile told her it was the right answer. That they would be fine.

Amazing how a few hours could change everything.

CHAPTER NINETEEN

Sage was asleep in the passenger seat when they arrived at the cottage.

Something about her exhaustion made him prideful, but he didn't appreciate having that reaction, so he forced it aside. He should be grateful. Yes, God knew he was that. To have a woman hold his hand and walk from the church with him so trustingly, allowing him the honor of buckling her into the seat, meant cherishing that duty. Not being boastful about sating her to the point of sleep.

Although it was difficult not to... enjoy how boneless she looked. The times he'd allowed himself to imagine pressing his cock into Sage, shame had come along for the ride. But she'd set him free of it tonight, and the result had been indescribable. He'd never known she could *speak* that way. Or force him to abandon his restraint. He loved it. A corner of Belmont's mouth ticked up when he realized he could still feel the nail marks in his ass. And he gave in, allowing himself a few beats of satisfaction for pleasing his woman. Thank Christ for that.

She'd given him even more than her body, though. Some of the ugly demons that were inside him when they walked into the church had been banished by the time they left. He wasn't fooling himself into thinking the mine would be easy to surmount. It wouldn't. Already the clock was beginning to tick loudly in his ears, counting down to tomorrow morning. But he'd go in knowing Sage loved him. If anything could help him face what lay ahead, it was that.

He climbed out of the Suburban, trying to be as quiet as possible shutting the driver's side door. He rounded the front fender, his blood pumping with the excitement of carrying Sage to bed. Laying her down in the sheets and removing her shoes, setting them in a place she could find them easily in the morning. His body weight would weigh down the mattress and wake her up, so he'd find a chair or bed down on the ground, like he did sometimes on the boat during a long job.

Just before he reached the passenger side, he stopped, staring at Sage through the glass. This was it. The last remaining hours before tomorrow crashed down on them. She didn't even know they'd been robbed of a day yet, and his throat wanted to cave in just knowing that. She was probably counting on the extra twenty-four hours to talk him out of going into the mine. Or maybe she'd accepted there was no way to stop him. Either way, he wasn't giving her that chance, was he?

Belmont rested his hands on the hood of the Suburban and breathed, battling the urge to climb back into the driver's side and speed both of them straight out of the town. A man was putting him down in the earth tomorrow, same way another man had shoved him into that well; they were just using different methods. He loathed another person having that leverage on him and Sage. But he would work and fight until they could see their way out of it.

His resolve was firm, but with only hours to go, he could do nothing to keep the blackness from drifting close, trying to surround and swallow him. Even with Sage asleep, he wouldn't violate this new understanding between them. Wouldn't take her comfort unless it was right. They weren't there just yet. So he paced around the Suburban until the disquiet went away and he could lift Sage from the passenger seat with the intention of letting her go.

When he eased Sage down onto the sheets and lit the hearth, Belmont fulfilled the dream of taking off her coat and shoes, covering her with the blanket, and stepping back. Marveling over the perfection of the woman who claimed to love him. *Him.* Someday he would sleep beside her, holding her through dreams and nightmares alike. But it wouldn't be until the secrets were gone between them. Until then, he wouldn't allow himself the joy.

Belmont paused at the doorway, swallowing the fist in his throat as he took a long look at Sage. And went to go face his hell.

* * *

Sage woke with a muffled gasp into her pillow.

She was warm, but she didn't feel safe. That made no sense, because Belmont would be nearby. If not in bed with her, he would be outside in the Suburban.

Trying to dismiss the cold dread building in her breast, she pushed up on one elbow and surveyed the room. Embers were glowing in the hearth and her shoes were arranged in front of it neatly, her stockings rolled up and tucked inside. But there was no Belmont.

Why was she panicking? She'd had the dream again, about Belmont walking into the darkness, but that was nothing new. The dream had been recurring for weeks. Maybe the story he'd told her last night had left her feeling unsettled. Yes, that had to be it. It would leave anyone feeling adrift, sorrowful for the boy who'd endured so much unnecessary fear at the hands of a grown-up he should have been able to trust. Her heart would never stop aching over how succinctly he'd told the story, as if he wasn't owed any sympathy. As if a grave injustice hadn't been done, the people he loved going on with their lives none the wiser, while Belmont suffered in silence.

No more. She wouldn't let him relive those four days again.

How to prevent him from taking her place at the mine, though? Belmont had never been capable of denying her anything, so she knew what it meant that he'd stood firm through all her pleading. There *was* no changing his mind. But what if she could change Augie's?

Last night, while Belmont told the story of being pushed into the well, then keeping it from his family, Sage had been too horrified to think of anything but his pain. But now, replaying his words, she saw her own plight much clearer. Belmont didn't deserve to carry the burden of what Lawrence did to him. Didn't deserve to feel guilt over potentially ruining the man's relationship with his children. But he couldn't see that.

The same way Sage couldn't stop beating herself up over leaving her parents.

Belmont had earned peace and happiness. Did that mean she'd earned it, too, by caring for Thomas and Bernie so long? Yes, she thought it might. They loved each other. *Love.* She'd watched it overcome so many obstacles on this road trip...and there was no love stronger than the one between her and Belmont. The squeezing organ in her chest told her so. Her sense of responsibility wouldn't desert her, however.

So what was the solution? Her parents needed support and Augie wanted his pound of flesh. Was there a way to manage both? If she could arrange a payment plan—with interest—to be fulfilled from California, they would eventually pay off the balance of her father's two remaining months in the mine. And she would send them money, whatever it took, to keep her place with Belmont in the sun. Just the possibility of going back to San Diego, something she'd never thought she'd do again, filled her with warmth. She and Belmont both deserved to be happy...and they wouldn't be happy without each other. Nor would they be happy in Sibley. So she would once again go to the devil and plead her case. She couldn't fail—she wouldn't—because this time she was bargaining for Belmont's life.

Feeling determined, Sage turned over and slung her legs over the side of the bed, anxious to lay eyes on Belmont. To...touch him. There was some discomfort between her legs where he'd been last night. For some reason, she wanted to tell him about it. Was that silly? This sudden need to confide the secrets of her body in him? She didn't know. And she didn't care, either. There was no room for doubt between them after last night. He loved her. She loved him. Everything was going to fall into place around that irrevocable fact.

"Belmont?" Sage called, pushing the fall of hair back over her shoulder. She listened for a moment and heard nothing but the drip of morning dew on the windowpane, the rush of wind outside. Again, the foreboding tried to form fog in her stomach, but she shook it off. Maybe he'd gone into town for breakfast. He would know she needed coffee first thing in the morning—it was her routine. And his routine was taking care of people. Her.

I'm going to take care of him, too.

Sage changed into her clothes, dragging the stockings up the sensitized skin of her legs, tugging a gray, long-sleeved trapeze dress over her head. And with a smile tickling her lips, she pushed open the door of the cottage—

An unfamiliar vehicle sat where the Suburban had been last night. It was a forest green SUV with shiny chrome wheels and a gold cross hanging in the window. And she knew. She knew to whom the vehicle belonged.

"About time you woke up," Augie said to her left.

Sage's head whipped around so fast, pain shot straight up the side of her neck. She braced herself on the door frame so she wouldn't collapse under the rush of denial and confusion. "What are you doing here?"

Augie leaned back against the front bumper of his car. "You and your boyfriend seem to be under the impression I have to explain myself." His smile was devoid of humor. "I don't. About time you both knew it."

"My boyfriend…"

She didn't like the way he sounded so familiar with Belmont when they'd spent all of two minutes in each other's presence. And she especially didn't like the casual way Augie perused her body, as if she were wearing a bathing suit instead of a dress and stockings. "Something tells me the prediction I made about you being grateful last night proved correct."

What was he talking about? The hair on Sage's neck was standing straight up. "He'll be back here any minute." She started to inch back inside, intending to lock the door and power up her cell phone to call the police, but Augie's next words made her freeze.

"No, he won't." He sucked air through his teeth. "Training at the mine doesn't let out until supper time, little Sage. You know that."

"He's not at the mine," she responded automatically, because her brain skipped reason and went directly into denial. There might not be any good reason for Augie to lie about Belmont being at the mine, when she could easily confirm otherwise, but Belmont wouldn't *do* that to her. He wouldn't leave without an explanation. "He'll be back any minute."

Augie laughed. Long and hard enough to make Sage think she might vomit. "Why don't you come out here and I'll tell you a little story?"

She shook her head. It was all she could manage.

"Suit yourself," Augie said on a smug sigh. "When I paid your man a visit at the motel yesterday, I had a feeling he wouldn't tell you."

"Tell me what?" she croaked.

"Your daddy did it again." He crossed his heels, left over right. "Spent all his hard-earned money on booze and cigarettes, without leaving a dime for the mortgage. Or your mother." He said the last word with a sneer, such breathtaking hatred in his eyes, Sage didn't bother trying to keep the dread at bay any longer. "You know, everyone in this town hates me until they need to be bailed out. Including you. Isn't that right? *Little* Sage."

Nausea built in her belly, splinters digging into her palms from gripping the door frame so hard. "Whatever it is, just tell me," she wheezed. "I don't have time for a speech. I have to go get Belmont."

Augie tilted his head. "You'll need to go pretty deep down into the mine to reach him. And seeing as how you're not an employee anymore, I don't think I can allow that."

The air crackled around her ears. No. He had to be lying. The devil was a liar, wasn't he? "Stop," she near shouted. "Stop this. He can't be in there."

She tried to rein herself in when it was obvious Augie was enjoying her distress, but her knees were threatening to buckle. "Your daddy owes enough to keep Mr. Clarkson busting his hump for another three years," Augie said, delivering the final blow. "He looked a mite shaky heading in this morning, I must say."

"No…" The world tipped sideways. Had her father really been prepared to let her spend three years in that dark hell? "Two months. It was only supposed to be two months." Sage gave in and sat down, her feet hanging over the ledge and sticking in the dirt. Shaky. Belmont had looked shaky. *Oh God no.* He'd known about the added debt and hadn't told her. He'd just gone and gotten started serving her penance. The vision from her nightmare was real.

"Chin up, now. I know when a man is easily broken, and he won't be one of them." His teeth shone white when he smiled. Too white. "Not without a little effort on my part. And something tells me he won't turn down all the overtime I aim to offer him."

"What do you want?" With a great effort, Sage lifted her head. "You didn't just come here to taunt me. What do you want?"

"Smart girl," Augie murmured, his sticky gaze running down her legs and back up. "Pretty girl, too. You might not walk around with all the trappings, but you resemble your mother in the ways that count."

Invisible ants crawled over Sage's skin, and if Belmont didn't need her, she would have prayed for numbness. Gone back into the cottage, lain down, and screamed into her pillow. But he did need her. At that very moment, he was suffering. She could sense it, like he was right there, whispering in her ear. God, she would give anything for that to be true.

"Yes, you sure are a smart girl, little Sage, so I won't insult your intelligence by pretending I don't have a serious quarrel with your parents." Red suffused his face. "They don't just use me whenever they fall on hard times. No. They've *taunted* me. Acting so goddamn happy even though they live like two pigs in shit. I could have given her anything she wanted, and she chose a lousy drunk who can't even perform his job right. A fucking *waste*."

"I'm sorry," she found herself saying, even though it pained her. "I'm sorry you were hurt by their actions, but so was I. I just want this over."

"Too bad, girl. You've put yourself in the thick of it." Augie pushed off the bumper and came to stand a few feet away. "You came to me for help. For a *solution*. You're just like them deep down and you'll be treated thusly."

Renewed guilt and an awful sense of foreboding made her muscles stiffen. "How so?"

His wing-tip shoes crunched on the earth as he shifted. "They made a fool out of me in front of this town.

Laughed in my face along with everyone else. So I worked and saved and made myself respectable. Something your father will never be. And she still didn't want me. Everyone knew it. The people of my town." He swiped a hand over his mouth. "Now I'll make fools out of them. You want your boyfriend out of the mine for good? You want me to sign off on Daddy's pension? You'll be my wife. We'll see who's laughing then."

The irony wasn't lost on either of them when a laugh broke from Sage's throat, hysterical and sad, all at once. "I wouldn't marry you if we were the last two people on earth."

"We'll see about that, won't we?"

When Augie turned on a heel and started to leave, Sage shot to her feet. "Wait." She raked nervous fingers through her hair. "I was going to come to you this morning—"

"Shocking."

"I was going to ask about a payment arrangement," she continued without breaking. "I have a good job back in San Diego and I'll pay back every cent he owes, with interest."

It even sounded lame to her ears, but more so when Augie only snorted in response. "Even if you could guarantee he won't come crawling to me for another loan, Sage, we both know this doesn't really have anything to do with money."

Sage stared after the SUV in horror as it backed down the path.

* * *

Belmont shoved the squishy orange earplugs into his ears, praying they would drown out the noise. Not the sounds of the underground machines he was training on. It wasn't the droning engine that was bothering him. His own boat motor back in California was equally loud. That familiarity was the only thing keeping his head from exploding.

No, it was the voices. The search party calling his name from a football field away. The tinny sounds blasted around his skull like rebounding bullets, breaking chunks of bone free so they rattled around. And then there was the soft scratching of the goat hooves at his injured leg, the soft whines of hunger. The dark. He'd never been anywhere as dark as it had been in the well at night. Even though there were spotlights and helmet lamps illuminating the mine, spots floated in his vision, trying to block them out.

The white walls he dug into looked like stone in the near-darkness, closing in on him, backing up, constricting tight again until he swore they were beating, like his erratic heart.

Sage. Think of Sage.

Belmont took a deep breath and closed his eyes, imagining her as she'd been lying in the bed last night, her hands tucked beneath her chin. In his mind's eye, she sat up and stretched, holding out her arms to him. And he pounced. He pounced and pinned her down, using her hair to angle her head, so he could bury his face in her neck. *Belmont, you're smothering me.* Bad. That was bad for her. He needed to stop thinking about the relief of having her crushed so tight to his chest. How he would draw on her warmth. How he wouldn't let her go until he was ready. Until he calmed.

No. No…he'd only been down in the mine for an hour, and already, he was sliding back on the algae-coated rocks. His pulse was haywire, spiking every time the walls closed in. A pounding had begun in the dead center of his forehead, like someone had stabbed him there with an icepick. He banished the image of Sage because using her, even with his mind, felt like a betrayal of her trust. And then he was left with nothing.

Nothing but the black. No way to breathe. His lungs were burning. His vocal cords, too. And they kept calling his name from too far away. He opened his mouth to shout back, but snapped his lips closed again before a sound emerged. Maybe he was meant to be down here. Two father figures had decided his life meant nothing and sometimes it *seemed* like nothing. He'd never been enough for his mother when she cried. Over the man who hadn't wanted him. The big, awkward one that didn't have the right words. The one that had different blood.

There was the scratching again at his leg and he kept quiet, so he wouldn't startle the animal again. Sage tried to climb onto his lap and offer herself, but he shook his head.

"No, Sage. No."

Belmont opened his eyes again and dragged in a breath, just in time for the walls to creep closer. Closer. The machinery juddered in his hands and he focused on the burn in his muscles, the smell of oil and exhaust. And he let himself drift into the darkness.

CHAPTER TWENTY

When Belmont arrived back at the motel that evening, Sage was waiting. Any hope she'd harbored over him conquering the mine was lost. He was a dead man walking. Such a contradiction in a man so alive, so teeming with energy and might. Every inch of him was the same robust maleness she knew like the back of her hand, but his eyes? They were dead. A dead sea of blue.

Unable to gain entry to the work zone any longer, she'd been sitting on the curb outside the motel's rental office since that morning, counting the seconds until he returned. Alternating between praying and cursing fate. Cursing her *father*. Being angry with Belmont for not telling her he'd met with Augie...and loving him through the sweep of every emotion.

That never ceased for a moment. No, it only grew stronger.

Now, she straightened on her feet, heart slamming in

her throat. Climbing out of the Suburban, Belmont was covered in white chalky debris and a mixture of dried sweat and dirt. Apart from the initial head-to-toe slide of his gaze, Belmont didn't look at her once as he walked toward his designated room. Or he did, but his stare went right through her, not really seeing. Not like he usually did, in that piercing, all-knowing way.

And she knew, right then. She knew it couldn't go on.

Hope tried to peek through again when Belmont paused at the door, cutting his gaze in her direction. "Do you need a ride home?"

His cold tone of voice fractured her heart down the middle. "No. No, I'm going to stay here with you."

"Not tonight." His tone left no room for argument. "It's not a good idea."

Realizing they were talking to each other from thirty yards away, Sage closed the distance between them, refusing to stop when alarm flared in his eyes. "Why isn't it a good idea?"

Belmont didn't answer her question. "I think it might be better if you stayed away for a while, Sage." He slowly flattened a palm on the door, as if it were the only thing keeping him standing. "Starting now. I need you to go."

Horrible pressure expanded in her throat. "I'm not going to do that." She ached to reach out and touch him, but if he rejected the gesture, it would kill her. "You should have told me Augie came to see you. We could have figured this all out together."

"There is nothing to figure out." He wasn't...Belmont in that moment. This closed-off man, speaking to her through clenched teeth, was not the man she knew so well. "Just give me a minute and I'll drive you home."

"Stop this," she pleaded with him. "Can't you look at me? *Please.*"

His head turned and Sage fell back a step. There was hell in his eyes. The kind she hadn't even known to be afraid of. She'd expected him to come out of the mine uncommunicative. For him to be back in the dark place he'd always been so hesitant to speak about. It was why she'd tried to keep him out of the mine in the first place. But she hadn't expected chaos. "I'm always looking at you, Sage. I never take my eyes off you." A line slashed down between his brows. "Don't you ever get tired of it?"

She was already shaking her head. "No."

A breath rushed out of him. "Please, just go. Nothing good is going to come from you being here right now."

"You're wrong," she insisted. "Nothing good comes from us being apart. Not now. I was wrong to get on the train and leave you. We should have worked through everything together. We've proven we can." Desperation forced her to play dirty. "Remember what it was like to be apart? How awful it was?"

"*Remember?* Do I remember not knowing where you were for two days and not being able to eat or sleep or think?" His laugh was barren. "Yes, I remember. I'll probably have nightmares about it for the rest of my life."

Sage tried to soothe him with a *shhh* through icy lips, but it emerged sounding awkward. She stepped closer and Belmont stilled in the process of turning the key in the lock. "Belmont, let me come inside and we'll talk."

"Please, sweetest girl..." He banged a fist on the door. "I don't have that kind of effort in me right now. We comfort with words. We comfort one another with *words* first, hands second. You can say it and I can repeat it a thousand times and it doesn't make me any more capable of keeping my hands off you when I'm feeling like this."

Her lungs emptied and yes, they weren't in a healthy place for the kind of touching her body suddenly craved, but the chemical reaction was defiant. Moisture made the flesh at the juncture of her thighs slick, her tongue thick with the need to tell him he'd made her sore. And that she'd liked being sore from him all day. Since returning to Sibley, she'd fought mightily to subdue her end of the dependency, but it woke up now. It sat up and saw its mate. All that soothing reassurance was hers for the taking. They were in a weak moment and it would be so easy to slip into that deep, quiet place. Let them hold and rock each other, drowning each other in wordless pity. Biting down hard on her bottom lip, Sage waited for the impulse to pass. Until it was manageable. "Belmont, we're not going to separate every time one of us feels overwhelmed, are we? That's not good, either."

"I just need time. Just give me some time." His hands were flexing and releasing on the door. "The longer you stand there, the harder it is to..."

Maybe she was tempting disaster by positioning herself against his warmth, by prompting more of an explanation, but she couldn't just let Belmont shut himself up in the room while anarchy rioted in his eyes. "The harder it is to what?"

Belmont didn't answer. He didn't need to. Maybe deep down, Sage had known all along that he was going to erupt sooner or later, but she'd been unable to stop it. Or allow him to go through it alone. Really, how could such a passionate human being remain quiet, keeping so much inside for years, without an explosion taking place? She should have seen it coming.

He kicked open the motel room door with a booted foot, the wood smashing off the opposite wall, splinters arcing to the floor. Sage barely had time to prepare before Belmont dragged her into the dark room behind him.

When he pressed her up against the door, Sage could admit to a thrill of excitement at having his huge body molded to her own, ashamed of it though she was. No. Yes. *No.* This was what they'd been working against. What she'd run away from. This way they could fade from separate people into a team of enablers in mere seconds, trading their problems for solace, without solving them first. His arms were banded around her so tight, those sounds of relief and agony so potent in Sage's ear, her vision blurred, her blood slowing. Their hearts boomed up against each other like two battering rams. *Just this once...just this—*

Belmont's hands hooked beneath her knees and slung them high, up around his hips, that rough mouth of his already attacking her neck, sucking it, raking his teeth beneath her earlobe. His erection was stiff and ready against the inside of her thigh, his hips working to thrust it higher, up toward the sore area between her legs.

Different. This was...other.

That's when she understood the root of the problem. Why she shouldn't have pushed Belmont into bringing her inside. They'd managed to separate the new loving part of their relationship from the dependent part. But right now the lines were blurring. They were losing sight of the boundaries they'd made out of necessity. He wasn't holding her like a coveted relic, the way he'd done once upon a time. Nor was he focused on giving them both physical release.

He was doing both.

Two other people might have gone down this path without looking back, but Sage knew in her heart of hearts, it led to *their* ruin. Her body didn't care about that foresight, though. It was hungry for the man, the unleashed strength being channeled through sex and frustration and dependency.

She wasn't even aware of Belmont unpinning her from the door, turning for the bed. Her back hit the mattress and he landed atop her, giving an eager thrust between her legs, her body excitedly accepting it. Common sense leaked out along with her equilibrium, soaking into the scratchy comforter. This was her drug. Being needed by Belmont. In return, he absorbed her guilt, placing her back on that pedestal. Making her the faultless woman she knew—and rationally, he now knew—that she wasn't.

They were fulfilling each other's needs in the wrong way, though. Did it matter? Yes, it mattered. It mattered, but he felt so *incredible*. His hands scraped up the outsides of her thighs, moving her skirt out of the way and hooking dirty fingers in the sides of her panties. He'd sacrificed his sanity for her and she could temporarily make him coherent again if she just gave in. If she unzipped his jeans and urged him on...

"Sage." He licked a path from one side of her cleavage to the other, burrowing his mouth between her breasts. "You wouldn't leave. What am I going to do? I can't let you go now. I don't know how."

Clarity tried to break through Sage's desire, but then his teeth were ripping the bodice of her dress down the center. Everything tightened below her waist, her nipples turning to aching peaks. Without a command, her hands threw themselves up over her head, a symbol of abandon, because what choice did she have?

Belmont tore open her dress from both sides, feasting on her breasts, her belly, with a frantic mouth. "I'll lose myself in my woman's body," he gritted against her right nipple, before raking his teeth on it lightly. "I'll take her with me everywhere. I'll never be without her. She'll never be without me."

His open mouth skated down over her belly, his hardened lips clamping around her femininity...and that shock of pleasure, his accompanying growl, told Sage they were at the point of no return. Maybe they'd already gone speeding over that line. Belmont was licking her through the cotton material, positioning her knees up near her elbows. And his words. They would never be without each other...she couldn't stop hearing them. On the surface, they were divine. She wanted that future. But the underlying meaning couldn't be ignored. They were feeding their dependent natures and it was bad. Bad for both of them.

Moisture leaked out of the corners of Sage's eyes, because she could already sense the difficulty of putting a stop to this. She would have made him forget his demons for a while, but then they'd be back to square one. Giving in would hurt him worse in the long run.

"Stop, Belmont." She blew a shuddering breath toward the ceiling. "We have to stop."

"No...no." He yanked her panties to the side, slipping his stiff tongue through her folds, and Sage's middle arched off the bed, lust climbing her thighs like vines. "I'll make you need it. Make you need me."

"I *do* need you, but not like this." She twisted her fingers around the wild, dirty strands of his hair and pulled him away. "Look at me. My eyes, Bel—"

With a haunted expression, he surged up, pinning Sage's arms above her head. "I am looking at you," he rasped, sounding out of breath. "I'm looking at the only thing that makes me forget." He reached a hand down between their bodies and unfastened his jeans. "Help me forget, Sage."

His despair stabbed her right in the center of her chest, because she shared it. It was theirs. They'd been born with corresponding needs that screamed out for each other, magnetic and undeniable. But deny it she must. Or they risked a lifetime of temporary satisfaction, instead of grabbing hold of the fulfillment she knew they could have.

"No." She pushed at his shoulders and attempted to roll away, out from beneath Belmont. "Wait…just—"

And that's when he broke and did something out of character. He tried to prevent her from leaving. He used his chest to hold her down and dragged down his zipper, his breath so labored it bounced off the walls. It only took a split second, that refusal to let her move, and it was so unlike Belmont, they sprang apart immediately afterward. Belmont stood on one side of the bed, both hands on his head, utter disbelief on his face. Sage faced him from the other end, fingers pressed to her mouth, yearning to hold him.

"Jesus. I don't know what…" He gave a quick head shake, but the horror in his expression didn't loosen its hold. "I won't make an excuse. You shouldn't accept one, either. I'm sorry. I'm so sorry."

There were a million reassurances in her head. *You didn't mean it. It's okay. You warned me not to come into the room.* But to know Belmont the way Sage did, she knew he would resent her trying to excuse his lapse of judgment. He wouldn't allow her to take any responsibility for it away from him. So she didn't try. "I'm going to go now. And tomorrow, we're going to try to talk again. We'll find a way through this together. Okay?" She rounded the bed, something inside her snapping in two when he backed away. "I know there's nothing I can say or do to keep you out of the mine. So I'm going to be right outside waiting for you. We're going to talk and get through this together, Belmont. Everything is going to be fine."

* * *

But it wasn't fine.

The following day, Belmont emerged from the mine looking haunted. His gaze was distant, his cheeks gaunt. And he didn't even stop when Sage called to him outside the motel. He didn't answer the door when she knocked.

The next day was the same. He moved right past her, as if she were a ghost, closing himself inside the room without a hint of recognition.

Her nightmare had come to fruition. Belmont was dying. She could see the bright blazing heartiness of him draining away, leaving nothing but a shell. And she could do nothing to comfort him without becoming one half of a relationship she knew would be toxic. She'd seen and lived it and she wouldn't let them become that. Wouldn't let Belmont diminish himself that way. She loved him too much.

This was *her* fight. She'd come to Sibley ready to battle and he'd tried to go to war in her place. But it was still her war. The stakes were simply higher now. If Belmont's spirit didn't survive the mine, she would never be able to live with herself. Already she'd lived with guilt over leaving her parents to the devil. She couldn't do the same to Belmont. It would kill her.

So she would set him free. There were no other options. Not for them.

The first phone call she made was to Peggy.

"*Sage!*" Even in her state of numb distress, Sage couldn't help but smile a little over her friend's trademark exuberance. "What the fuck? We've been combing the Interwebs and calling your phones and *nada*. We thought you guys fell into a giant sink hole. Please tell me you've been shacked up in a swanky hotel making up for wasted time."

Sage's heart twisted, wishing life could work itself out so easily. "No." She cleared the rust from her throat. "We're in Sibley, Louisiana. My hometown."

Silence throbbed on the line. "I should have known where you were from, Sage. We're best friends."

"I know." Sage stared back at her reflection on the hearth's glass door. "There's probably a lot you should have known, but I don't have time to explain any of it now. And I'm so sorry. You'll have every right to hate me after I tell you this."

"You're scaring me here." Peggy's chuckle was packed full of nerves. "Whatever it is, we'll fix it. I've got freaking Aaron on standby, and boy, if you thought he was a machine before, you should have seen him after that call from Bel."

"What call?" Sage tried to massage away the sudden headache, but the searing discomfort only worsened.

"Never mind. Belmont...he's in trouble, Peggy. You have to get everyone down here. You have to force him to go home."

When her friend spoke again, it was all worry, no teasing. "Sage, is my brother hurt?"

"No. Not in the way a doctor could see." She needed to get off the phone. The longer it went on, the more she would have to explain, and God. God, after three days of not being able to reach Belmont—even with him standing right in front of her—she was empty. She'd been drained of all her energy and there was nothing left but misery. "He's in the motel in Sibley. Room seven. You need to come right away, Peggy. Tomorrow morning, if you can."

"I'm already packing." Peggy was crying now, drawers slamming in the background. "*Elliott!*"

Sage hung up and stared at the phone, wondering if it would be the last time she ever spoke to her best friend. Her next phone call made that a possibility.

Augie answered on the first ring. "This is Augustine Scott."

She ignored the voice at the back of her mind, begging her to disconnect the line. "I have three conditions," she said. "And then I'll...marry you."

"And what might they be?"

The amount of glee in those five words made Sage's stomach rebel, so she breathed in and out through her nose. "You don't let Belmont go back into the mine. You revoke his access."

"Normally I'd say that wouldn't be a problem, but he's one big, stubborn problem."

Nerves rose up, threatening to swallow her whole. Augustine referring to anyone as a problem meant that person was in danger. "He'll be leaving tomorrow morning. Afternoon at the latest. Just...let him leave on his own. Don't you go anywhere near him."

He didn't speak for a moment. "What are the other conditions?"

"This wedding happens as soon as possible." Eyes squeezed shut, she forced the words out. "Arrange whatever you need to arrange. Just have it done by tomorrow."

"Did you think I would give you time to back out?" He snickered. "And lastly."

"Lastly..." Needing movement, Sage shoved to her feet and paced to the cottage. "Once we're married, this is over. You sign off on my father's pension and leave my parents alone. You don't know them anymore. If they come to you with a problem, I'll find a way to fix it."

Amusement trickled down the line. "I'll gladly agree to that, little Sage, but we'll just wait and see how you propose solving their problems without me." His hum kicked off a round of bomb blasts in her stomach. That was it. It was over. She'd surrendered.

"I'll see you tomorrow," Augie murmured down the line and the illicit promise in his voice was so repulsive, Sage ended the call by smashing the phone under her booted heel.

CHAPTER TWENTY-ONE

When the knocking started on Belmont's door the following morning, he was already sitting on the edge of his bed, staring at the blank television screen. He must have been parked there since arriving back from the mine last night, because his clothes were still caked in filth, along with his hands and face. A shower would have helped clean him on the outside, but nothing would have stopped him from feeling dirty, so what was the point?

He turned and glanced at the bed behind him, wincing at the memory of what he'd done. Every time he replayed what happened, it only got worse. How many times had she told him to stop? Said no? He'd been so fucked up over the hours underground, he couldn't hear a thing over the machine roaring in his ears. And the calls of his name. They were never-ending. Everything had slammed to a halt when he registered her struggling, but it had been too late. He'd . . . denied Sage a right. He'd betrayed her trust. Sage. His *Sage*.

Instinct prodded him in the spine, the gut, insisting he find her and apologize over and over again, despite the fact that he'd already done it once. He would bring her coffees, dresses, and scrapbook materials. Anything he could think of to make her happy, even if she didn't forgive him. Thing was, she *would* forgive him. Sage was incapable of holding a grudge. There would be talking and nearness between them. Her voice would wrap around him like a scarf. And right now he wasn't able to accept her solace.

The mine and all the suppressed memories he'd shoved down into the bottom of his barrel were floating to the top. Every inch of him was scoured and raw. Being around the one person who could balm his wounds was too hard. When she was close, he wanted to latch on for dear life and never let go. She didn't want that. He didn't want that for her, either. So he stayed away from Sage. Couldn't even bring himself to look in her direction.

Eventually, he would overcome this broken part of himself. He *would*. Because Sage was suffering just as he was suffering, and that was unacceptable. There was time, though. As long as Sage was safe from the mine, he could continue to toil and beat these demons in himself. She would wait for him. Wouldn't she?

Belmont stood to answer the door, but couldn't resist one more glance toward the bed.

Help me forget, Sage.

Who knows? Maybe she wouldn't forgive him. He'd proven himself to be exactly what she wanted to avoid. Proved he wasn't good for her. Would she wait?

Belmont stared down at his hand, willing it to lift and open the door, but it just hung there by his side. Smart hand. If Sage was standing on the other side, he might not be able to send her away this time. He was so damn tired, he swayed on his feet. His heartbeat was pumping slow, slower…slower, like it couldn't find a reason to keep working without Sage around.

A fleeting thought meandered through his mind. What if he was still beneath the surface in the freezing motel pool he'd jumped into all those days ago? All of this could be one awful dream conjured by a lovesick man. If that were true, he hoped he dreamed up Sage on the other side of the door. He wouldn't be able to hurt her if she weren't real.

Suddenly eager, Belmont turned the knob and threw open the door.

It wasn't Sage.

There were…one, two…seven men, only one of whom he recognized from the last time Augustine had paid him a visit at the motel. And Belmont didn't know what they could possibly want with him, but intuition told him their presence was a very bad thing. Very bad. In the last week, he'd slept only a matter of hours and his muscles were strained from mine work. His heart was barely performing its function by pumping blood and he ached head to toe. He ached for Sage. What he'd done. How he'd fix it. Whether trying to do so was even the right thing for her.

But his mind was alert enough to know if seven men were there, they anticipated a problem. And the only way Belmont would give them a problem was if Sage's safety or happiness were in question.

His hands flexed into fists, his back teeth grinding together.

"This is the guy?" one of the men said. "What's wrong, man? Are the showers out?"

Laughter kicked up from someone he couldn't see.

"Can't we find him a hose or something? I don't want him fucking up my leather seats."

Belmont's eye started to twitch. "Why are you here?"

The familiar man in front—who Belmont decided must be the leader—wasn't smiling. No, he looked...wary. Prepared. "We're going to need you to come with us, all right?" He tilted his head toward the parking lot. "No one has to get hurt, but your visit in Sibley ends this morning." His shrug was tight. "No hard feelings, but you kind of wore out your welcome."

Fury shot through Belmont's veins, branching out into his limbs, his fingertips. "I'm not going anywhere." An ache started in his jugular. "Where is she?"

That laughter he couldn't pinpoint painted the air with red. "Probably getting ready for—"

"Hey," the leader shouted, turning around. "Why don't you shut the fuck up, huh?"

Belmont had the leader by the throat while the question still hung in the air. The men around him braced, reaching for the insides of their coats, but Belmont only registered those actions dimly. The sense of wrongness with which he'd answered the door was now booming in his ears like cannon fire. He was looking directly into the man's nervous eyes, but suddenly all he could see was Sage outside the motel room door yesterday, looking pale and...resigned. He'd been so focused on getting himself out of her beautiful orbit, he hadn't really allowed her appearance to process. Not as deeply as it was now. And there was no comparison to the new kind of pain that rammed into his midsection, almost doubling him over.

"*Where is she?*" Belmont roared, sending some of the men scattering back. "What is she getting ready for? You have five seconds before I break your neck and ask the man behind you."

Belmont didn't realize the man was dangling. Not until his toes tried to find purchase on Belmont's boot. "She's getting married today. And not to you," the man spat. "Augie isn't taking any chances on you busting up the proceedings, so you're taking a little trip. Don't worry, though, it's not forever." A breath wheezed out of the man. "We just need to get you out of Sibley until it's over. Then you can go on your merry fucking way."

Another voice. "Be sure to send congratulations to Augie. He loves a good greeting card."

Those words made Belmont's arm go slack, sending his prisoner crashing to the ground. Half of him was now even more convinced he was still in the freezing motel pool, but common sense rose up and obliterated that theory. His throat wouldn't work to ask why. Why? *Why?*

Because he knew Sage through and through. And she'd found a way to keep him out of the mines. There wasn't a single doubt in his head.

Searing agony ran him through like a sword.

It appeared he'd failed her in yet another way. The ultimate way. Because she'd saved him…at a cost to *herself. NO.* He hadn't anticipated that and now…now she'd made herself the sacrifice, instead of the other way around. Instead of him.

He had to stop it. He couldn't let her—

Belmont's lack of focus left him temporarily vulnerable, so he didn't see the wooden bat swinging toward his head. It connected with a horrendous *thwack,* blinding him in one eye and jolting him back a step. That opening allowed the men to pour inside the room, surrounding Belmont. One still held the bat up, obviously looking for an opening to swing again, but Belmont shocked him by shooting out a hand, closing it around the wooden barrel and yanking it away. His skull throbbed as he crunched the bat over his knee, snapping it in half and tossing it aside. "Fight me like men," Belmont growled, knowing the distorted sound of his voice was a bad thing. More so when blood began trickling into his eye. "Fight me like the kind of men who wouldn't make a woman do something against her will."

The command was laced with misery because they made him a hypocrite. Hadn't he tried to love Sage against her will? Right there on that very bed?

"Oh, something tells me she'll at least act willing," one of the men snickered. "If she wants to hold up her end of the deal."

Belmont bellowed, not only at the idea of Sage with another man, but at the confirmation she'd struck a bargain. He lunged toward the closest man, swinging his fist and sending him staggering back. One by one, he took them all on. Blood spewed onto the walls and carpet. Cheap furniture was cracked in half, clothes were ripped, and epithets were shouted. But in the end, the odds weren't in Belmont's favor. While he was focused on a frontward attack, someone brought a chair down on his head from behind, rendering him unconscious.

As the blackness claimed him, denial rocked his very soul.

* * *

There weren't many people in this town who were kind to Libby.

Memories in Sibley were sure long when they wanted to be, but short when it came to her. Folks chose not to remember that she hadn't *always* needed to sell her body for money. There had been a time when she'd lived happily with her husband, Colburn, on the outskirts of town, working in the beauty parlor as a shampoo girl. But hard times had fallen on them when Colburn got sick—and God knew, the mine company's insurance wasn't for shit.

Some of her friends had stuck around and offered a lending hand when Colburn passed, but they'd vanished lickity split when Libby's well of cash dried up. Even after she'd downsized from a two-bedroom house to an apartment behind the supermarket, most of the money from the sale had gone to medical expenses. Now, Libby didn't blame her poor husband for her predicament, but it turned out, humans found a way to survive, even at the cost of their pride.

Her first customer had been the town preacher some twenty years past. He'd climbed the rickety stairs to her apartment under the guise of offering condolences. While she'd poured the coffee, he'd slid a fifty-dollar bill across the table. Libby had always been quick on the uptake, so she'd knelt in front of the man of God and done a whole lot more than pray, because fifty dollars was fifty more than she had in the bank.

She'd only meant to do it once. The guilt when she'd walked into church on Sunday had been awful. But the money had come *so easy*. So she'd kept on, and on, until twenty years had sped by in a blur of sweaty men and her evening bottle of wine.

But hell if she didn't walk through town with her chin up. They wouldn't make her ashamed of what she'd done to make ends meet. To stay sheltered and fed. *No sir.* At least, that was the attitude she'd kept until walking into the convenience store and meeting that gentle giant. The giant that required seven men to carry him out of the motel room and throw him without ceremony into the back hatch of his Suburban. *Belmont.*

Not the kind of name one forgot. Not the kind of man one forgot, either.

When he'd conversed with Libby, she'd realized how long it had been since someone spoke to her without disdain. Or judgment. Had it been years? Sometimes she took the bus to Shreveport when she needed new, inexpensive clothes, and *those* store clerks were polite to her. But only because they didn't know she was the prostitute of Sibley.

Most of the men wrestling Belmont's lifeless legs into the Suburban had visited her at some point over the years, and not one of them acknowledged her on the street. Or even in private. They didn't see her as a human with feelings, but Belmont... she thought he had.

And she desperately wanted to repay that simple kindness.

So she watched and waited, her body tucked back behind the rental office. A wrench turned in her belly when the Suburban left the lot, because there was nothing she could do to stop them leaving.

When a white van pulled into the motel parking lot half an hour later, however, hope rekindled. Six people poured out of the vehicle and none of them were smiling. A gorgeous man in a suit, his hand lingering on the back of a young girl with wild hair. An older, authoritative-looking man watching a wide-eyed beauty with concern. And a flannel-wearing cowboy, helping a stricken brunette from the far back seat. They were there for Belmont. Libby could feel it all the way down to her toes. Something about the...*light* they radiated. The palpable concern. They were the type of folks Belmont would care about and vice versa.

But even though she was fresh from having such a pleasant conversation with Belmont, she was still a little gun-shy about approaching people. Over the years, she'd given up on being discreet and become a walking advertisement for her profession. So she hung back and lit a cigarette, watching as they approached room seven, walking right through the still-open door.

The high-pitched wail from one of the women got Libby's feet moving. She stopped in the doorway, though, shifting side to side as she waited for their attention.

The wide-eyed girl with curly hair was kneeling down, picking up pieces of the broken chair, and the suited man—they resembled each other, those two—was pacing and cursing, fingers punching at his cell phone. "He's not hurt, is he? Who would want to hurt Bel?" the dark-haired girl murmured. "He's...Bel."

Curly hair started sobbing, and the older gentleman who oozed respectability lifted her into his arms and sat down on the bed. Everyone sort of gravitated toward the pair, laying hands on the crying girl, almost as if they didn't have to think about it. Who were these people?

"We need to find Sage," Suit said. "We find Sage, we find Bel. That's all there is to it."

"No..." Libby piped up from the doorway. When all six sets of eyes swung in her direction, she almost ran for it. Truly, she did. But in the same way Belmont had grounded her and made her feel like someone in that store, these six people did the same. "Little while ago, some men took Belmont in that old Suburban. I don't know what Sage looks like, but there wasn't a woman with him."

"Took *our* brother?" Suit prompted, stepping forward with an incredulous expression on his handsome face. "There must have been more than a few men."

Regret tilted in Libby's chest. "Sounded like they were having some trouble with him in here, but…he wasn't moving when they put him in the car."

The dark-haired girl dropped onto the bed, her face white as a sheet. "Did you hear what they were talking about?"

"No, I was too far down." Libby shook her head sadly. "But I know where they might have taken him."

Everyone on the bed shot to their feet. "How?" asked the older gentleman.

Laughter from days gone by filtered into Libby's mind. The clinking of bottles and the haze of smoke. Sore joints and smarting skin. Creaking springs under her abused cheek. Thankfully, the six interpreted the meaning behind her silence. The girl with the wild hair had been hovering to the side, but she stepped closer to Libby now and laid a hand on her shoulder, sending a shock of warmth down Libby's arm. Real human contact. The good kind. "Will you please take us there?"

CHAPTER TWENTY-TWO

Sage.

Belmont's eyes flew open, and immediately, he started to struggle.

His whereabouts became clear right away. The ripped felt of the ceiling that hung down in a patch the shape of Texas meant he was in the Suburban. The backseat, to be exact. When he attempted to turn onto his side and sit up, his wrists burned. Tied. They were tied together so tight, he'd lost feeling in his hands. No. *No. I have to reach Sage.*

He threw back his head and released a roar through clenched teeth, not caring that the action made his head feel like it was splitting down the center.

Give me the pain. Give me all the pain.

What time was it? For all he knew, the ceremony between Sage and Augustine had already taken place. This couldn't be happening. *Please Lord, I'll do anything.*

Belmont's vision doubled as he sat up, the urge to throw up burning his esophagus. His muscles strained as he tried to free himself from the rope. Moisture trickled into his palms and he knew it was blood, could feel the tearing of his skin.

"*Fuck*," he shouted at the ceiling, blood and sweat mixing together and running into his eyes, stinging and obscuring his vision. Blinking as fast as possible, he whipped his head toward the window, trying to determine the time of day. Could still be morning…or afternoon. Or early evening. The cloud cover gave him no clue. He needed to move. Now.

Hunched over, Belmont forced his body through the narrow passageway near the back door, turning so he could open it, but his hands were dead. He couldn't feel anything, so he flipped around, lying back on the seat, and opened the door with his feet. A moment later, he hurled himself out of the vehicle, landing on his knees.

"*Belmont.*"

"*Bel!*"

No. Not the voices again, calling his name while he crouched in the well. He couldn't go through this routine again, where he alternated between wanting to be found and afraid of the same outcome, at the same time. His vocal cords wouldn't work anyway. But like that drowning person whose brain wouldn't allow him to succumb without a fight, he kicked for the surface. "*I'm here*," he yelled, knowing it was futile. "*I'm right here.*"

When hands and faces and silhouettes surrounded him, it was so unexpected that Belmont didn't believe they were there at first. He was too far down in the earth. They were searching so far away. How could they have found him?

But...they were there. He wasn't alone. There was his little sister, Peggy, crying. And Aaron was pissed off, shouting for a knife to cut the ropes. Rita stood in his line of sight, juggling a water bottle and a flannel shirt, then diving to her knees to wipe the stinging mix of blood and sweat from his eyes. Behind her stood a familiar woman. Or at least, he thought she looked familiar, but her form kept fading in and out in the sunlight. There were others there, too—Elliott, Jasper, Grace—running toward the nearby house and looking inside, making phone calls...they'd all come for him.

Something inside Belmont righted itself. The part of him that had never been rescued from the bottom of the well reached up...and three hands grabbed him by the forearm, pulling him to the surface. Even as he realized the rescue he'd been waiting for since he was ten might be all for nothing, hope rushed through him. Enough to fire him into action. "Sage," he gritted out, just as his bound wrists were set free. "Please, I need to get to Sage."

He sat up and tried to stand, but too many sets of hands pushed him back down. Rita held a bottle of water to his lips, but Belmont knocked it aside.

"She's marrying someone else." Belmont found his brother's slightly dazed eyes and held, all while struggling to his feet. "Sage is marrying *someone else*. I did this. It's my fault. I need to get to her. I'm losing her...I'm losing her...and I can't use my hands."

For a moment, Aaron only stared. Belmont could see that he understood. Belmont's health didn't matter; the people who'd left him to die meant nothing. If he didn't find Sage, he would *wish* he had perished in the back row of the Suburban. When Belmont ground out his brother's name a final time, Aaron snapped into action. He threw an arm around Belmont's shoulders, striding beside him toward the Suburban. "*Let's go.* I'll take Bel and Grace in the Suburban. Everyone else follow in the van." He assisted Belmont into the passenger side and slammed the door. "We've got a fucking wedding to crash."

* * *

Sage thought Augustine would bring her to town hall to trade their vows. Or arrange to have the preacher perform the ceremony behind the gates of his home. What else could someone plan on a day's notice? She should have known better. This wasn't about Augustine settling down with a woman he respected or cared about. No, this was about restoring the face he'd lost with the people of Sibley. Her parents.

Her parents, who were sitting in the second row, their stiff bodies communicating how shell shocked they were. How horrified. From the back of the church, Sage could see Bernadette's slim shoulders shaking as she cried into a tissue. Miners packed the church with their families, having been given the day off to attend the nuptials. She'd overheard one of the men explaining there had been a sign posted on the fence surrounding the site that morning, alerting the workers to the wedding and inviting one and all.

Since Sage hadn't directly invited her parents, wanting to spare them the inevitable misery as long as possible, she surmised that Augie had invited them personally. Her stomach turned over at the reality of that. This man knocking on her parents' door—the same door Belmont had knocked on just days earlier—and informing them their weakness had come to roost in the form of their daughter's loveless marriage.

Sage flinched at her own bitterness. No, she wouldn't allow the man or the situation to alter her way of thinking. Her values. She would go through with the ceremony and deal with every day, one by one, as they came. No self-pity would pass.

The organ music started—the same refrain she'd heard hundreds of times—and Sage's heart leapt into her throat, clutching the flowers in her hands until some of the stems snapped.

They were beginning early. Good. This was what she wanted. To get it over with. The Clarksons would have retrieved Belmont early this morning, and even if he balked or refused to leave, he would be distracted until the wedding concluded.

Oh God. *Oh God*, had anyone ever had to make a choice like this? Save the life of the man she loved, but break his heart in the process? Or stay with him, love him, while he slowly killed himself? There was no choice, was there? The very idea of spending another day watching him float into the motel room without his usual, visible strength...it would kill her, too, in the process. *Might as well die for a good cause.*

A tear slipped down Sage's cheek when Augie appeared at the altar, through the side door. Right in front of the pew where Belmont had made love to her for the first and last time. Augie sent Sage's parents an exaggerated smile and she almost fled, then and there. Sheer willpower kept her rooted to the ground. And the knowledge that if she backed out now, her life and the lives of her parents would be a living hell until they died.

The organist was now on her third round of the bridal march, but Sage still hadn't moved. A woman, probably one of the miners' wives, was sending her a sympathetic look from the back row...and that was what finally got her moving. This town was built on strong women. The wives of miners, who faced the possibility of losing their men every single day. She was one of the ones who'd lost. Dear God, had she lost. The most incredible man in the world. A man who'd been willing to face the darkness every day to have her love. And he did. He would have it now and straight through to eternity, no matter who she married.

Sage started down the aisle on wobbling knees, winning a small victory inside when Augie scowled at her choice of attire. A black dress that covered her, neck to toe. She tipped up her chin and kept walking, taking heart at the nods of understanding from the congregation. Taking her father's place in the mine had earned their respect, if nothing else. She was one of them now, as she'd never been before, even though she would trade vows with the man who kept them trapped beneath his thumb.

When Sage reached the altar, she stood and faced her future husband, but couldn't help casting a long look at the front pew. For a too-fleeting moment, before the preacher began to speak, she felt Belmont's breath on her neck.

"I love you, too," she whimpered. *"It doesn't hurt when you're looking at me."*

"Then I won't stop."

"Are you here with me, little Sage?" Augie murmured, his mouth smiling, but his eyes hard as stone. "I'd hate to quarrel on our first day as man and wife."

The center of her chest was smoking with devastation.

Was he so soulless that he didn't see it? Or did he simply not care? This was the man she would live with. Share a bed with. By pledging to be Augie's wife, she was giving up her chance to marry Belmont someday, and God, oh God, it was like she'd jumped off a bridge and now ached to be back up on the ledge. *This is the right thing. I'm saving Belmont, my parents.* Tears leaked out of her eyes, falling and disappearing into the bouquet of orchids she clutched in her hands. Their purplish tint reminded her of a funeral. Hers. That's what this was.

"Dearly beloved…"

Sage stopped listening after that. Couldn't make out a single word over the white noise crackling in her ears. *This is a dream.* If she just pretended that blessed morning would come in a few hours, maybe she could get through the actual words.

When the church doors crashed open, Sage was still trying to live inside the dream, so she didn't believe her eyes at first. In fact, the Clarksons appearing at the top of the aisle was exactly the scenario her grieving mind would conjure up to save itself, so it had to be an illusion. Especially when their familiar figures parted, allowing Belmont to step through and stride down the aisle, looking like a man possessed.

Sage dropped the bouquet, the crackling in her ears thinning into nothing. A void of sound so thick, she could hear a distant ringing. Blood, there was blood on the man she loved and his eyes were riddled with pain. Stark misery. And she'd put it there. She'd done it. While she could feel the answering agony in her own expression, shooting straight down to her laboring heart, witnessing how badly she'd hurt Belmont was far worse.

"I had to," she whispered, not even sure if he could hear her. "I had to. You were fading on me. You were going to keep fading."

Belmont's right eye tugged at the corner, an acknowledgment that he'd heard her, but it only seemed to upset him more. "You don't think this would fade me out, Sage?" His voice was hoarse. "I'm already half gone just seeing you up there. Without me."

The entire congregation had risen once more to their feet, murmurings passing among them. She didn't have to look at Augie to know he was seething. Couldn't look anywhere but Belmont. How had he gotten injured? In the mine? No, this looked like the result of a fight. And none of his siblings would lay a finger on him. Not even Aaron, after everything they'd overcome. Augie? Yes. She was suddenly positive that the man forcing her into marriage was responsible for the blood on Belmont, the discoloration of his jaw and around his eyes. Which meant… which meant, *she* was responsible.

Denial ripped through her. "*No.*"

Without thinking, Sage went toward Belmont, who'd stopped beside the first pew, clearly trying to discern how far they'd gotten into the ceremony. But Augie grabbed her by the elbow to keep her from going to Belmont.

"*Let go of her,*" Belmont roared. "Let her come to me."

Augie's face whitened over the deadly demand in Belmont's tone. But instead of responding, he tipped his chin toward the acting best man, who looked more like a bodyguard. The man hesitated, but went toward Belmont with the obvious intent to escort him from the church—and received a stunning right cross for his trouble. And he didn't get up.

Since she'd never seen Belmont commit an act of violence, Sage's chin dropped. But it energized something in her. She'd been asleep, trying to court numbness, but the action started a buzz in her blood. When she attempted to pry her arm free of Augie's grip one more time, he jerked her back. "You're already forgetting your place, little Sage."

And that's when all hell broke loose.

Belmont lunged, his big hands closing around Augie's neck. "What did I say about calling her that?"

The older man stumbled back, tripping on the altar steps and going down, still being held by Belmont. His eyes bulged, spittle flying from his mouth, his body shaking with the force of Belmont's strength. *No one* moved to help the mine owner, except for the Clarkson siblings and their significant others, pouring down the aisle and shouting at their brother. He wouldn't let go of Augie, though. Sage could see in the determined line of his jaw that it would take a miracle to break him free of the rage. So Sage fell to her knees and did the only thing she knew would actually work. She crammed her body in between the two men and wound her arms around Belmont's neck.

"Belmont," she ordered, right against his filthy ear. "You stop this right now."

"Can't."

"You can." She stroked his neck and watched his eyelids flutter, felt the tautness of his muscles loosen just a degree. "This isn't you."

"You don't know what I would be like without you," he said through clenched teeth. "Maybe this is only the beginning."

"That's enough, Bel," Aaron shouted. "*Come on*, man.

Get off of him." Along with Jasper and Elliott, they hooked hands beneath Belmont's arms and pulled, pulled, but being removed from Sage made him more frantic and he wouldn't budge.

"Please," Sage whispered, a shudder passing through her. On the ground, Augie's kicking feet began to slow and now it was real, now Belmont could end up in prison. Another small space he wouldn't be able to stand. "Belmont, *please*."

His body slumped, his forehead grinding gently into hers. "I won't let you do this. I'd die first. Come away from here, Sage. With me."

"Okay. Yes."

Augie gasped for air behind her and Sage breathed a sigh of immense relief, extricating herself from Belmont, even though it was visibly difficult for him to let her go. Belmont helped her back to her feet. Side by side, they watched Augie roll to his hands and knees, his body heaving with the effort of replenishing his lungs. The hatred he turned on Sage knocked her back a step, but it eventually swung to everyone. Belmont, the members of the congregation. Her parents. Especially her parents.

Augie staggered to his feet, his laughter sounding like a scratching record. "You're only delaying the inevitable," he wheezed. "Someone has to satisfy the debt. It's only a matter of who and when. This little act of"—he waved his hand around—"true love or chivalry or whatever the fuck doesn't change the numbers."

"You said this wasn't about money," Sage shot back, sensing Belmont move closer by his body heat. But she stepped away, into her own space, facing the man who'd had far too much bearing on her life. "Which is it? Is this about money or making people suffer? You can't have it both ways. So *which is it?*"

"It's whatever I decide," Augie spat back, eyeing first her, then the Clarksons, with disgust. "Everyone is so worried about one another. So *loving*. So full of shit." He yanked at his tie, loosening it and leaving it askew. "But who's the one you come to when love doesn't pay the fucking bills and you need a loan or some overtime? Me. That's right. *Me.* And you all hate depending on Augustine Scott, but you know who hates it more? I do. I could empty my bank accounts and I'd still eat dinner alone."

Silence dropped like a heavy velvet curtain over the church. Everyone stared, including Augie, who seemed shocked by his own revelation.

"You know what I think you hate most? The more you try to prove money rules everyone, the more difficult it becomes to escape the fact that you're wrong." Sage flung a hand out at the congregation. "Look at these men. They go into the mine every day. And it's brutal. So brutal. You think they do it because they're scared of you? No, it's about love. It's about feeding their families and having a roof to live beneath. It's about pride and duty." Sage hardly recognized her own voice, it was so clear and confident, but she couldn't stop to consider why. "You think making threats and collecting favors will take those things away from them? It *won't.* I almost let you take my pride, my *love*, from me, but look. Look around. You lose." Her heart thundered in her ears. "If you decide this is about money, we'll find a way to settle the debt, but it won't make you happy. You won't be happy until you stop trying to make everyone as miserable as you are." Once again she gestured toward the people filling the pews. "You won't succeed, either. They won't let you."

Sage didn't know what would happen next, but she needed to be free of the church. She needed her friends. And Belmont. Always Belmont. She took his hand and started down the aisle, but someone stood in the middle of the congregation, bringing her to a halt. "I'll donate a day's worth of pay toward Thomas's books." The stocky mine worker shifted on his feet, looking uncomfortable by the attention wrought by his announcement. "I'd do more if I could. That girl, going into the mine like she did for her daddy...we all hope our daughters grow up like that. And bring home the kind of man who'd take her place, even though...well"—he nodded once at Belmont— "even though. She's right. This is about pride. And she's one of our own now. I don't mind working a day on their behalf."

The man sat down and tugged his Saints cap back on.

Sage watched through blurred vision as man after man stood—there must have been two hundred—pledging a day or two's worth of work to her family's cause. A family they'd never embraced, but somehow she had changed their minds.

"It was you," Belmont whispered in her ear. "This is all for you."

As men continued to stand and offer up their physical labor, Belmont took Sage's hand and walked her down the aisle, toward the back of the church. She called thank-yous to the men as they went, knowing nothing would ever be sufficient. There was no way to express what the outpouring of love meant, but she would find a way to try.

Steps from the door, she turned to find her parents watching her with something that looked like astonished pride, but it only lasted for a fleeting moment, before they curled their bodies into each other. Sage wasn't surprised by it. Not hurt, either. Not anymore. Watching the familiar sight only strengthened the realization that she'd returned to Sibley with a lot of guilt she'd never deserved. She didn't want her parents to shoulder it, either, so in that moment, she shed it and left it behind, along with the fear that she and Belmont would ever be like them.

And the friends who followed her from the church— her beloved Clarksons—they would help. There wasn't a question in her mind. Combined with the money she had saved in the bank, the debt would be settled and her father would have his pension.

Her parents were free. Which meant *she* was free. Bernie and Thomas would always be a concern. There was a very real possibility they could find themselves in financial trouble again. She would help them. No. *They*, she thought, feeling Belmont's hand holding hers so tightly. *They* would work tirelessly to find a solution. But that help would come from California or occasional trips to Sibley, because she couldn't sacrifice her own happiness anymore. The first step was getting back in the Suburban and driving.

God, she couldn't wait.

Just before exiting the church, she turned to find Augie watching his employees with awe, and something inside Sage told her it was the beginning of a change. A good one.

As they walked down the steps, however, into the cold morning drizzle, Sage looked up at Belmont and saw his eyes remained unsettled. Their hands were connected, but somewhere between them, a link in their chain had snapped.

CHAPTER TWENTY-THREE

Belmont stood inside the shower steam, his hands flattened on the door of the bathroom. He'd gotten to the church in time, but he hadn't won back Sage. Not yet. Not even close. Was there relief that she no longer needed to become a martyr? Lord yes. The hot water from the shower had washed away the blood and dirt, and it had managed to ease some of the monumental tension, too. But the way she'd looked, standing up on the altar like a sacrifice, would stay with him forever. *I'm too late.* He *had* to be too late. Who wouldn't want to speed up the process of marrying Sage? It had to be over.

Maybe those prayers he'd whispered in the bottom of that well had finally reached God's ears decades later, because he'd walked out of the church holding her hand.

Now she sat inside the motel room on the bed, waiting for him. To talk.

Even if she agreed to forgive him for what had taken

place on that very bed days before... she still wasn't going to like what he had to say.

Stopping the wedding had only been a temporary fix. They'd come a long damn way in making the love between them something that would help them grow. As people *and* as a couple. She'd shone so brightly in the church today, her courage and honesty almost taking him to his knees. Watching Sage overcome her own demons made him realize he hadn't done the same, though. Not completely.

That night they made love in the church, telling Sage what happened with Lawrence had set some of his past loose, along with doubt. Having his siblings arrive like a mismatched dream team had given him faith, something he'd been lacking for a long time. Now it was time to put some of that faith in himself.

If he and Sage were going to face each other on equal ground, there was still a mountain he needed to climb. Or a pit he needed to descend into, rather.

Growing anxious over not having her in his sight, Belmont made sure the towel was tucked securely around his waist and pushed out of the bathroom. Steam followed him into the room, swirling around Sage, making her look like even more of a fantasy than she already did. Peggy must have brought her over a change of clothes while Belmont had been showering, thank God, because her black dress had been replaced by a soft blue one. He gulped over the way the top button sat between her breasts, lower than usual. The way her hands gripped the edge of the bed, knees pressed together as she looked up at him. So sweet and serious.

Belmont stooped down near the dresser, snagged a pair

of briefs and the closest jeans from his suitcase, and put both on beneath the towel, before letting it drop. He didn't want to put on a shirt, though, because even a thin layer of cotton would be a barrier between Sage and his heart—and he couldn't stand the idea of that.

He went to the window, keeping his back to the curtains. Sage stood. She took a sidestep. So did Belmont, but in the opposite direction. Sage backed up. Belmont eased forward. They orbited each other through the room, like Earth and the sun. The way they used to do before. Before Sibley.

There was a weight in Belmont's pocket and he recognized it as his pocketknife. One he needed often on the boat and had gotten used to carrying. And he was grateful for it now, because before anything else happened, he needed Sage to understand something. Keeping his gaze locked on her, Belmont removed the pocketknife, flipped open the blade, and dragged it across his palm, causing a flash of pain and a gasp from Sage. When the blood began to well, he turned his hand over, allowing the red stickiness to drip onto the center of the bed.

"I'll never again hold you down against your will, Sage." He swallowed the burgeoning ache in his throat. "Tell me you believe me."

"Of course I do," she breathed, floating toward his discarded towel on the floor. She stirred the air as she passed him, kicking off a fit of need in his belly. *So strong.* Stronger than ever because he'd almost lost her, and despite his common sense, there was no humanly possible way to deny the possessiveness. It was wrapped around his intestines like masking tape.

There was a slight hesitation when Sage approached

Belmont with the towel, probably because every inch of him was flexed, aware of her. He forced himself to relax, breathing deeply through his nose as she wrapped the towel around his hand. "Thank you for changing your dress. Thank you for wearing black."

A hitch in her ministrations. "Why are you thanking me for that?"

"It was a signal to me that you didn't want to go through with the wedding." Her clean smell slipped along his senses. "I knew you didn't, but... after how I behaved with you, I got confused here and there, wondering if you just wanted to be free of me."

"No. That wasn't it, Belmont. You know it wasn't, you just have to think." She shook her head, forcing him to notice her hair was coming loose. Strands were curled against her sweet neck, into the back of the dress. It was hard in places, as if she'd used hairspray or something, and he quelled the impulse to carry her into the bathroom and wash it out. "You just have to think back," she whispered, closing her hands around the towel and holding, soaking up his blood. "You have to remember me telling you I loved you."

Flashes of her mouth in the dark, her hands tracing his chest. "If I come back with a new body and mind in the next life, I will still remember that, Sage Alexander."

Her eyelashes swooped down to hide her eyes, but he caught the glimmer of happiness and clung to it hard. "I would remember you telling me, too."

"You've forgiven me for holding you down, then."

"Yes. *God*, yes."

"There's no excuse."

"No. I know you won't let me make any for you, either."

"Thank you." He leaned down and let his nose hover an inch above her hair. Let himself inhale. "Thank you for knowing me that much."

She was waiting for him to touch her. Belmont could sense it. Or maybe she was trying to work up the courage to touch his bare chest, which was lunacy, because his skin was starved for her hands. But perhaps it was better they were both waiting. Waiting. Because there was more to be said and nothing—especially not another lie of omission—would lie between them ever again.

"I'm staying here, Sage." His heart cracked at the fear that flew into her hazel eyes. "I'm going back to work the mine."

"No. *No*, Bel—"

He brought their mouths together and pressed, pressed hard, to quiet her protests. "I don't know how long it's going to take, but I will not make you the wife of half a man. I won't have a single weakness when you lay down beneath me every night in our marriage bed. And I won't raise our children knowing there's an ounce of fear left inside of me. I will be the strongest man I can be. I will better myself in order to give you the best. And I will celebrate knowing that I can protect you and our children from *anything*. Darkness won't be able to stop me. Nothing will. Not as a fearless man with a fearless woman as my wife."

"I am not fearless right now. I'm scared." Her voice wobbled, puffs of her breath landing on his lips. "There won't be any more darkness, Belmont. It's over. Get in the Suburban with us and go to New York. It's what your mother wanted."

"Miriam would understand, and I need you to try to do

the same," Belmont said, hating himself for making her afraid, even if there was no other course for him. "You almost married another man today because you didn't trust me enough to wrestle my demons. And I don't blame you, Sage. I *won't* blame you. But I *will not* live our life together wondering if you'll sacrifice yourself again on my behalf. Next time you'll trust me. I won't have it any other way." He laid a kiss on her cheekbone. "Tell me you understand."

The conflict in her was huge. And there was a chance she could have broken him down if she tried hard enough, because a crying, pleading Sage would have sliced through him like a saber. But this was what made his woman the ultimate prize. What would make their life together timeless and full of untarnished beauty. They loved the worst versions of each other. And they loved the potential best, just as much. "Okay, Belmont." She tucked her head underneath his chin. "Just as long as you know I would wait forever this time, if that's what it takes. Forever and a day."

Relief blew into Belmont's stomach. Gratefulness, too. And yes, there was anxiety over being separated from the woman who owned his heart and soul, but there would be no reversing his decision. It *would* be worth it when he saw the absolute trust in her eyes. That was the *only* way he could watch her drive away.

They still weren't touching. Nothing below the neck anyway, but Belmont needed Sage to initiate this time. It would be a damn long while before he forgot that split second of her struggling beneath him, so although it was difficult, he waited. The flesh behind the zipper of his jeans thickened and grew long, stretching the denim, his nipples turned to points, and his mouth hungered, but still he waited. And waited. He couldn't see Sage's face when her fingertips finally danced down the trail of hair leading to the button of his jeans, and he needed to judge her expression. So he pinched her chin between his thumb and forefinger and tilted back her head. There. Thank the Lord. There was eagerness and excitement and...curiosity.

"You have some kind of look in your eye." His thumb brushed back and forth on the crease of her chin. "I'd like to know what it means."

"It means, I want to take off your pants." Her eyes were trained on his chest, wide and a little cloudy. "And I want you to take off my dress. I...we haven't been naked together and you just talked about having children with me. I know why we've gone slow, but I—I don't want to go slow right now."

"Yeah." The organ housed in his rib cage knocked louder, and nothing could stop Belmont from dropping the towel wrapped around his hand and easing the top buttons of her dress free of their holes. "Me either."

"I want to..."

He moaned when she started to unfasten his pants.

"I want to give certain things to the man who will be my husband."

Belmont knew what she meant, but since he'd only ever considered the idea of Sage on her knees fleetingly, before shame shut him down, he'd never really imagined it happening. Or what being in her mouth would feel like, for longer than one or two licks. *Be sure that's what she means.* If he put expectations on her she wasn't comfortable with, he wouldn't be able to live with himself. "What are you aiming to do once my zipper is down, Sage?"

Her answer was to fall into a kneeling position and Belmont swayed, using his own hair as an anchor for his hands as Sage tugged off his jeans. As she peeled down his briefs and released a rush of breath onto his hot flesh, she said, "I want to make it so you can't hold back." Her lips coasted up the entire length of him and Belmont's vision blurred. "I want to give you every reason to hurry back to me."

"No, Sage," he rasped, dropping his hands to her hair, curling his fingers in the strands. "I can't live without you. I *love* you. I don't need another reason—"

"And I want to know the feel of you in my mouth," she interrupted, her voice like a calm lake before a storm. "I've thought about it so long. How deep I'll be able to take you."

"You've thought of me in your mouth." His molars were ground together so tight, his words were almost indiscernible, even to his own ears. "All this while, I was trying not to."

Hazel peeked up at him from beneath her sweep of eyelashes. "Is it crazy if that's another one of the reasons?"

Belmont didn't have another chance to answer because pleasure plowed into his middle like a battering ram wrapped in silk. He watched in disbelief as the top of his cock disappeared into Sage's gorgeous mouth, a groan ripping from his throat as it slid back out. And then... then she surged forward again and took more. "*God, almighty.*"

Her nails raked through the hair on his thighs, and after that, Belmont's focus was split between incredible suction and trying not to come. The way she looked up at him didn't help the situation at all, because her eyes were... lusty. She *liked* having him in her mouth. He'd never expected that. The times he'd pictured Sage taking him past her lips, there'd been uncertainty and shyness. No such reactions were anywhere to be found as she moaned her way up and down his inches, raking him with her teeth by accident and setting off a bonfire of need that would never go out. Never. No matter how many times she sucked him or made him come.

"The motion of my boat," he said on an exhale. "The way it *rocks*. That's what made me think of you the most like this. I would go crazy on the water sometimes. The way the water rolls is me inside you. The way the water laps the side of the boat makes me think of your tongue—"

"Doing this?" She flickered her pink tongue against his engorged head, but before he could answer, she lifted his fisted cock and tilted her head, wetting his balls with quick licks. "Or this?"

"*Yes*," he managed, his abdomen squeezing. "All, Sage. You're the tide. You're everything."

His words broke off into nothing when she sucked him deep, her lips moving far past the point she'd gone before. When his tip met resistance, black speckled his vision and he knew it had to be over. If his sensitive cock met her throat one more time, she'd be drinking him. And if he didn't make love to this woman, his world wouldn't be right when she left.

He was letting her leave? Belmont's heart constricted. *What am I thinking?*

With a strangled sound of pure torture, Belmont lifted Sage to her feet, holding on to her when she proved unsteady. Pulling her up against his chest. Close. So close. Her lips were red and shiny from sucking his cock and it riled him. There was no room for jealousy between them.

Oh no. But the shards of it were still there inside Belmont, lodged in secret places. Sage was his. Irrevocably. But she almost hadn't been. She would forever be the one he confided in and trusted, so she needed to know how deep his devotion ran. When she drove out of Sibley, it would be ringing in her ears.

Belmont looked down and realized his fingers had been busy unhooking the buttons of Sage's dress. The garment was wide open, straight down the center, allowing him a view of her black underwear and matching bra, the hollow of her belly, her pushed-up breasts. Seeing what had been waiting beneath the dress had the possessive male inside him bristling, scratching to get loose. Sage seemed to recognize the change in him, too, because she whimpered and pushed the dress off her shoulders. And Belmont pounced.

Her underwear became a scrap in seconds and cast aside. The bra was left on, purely because he couldn't wait another second to be connected with her. They moved like one fluid unit, Belmont stooping down, Sage leaping, wrapping her legs around his waist. Lord, he loved holding all her weight. Wanted to carry her through deserts and rainstorms and over thresholds. Her heat settled on top of his erection just as Belmont moved to claim her mouth and they groaned in unison, hips rolling, tongues mating.

Sage's eager mouth was paradise, her knees writhing on his hips to keep her aloft. He leaned back and let her climb his body, slip down, scale him again, the slick moves rubbing her pussy up and down the length of his cock. His cock, which she finally trapped between their bodies, beginning a rough humping rhythm, little sobs killing him as she sent them into his mouth.

Between the slide of Sage's curves and the images of

her on the floor, looking up at him, Belmont needed to get inside her. The need was immediate and consuming. By the time he reached beneath Sage's bottom and guided his length to her pussy, easing in the first few inches, he was chanting her name like a prayer. His voice got louder when she dug her nails into his shoulders and tossed her head back, working her hips, working, working, until he was firmly planted. All the way inside his woman and still not deep enough.

"God, Sage. God," he gritted against her throat, unable to resist bouncing her once, trying to sink another inch inside her tightness. "Before I fuck you, listen to something for me. Look at me and hear my words."

"Yes. Tell me," she said unevenly. "Yes."

He took one step and propped her backside on the closest piece of furniture, jostling her on his cock and making his breath go choppy. Taking the sides of her face in his hands, he leaned in and brought their faces an inch apart. "Nothing in this world would have stopped me from fighting for you today. No one could drag me away. Do you hear me?" He waited for her stilted nod. "If I'd come too late to the church, and you had married that man today, I would have stayed in Sibley and fought. Every day for the rest of my life. Nothing and no one can test my love or take it from me. Take *you* from me. Do you understand that?"

She sucked in a gulp of breath. "Yes." Her arms wrapped around his neck, her fingers tunneling into his hair. "I wouldn't have been able to keep myself from fighting, too. For us. I wouldn't know how to see you and not touch you. Not feel you touching me."

"It's even better now, isn't it? The way we touch."

His mouth raked up her ear, burrowing in the strands of hair near her temple. "We know each other more now. Your thoughts aren't a mystery now and I love it. This is right."

He missed her answer because his body began moving without permission. There were these little muscles between her thighs that kept flexing and making his blood pound. And he thanked God he'd pinned her to the furniture, because without every ounce of available friction, he would have gone crazy. Out of his mind. But it seemed as if he might reach that point anyway, because that first drive...God in heaven, it sent his balls up into his stomach.

Belmont hissed over the sweet agony. "Are you...did I make you wet enough? You feel slippery, but I should have—"

"I'm perfect." Her eyelids drooped, her puffy lips in the shape of an O. "Don't stop."

"Condom, Sage." He fell forward, burying his face in her neck, misery leaking from his every pore. "I forgot the condom."

The words sounded so out of place between them when they were the only two people in the world. Weren't they? Hadn't they always been, in a way? But this was Sage and protecting her was his job. His way of life.

"I need to put one on. Just give me a little time." She shifted beneath him, wrenching a growl free from his throat. "Please don't move."

"Belmont." Her beautiful eyes held him captive, her thighs gliding up and down his hips in a seductive tempo. "Give me sons. Give me daughters. That's how it was always supposed to be. From the very first minute."

Belmont could barely stand the beauty those words unleashed inside him. It was an exhilarating rush through an endless field, Sage at his side. And there wasn't a single barrier in their way. "I love you so much," he managed, his hips beginning to flex...and then pump. "Marry me, have our children, never want for anything. Say yes to me, Sage."

"Yes, yes, yes."

Sage's back arched on the furniture, a bead of sweat sliding down between her breasts. Her teeth chattered, her nipples peaked until he couldn't resist using his mouth on them. Sucking her like their children would do someday. Their bodies made wet sounds, meeting on rough plunges and sliding free. Belmont couldn't get her legs high enough, couldn't keep his hands from pushing her knees wide to give himself room, the fever to go deep taking over. Hot, thorough grinds of his cock into Sage were the ultimate high, this certainty that once he planted his seed inside her, it would take hold. It would begin something extraordinary.

"Belmont..."

She didn't have to say anything except his name and he knew what she needed. He pressed his thumb down on her clit, catching the tiny nub between his digit and the base of his cock, massaging her from all sides.

"Oh...my God," she screamed, her stomach shuddering.

Her reaction made him thrust out of rhythm. But then he drove even harder, the urge to satisfy tightening his muscles, swelling his cock that final, painful degree. The intensity of his need loosened his tongue, almost made him delirious, and when Sage dug her fingernails into his ass and spread her legs wide as they would go, every word inside him flowed free, like his inner dam had cracked. "So many little things you did on the trip...and I didn't know what they meant." He bared his teeth at her neck. "Like the way you always fingered the buttons of your dress around me. Or gathered your hair to one side, so I could see your neck. Your pulse. I know what you were after now. I was after it, too. I'm going to be after it *every day* of my life. Except I'll be the one fingering your buttons and pulling your hair to the side, giving my mouth a place to lick and kiss your neck." His thumb circled her clit, teasing it by slowing down and moving fast again. "This is all mine. Your body. Your heart. Tell me you're giving it to me, wife. Tell me while I'm fucking you. Tell me while we're making our first child."

"I'm..." She heaved a breath. "I'm g-giving it to you."

Sage was slipping on the furniture due to the sweat they were working up together, so Belmont dragged her back upright, hooking both arms beneath her knees so she could ride him standing up. And Lord, she rode him hard. The soles of her feet curved around his ass, her breasts rebounding with every downward twist of her body. They were staring at each other when the end came. Maybe they gave each other permission without speaking, because at once, they both held their breath...

"Oh my God, *Belmont*."

He trapped her gaze by pressing their foreheads together. "Husband."

"Husband."

"Wife."

When her pussy started to constrict around his flesh, Belmont threw Sage back down onto the furniture and lunged, driving deep as possible, letting loose his own shout of ownership between her breasts. She batted at his shoulders, dragged him close, scratched him, soothed him. His own orgasm was secondary to Sage's pleasure, but when it came, the sensation was like being reborn. A giant, invisible hand clamped down on the back of his neck, the bottom of his spine, and squeezed, until he could only grab on to Sage and wait out the relief. Chant prayers and curses and names of their future children into her shaking body.

They didn't move for a long time, neither of them finding a use for words as the sweat cooled. Belmont supported himself on an elbow so she wouldn't be crushed while he memorized every inch of their bare skin pressed close, their hearts in sync, kissing one another with each beat.

His mouth curved into a smile when he realized Sage had fallen asleep. The idea of her leaving him in the morning made Belmont want to claw off his own skin, but there came a time when a man needed to trust his gut. And trust the family he knew would protect his future wife in his absence. He wouldn't torment himself tonight, though. Tonight they would finally sleep together.

Kissing her forehead once, Belmont lifted Sage into his arms and set her down gently on the bed. He gave himself a moment to savor the freedom of lying down beside her, before getting into bed and aligning their bodies. The curve of his arm slid into the valley of her hip like it was always meant to be there. There was a sigh deep, deep inside his body that only grew louder when he pressed close, drawing her back as tightly as she would go. A knot formed in his throat, expanding until he was forced to breathe through his nose. The privilege of going to sleep protecting his woman was one he'd never take for granted. Never.

When Sage turned in his arms, folding her hand between their bodies and tucking her head beneath his chin, euphoria slipped in with the darkness and claimed him.

CHAPTER TWENTY-FOUR

Sage woke up beside Belmont.

She'd never seen him asleep before, and it was such a quiet, important moment that she slapped a hand over her mouth to keep from breathing too fast and waking him up. He was a giant man, not only in stature but in character, and not even the softness of sleep could steal those qualities. He was shirtless with the white, starchy sheet twisted around his waist, leaving his sea captain physique bare to Sage's gaze. One arm hung off the bed, the other buried beneath her pillow, the crook of his arm creating a cradle for her neck.

What time was it? She hoped it was the middle of the night, so they could put off his leaving for a matter of hours. The strip of light on the wall made it unlikely, but she wouldn't be his wake-up call. Seeing him like this was a gift and she wouldn't squander it.

Unfortunately, that was the moment she realized Belmont had hair under his arms. Such a stupid thing to make her giggle, because obviously he had hair there—he was the most masculine man on the planet—but that didn't stop Sage from laughing into her pillow. When she finally came up for air, she found Belmont watching her with amusement.

"What is it?"

She didn't trust herself enough to speak, so she reached over and tickled the patch of black in question. And he laughed. But it wasn't just a laugh. It was a throaty, sleepy, Belmont laugh that lit up the dim room and she never wanted her ears to encounter anything else. Not as long as she lived. "You have armpit hair *and* you laugh."

He turned onto his side, propping his head up on a fist. "Your bangs are messy when you wake up. They look like pick-up sticks." A smile curved his mouth. "I love it."

"Now I want to go fix them," she sighed around a grin.

"Don't." They stared at each other for long moments before Belmont spoke again. "If we were home right now, I'd make you coffee. I know your habits. They're going to become mine."

"Just not yet," she whispered, trying to keep her eyes off the clock.

His easy demeanor slipped a little. "Just not yet, sweetest girl."

She scooted closer. One inch, two, three. His chest started to rise and fall faster, but he maintained their eye contact. "What about you? What was your morning habit before me?"

He clearly had to think about it. As if the notion of *before her* was a foreign one. "Orange juice and push-ups."

"Oh." Her nipples went stiff beneath the sheet. "I'd like to see that sometime."

"You're going to see it every time." Reaching out with his free hand, Belmont pulled the sheet down and exposed her naked body. She was still new enough at being unclothed with him that her face turned hot. But any shyness vanished in the presence of his hunger. It flared in his expression, followed by the visible tightening of his muscles. Barely a second passed before Belmont prowled over her, ripping the remaining sheet out of their way. When he settled between Sage's thighs, her hands flew up, fingers clutching at the pillows. "You're going to be my new morning habit." He dragged his tongue along the seam of her lips, catching the bottom one with his teeth. "Understand?"

It was more than a show of dominance, it was a promise of things to come, and Sage responded to it like a rose being watered, something new thrilling inside her. "*Yes.*"

He moved his hips, the molten look in his eyes telling Sage he felt her wetness. And with a gritted version of her name, Belmont seated himself, knocking the headboard into the wall. "*Mine.*"

* * *

A few hours later, Sage leaned back against the bumper of the Suburban with Peggy, the other Clarksons, and their companions loitering close by. After she'd made love with Belmont, he'd asked her to stay in bed while he showered and dressed, saying he wanted to remember her with messy bangs and a rosy mouth. She wanted him to know how confident she was in him, so she'd given him a brave smile after he kissed her a final time. And left. Not crying and begging him to get behind the Suburban wheel where he belonged was the hardest thing she'd ever done. Actually driving away without him would be the second most difficult.

None of them were okay with leaving Belmont behind. Not remotely. Aaron hadn't shown a hint of emotion upon finding out, which spoke volumes in itself. Now they waited. For what? Probably for someone to do the wrong thing, so everyone else could follow suit. But going on a search for Belmont would yield no results, if he didn't want to be found.

"We have to go," Sage said to Peggy. "This is what he wants."

"I know." Peggy nodded and sipped her paper cup of coffee. "It's just kind of funny..."

Sage looked at her best friend. "What?"

Peggy leaned into Elliott's touch when he approached, smiling sadly, but gratefully when he cupped her cheek. "Bel is the reason we're all here, isn't he? He's been nudging everything into action this whole time. Aaron and I weren't going to come on the trip until he agreed."

Aaron nodded. "Outside Wayfare." He rubbed his eyes. "Seems like that morning happened a decade ago."

Rita gave a wry laugh. "Feels a little fresher for me." She leaned into Jasper. "But yeah...Belmont left my luggage in the kitchen of Buried Treasure, didn't he? Made it so I would have had no choice but to go back to Jasper."

The man in question squinted into the sunlight. "Not to mention, he suggested I get my shit together on more than one occasion."

"Same here," Elliott said gruffly, brushing a curl back from Peggy's face. "He told me I didn't see Peggy. He was right. I owe him for that. And I'll never repay the debt."

"He knocked me on my ass once, too," Grace said, her wide smile revealing that front crooked tooth, only one of the traits that made her irresistible. "Literally."

Aaron pulled Grace into his side. "Better than having a tooth knocked out." The group laughed, but it was short lived. They were all still looking over their shoulders, hoping Belmont would appear. "Yeah, our brother has been pulling the strings all along. Hard as it is, we have to let him pull one more. Sometimes he does things that don't make sense until later. Much later. He's kind of like Miriam in that way, isn't he?" His throat worked. "We're heading out in five minutes. Use the bathroom, refill your coffee, whatever."

"Shotgun," Peggy said with a wink.

They started to disperse, but were brought up short by the appearance of a woman. It took Sage a moment to recognize Libby, the only other woman in town beside her mother she'd seen ostracized. They'd never spoken, but once upon a time, Sage had fancied them kindred spirits, silly though it was. "You're Belmont's Sage?"

Hearing his name was like an ice pick to the heart. "Yes."

Libby wrung her hands at her waist. "Well, I just wanted to stop by and make sure everything was all right for you folks. I'll be heading home now."

"Wait," Aaron said, then turned to Sage. "Sage, Libby is the one who helped us find Belmont this morning."

It only took a split second for Sage's lungs to empty, gratefulness inflating her chest instead, like helium. She pushed off the bumper and went to the startled-looking woman, wrapping her arms around her. "Thank you."

Slowly, Libby's arms lifted to return the embrace. "Trust me when I say it was my pleasure." She stepped back from Sage, running shaky fingers through her hair. "What is it about the eight of you anyway? You all seem to...put a change in the air or something."

Sage turned to look at her friends, but the sun was so strong, she could only make out their silhouettes. Aaron cocky with his arms crossed. Grace beside him, her hair flying in seventeen directions. Jasper and Rita pressed together, her head lying on his shoulder. Peggy twirling a curl around her index finger, Elliott observing, his legs braced apart. Ready to take on the world. All of them were. And she was one of them now.

When Sage saw a shadow move on the ground, she realized Libby was walking away. She turned and caught the woman's arm just in time. "You should come with us to New York."

Was it her imagination or did the lines on Libby's face seem to soften, almost fade? "I couldn't, I..." She glanced around, at the town in general, it seemed. "I wouldn't know where to begin."

Grace stepped up beside Sage. "We can help with that."

"Yeah," Rita chimed in. "We specialize in fresh starts."

There were a few beats of silence before a smile bloomed across Libby's face. "Can you give me half an hour to pack?"

* * *

On the second day in the mine, the walls stopped closing in.

Yesterday, Belmont's anxiety had stemmed mostly from the knowledge that Sage was traveling without him, so he'd had trouble separating the nausea that created with his fear of being penned in. He'd sent away the woman who could very well be carrying his child already. That thought *would not stop* occurring, to the point where he wondered if Sage had encouraged him to make love to her without protection on purpose. Subconsciously, of course. His Sage didn't have a calculating bone in her body. Either way, it had worked. The urgency to pull himself together was so high, he couldn't see the peak.

Maybe that was why on day two in the mine, Belmont rode the transport into the bowels of the earth...and no longer experienced the memory of voices calling. His muscles still locked up, dread clawing up the inside of his throat. The insides of the mine beat and pulsed, as if he were trapped inside a giant heart. But the voices were gone and that was a start.

A vision of his siblings crowding around him on the ground, wiping blood and dirt from his eyes, flashed. And even more calm invaded. More and more, when he remembered his brother's steady reassurances during the drive that they would make it to the church on time, come hell or high water. And still more calm—the *most* of all—coasted down his raw insides when he thought of Sage dropping her bouquet and coming toward him in the church. Rescuing him from going insane over her standing beside another man in front of the eyes of God.

Belmont hopped off the vehicle once they reached the deepest point of the mine, breathing through his nose to combat the urge to throw up. The smell. It was damp and dank. The opposite of fresh. The cloying scent of gasoline from the equipment was welcome, because it saved the workspace from feeling like the bottom of a well.

He swallowed hard when the ceiling appeared to cave in, but held his ground. The scratching hoof noises rubbed the inside of his ear canal, but he shook them loose and breathed. He breathed.

A few feet away, the white wall of salt mocked him, moving like a fun house wall.

The pickax was in his hand before he registered the weight. Twirling the cold metal once against his palm, he lifted the tool up over his head and swung it down with all his might. Which turned out to be a lot. Salt rushed to the floor like a waterfall. And his nerves did the same. They were still there, jangling and sensitized, but with every fall of the ax, a weight lifted from his shoulders, his heart.

Something was different inside of him. Wasn't there? There'd been a shift. He couldn't pinpoint where, though. He was alone in this section of the mine. In a sense, he'd always existed inside his own space by himself. But he didn't *feel* alone. At his back, he could feel five sets of hands, supporting him, encouraging him. He could feel the cool water on his face from Rita and the crushing arms of his brother. He could hear Peggy's laughter and tears and sarcasm. He could taste the pride in his mother's food.

And God knew on top of everything, Sage shined bright as the sun. Leaving him behind on the train platform because she loved him too much to let him turn outward, instead of inward, to beat back the darkness. Forcing him to be a better man because she believed in him. Yes. That was when the shift had started. Where everything else began. With Sage.

Belmont removed his hard hat so he could strip off his sweatshirt and T-shirt, leaving him bare-chested. The red streaks left behind by Sage's nails caught his attention and he let the wall see them. Nothing was insurmountable when he could win a woman like that. Make a woman like that his wife.

He picked up the ax once more, cocked his head, and listened. His ears were greeted by nothing but silence, nothing but the quiet walls around him that *could not* hold him any longer than he desired. He was down there in the earth by choice. And he would walk out and go find his woman the same way he came in. Standing on his own two feet.

With five sets of hands at his back.

By the hundredth swing of the pickax, Belmont was laughing.

CHAPTER TWENTY-FIVE

Sage huddled her body around the heart clock, leaning down to listen to the ticking. Beneath her toes, the sand was freezing, but she burrowed them through the hard-packed granules anyway. Her surroundings were familiar and unfamiliar all at once. She'd envisioned this moment in Coney Island so many times—the white-capped water rolling in, New Yorkers blowing into their hands and stomping their feet to keep warm—but Belmont had been a part of those imaginings. Big and steady, arms crossed as his siblings revolved around him.

The unfamiliar part was the Clarksons. All those traits that made them extraordinary were a shade duller. They sat in a straight line on the beach, Peggy, Aaron, and Rita clutching at the fronts of their Walmart-purchased robes, bathing suits beneath, waiting for the whistle to sound. Occasionally, one of them would offer the others a smile, or accept a kiss from their significant other, but it was forced. They were forced.

Since the road trip started, Sage had been so sure that this morning—New Year's Day— would be magical, although she'd never expected to witness it with her own eyes. Miriam's illness hadn't given Sage much time to get to know her, but she would never forget the woman's wise, if slightly whimsical, personality. Through stories, Sage knew Miriam had often employed a little mischief to teach her children lessons. So...this couldn't be it. This moment couldn't really just be about jumping into the ocean, could it?

Hundreds of Polar Bear Club members milled on the beach, ribbing one another and stretching. They took pictures and reminisced about years gone by to the handful of brave news reporters. Sage bent down and placed her ear on the clock, listening to the steady beat. Hoping the heartbeat of the extraordinary man who'd given her the gift was pumping with the same unquestionable sureness.

"I can't picture Mom doing this," Rita said, her long, black hair whipping against her cheeks in the wind. "Even if she was drinking."

"Me either," Peggy murmured, leaning into Rita's side. "She was an indoor person, just like the rest of us."

"Except Bel," Aaron said. "The ocean is his jam. He shouldn't be missing this."

Listening to them speak about Belmont was painful for Sage, but she knew they needed to. God, the fact that the siblings were talking at all was a miracle. They'd started the road trip at odds and now they were huddled together on the beach like the survivors of a shipwreck. Maybe that was Miriam's grand design. If so, it was a noble one, but

Sage couldn't help thinking they were missing something. Something besides Belmont.

"Since this was your mother's idea," Sage started. "Why don't you read something from her journal?"

Elliott, who'd been standing guard behind Peggy, slid a hand into her curls. "That's a good idea. Who has it?"

"Belmont," Aaron answered. "He's had control of it this whole time."

"What do you mean?" Rita asked, turning her head.

"Don't you see?" A smile made its way onto the ex-politician's lips. "When Rita needed it, the damn thing appeared in her suitcase. It fell into my lap from the Suburban's sun visor, marked on the perfect page, when I needed a kick in the ass. And Peggy…"

"Bel…" She shook her head. "I didn't know why until now, but he kept reminding me it was in my purse, the whole time we were in Cincinnati."

Aaron blew a breath toward the Atlantic. "There you go."

Sage railed against the guilt, but it wouldn't be ignored. Not completely. Belmont had to stay behind for himself and she respected him for that decision, but there was no way around his absence lying squarely on her shoulders. Subconsciously, she'd wanted him to come find her in Sibley, which was why she'd left behind the scrapbook. Some part of her had known she couldn't live without Belmont Clarkson. Had she been selfish?

"I know what you're thinking, Sage," Peggy said, tugging her into the cluster of Clarksons. "And you knock it off right now. Or we'll drag you into the frigid pit of despair with us."

"Actually, that's not a bad idea." Aaron sent her a calculating look. "If we expose her to hypothermia, Belmont would probably get some kind of Sage batsignal and show up. If for no other reason than to whoop our asses."

Sage laughed, then let her eyes drift shut with a sigh. "No, I think he knows I'm made of sterner stuff now. It would drive him crazy, but he'd let me go in."

"Is that a yes to taking the plunge?" Rita asked.

"Hell no," Sage replied.

The laughter felt good, but once again it faded into silence. And with the loud conversations and camera clicks going off around them, they stared out at the water, each lost in their own thoughts. Sage's were of Belmont, yes. He would forever be there, casting a long shadow and marking everything with his presence. But there was more. She had a sense of...accomplishment. Perhaps in the beginning of the trip, she'd taken some slides backward, along with Belmont. They'd depended on each other in a way that she couldn't live with. So she'd made it right. *They'd* made it right. And in the process, she'd left Sibley behind. But when she thought back to her hometown now, it wouldn't be with shame or regret.

It would be with pride.

Sage didn't know what caused her to look down the beach, through the throngs of Polar Bear Club members and people who'd come as guest plungers. Intuition climbed the back of her neck and whispered in her ear until Sage set down the heart clock and rose to her feet, obeying a call that wouldn't be denied. Weaving around people and squinting into the morning fog, she could only hold up a finger when Peggy called her name curiously. But Sage kept going, going, until she was clear of the crowd.

And then there he was.

Belmont walked toward her, not a single hitch in his

stride. He was smiling. Smiling in a way she'd never once seen him do before. Glorious and substantial and...new, somehow. His black coat blew out behind him in the cold wind, but he seemed untouched by the weather. He was the weather...he was everything. And his arms were wide open for her.

Sage broke into a run, her feet sinking into the sand with each step. Tears that felt as if they'd been saved up for weeks chose that moment to stream down her cheeks. The tide rolled in and she ran right through the thin glassy layer of it, water splashing up onto her shins. It seemed to take forever to reach him, her missing other half. But then she was finally there, arms of steel banding around her, lifting her straight off the sand. Into warmth that couldn't be described. It was home. It was life. It was beauty and magic and power and love.

"How have I been breathing without you, Sage?" Belmont's voice vibrating against her head. "How did I manage it?"

Even though she wanted to burrow into his neck and never come out, Sage pulled back and searched blue eyes that put the nearby ocean to shame. "You managed it because you're a fearless man." Yes. *Yes.* She could see that was the truth. Impossibly, he seemed to stand even taller than before. His gaze was clear and full of affection, with none of the ghosts. Not a single one. He was there with her, completely and irrevocably. And there he would stay.

Belmont cradled the back of her head and brought their faces close. "A fearless man for a fearless woman, Sage. All of me is standing on this beach in front of you. All of me will stand beside you for the rest of my life."

"I want nothing more than that," she whispered. "I want it with my whole heart."

"You have it." He laid a soft kiss onto her lips. "Same way you've had my heart. Same way you've made it beat. Made it strong."

Sage lost her breath, so when Belmont kissed her, she needed to pull away for air almost immediately. Her inhale sounded more like a sob, but Belmont kept planting kisses, smiling ones, *shh*-ing ones, humming ones, until she finally filled her lungs enough to give him a proper kiss. Oh, and he took *advantage*. With one hand lost in Sage's hair and the other bracing her lower back, Belmont gave her the kiss of a lifetime, drawing on her, slanting his mouth over hers one way, then the other, so fluid and hungry, she would have swooned...if her feet were on the ground. But they were dangling in the air, symbolic of how she felt, and she never wanted to come down. With Belmont, she would never have to.

* * *

Belmont wanted to go on kissing Sage until the sun set.

She'd missed him. He could taste it in the way she tugged him back for more every time he attempted to give her breath. Lord, he was grateful for Sage missing him. And while he would give thanks for it every day, he would never give her cause to grieve his absence again. He'd be a landmark for her, same way she'd become one for him. A constant. A tide.

Having his mouth move with Sage's in tandem had been a mind-blowing experience every single time. But confidence flowed in his veins now, lighting him up like a sky during an electrical storm. Yes, he was huge in size, but he'd never completely felt unshakable on the inside. That had changed. He kissed Sage now—her delicious, giving mouth—and felt just a little more deserving this time around. As long as he remembered he would *never* stop needing to earn Sage's love, that was acceptable.

This time, Sage pulled away from the kiss and Belmont dragged her back with a groan, because now his whole body was involved. At one time, had he really been capable of holding her body against his own and not making love to her? She was angled back over his arm now, her thighs writhing on his...and she was pulling away again.

"*Belmont*," Sage breathed, putting a hand to her throat. "I...you..."

He gathered her hair in a fist. It was flying around and blocking his view of her face. "I have to go jump in the Atlantic. I know." He leaned down and licked into her mouth. Just once. Enough to keep that blush on her cheeks. "Maybe some cold water isn't a bad idea when I'm feeling like this."

"Like what?"

His pulse flowed hot. "Like we haven't even begun to make up for lost time. And I need to get started on that. Badly, Sage." She exhaled and he sucked it in. "So badly."

Her hazel eyes were wide on his. "No more waiting to touch now. Everything about us is...right." She laughed and shook her head, a tear sliding down her cheek. "Isn't it?"

Belmont pressed his mouth to her forehead. "More than right, sweetest girl. It's us."

They stood like that, ocean air trying to tunnel through them, before giving up and going around, until Sage stepped back. "There are three other people that need you, too." They took each other's hands and turned toward the crowd, walking back down the beach to where the trio of Clarksons waited. The sight of them put a lump in his throat. Would they ever know they'd been there with him in the mine?

Yes. He wouldn't keep it to himself. Someday soon, he would tell them.

Peggy broke free of the pack first, as expected, throwing herself into his arms in a tangle of limbs and curls. "Quite an entrance, big brother."

"Yeah, real dramatic, Bel." Aaron wasn't looking at him when he spoke, and Belmont understood. They were still working on being brothers. The real kind. The kind that could look at each other and acknowledge that they had a bond, whether they denied it or not. But maybe they were further along than Belmont realized, because Aaron turned to look at him, his eyes glassy. "I'm really fucking glad you made it, man."

"Me too," Rita said, swiping at her nose and burrowing into his chest, next to Peggy and Sage, who he'd tugged back into his side. "But a text wouldn't go unappreciated next time."

Belmont pulled his sisters close with one arm and extended the other one to Aaron, who rolled his eyes but came nonetheless. Behind him, Elliott, Grace, and Jasper each laid a hand on his back, then moved away without saying anything.

And there they stood on the shores of the Atlantic, as Miriam had wanted. But they weren't the same people who had left San Diego four weeks earlier. They were five forces of nature . . . and one unstoppable unit that had found their way back to one another. They'd barreled through obstacles and overcome their limitations and something told Belmont that life wasn't going to go back to normal.

This—the Clarksons *together*—was going to be the new normal.

Aaron broke the group hug first, finding Grace close by and throwing an arm around her shoulders. "You better get changed, Bel. I think they're going to blow the whistle soon."

He nodded, following the pack to where they'd been sitting before. Since he'd driven like a bat out of hell to reach New York in time, he hadn't stopped to buy a bathing suit. So with a shrug, he took off his coat, which had Miriam's journal stowed in the inner pocket. He handed it to Sage with a wink... and then stripped down to his boxers.

Lord, it was worth it just to see the blush climb her neck.

"There's something different about you, Bel." Peggy giggled, but there was still moisture in her eyes. "It's good. It's really good."

Peggy and Rita let their robes drop, their teeth beginning to chatter immediately. Aaron followed suit with a heartfelt curse.

The whistle blew and everyone around them ran. But the siblings didn't move.

Belmont got the odd sense they were waiting for a signal from him. An intuition he'd had before, but never believed. Until now.

"For Mom," he said, taking Rita's hand on one side, Peggy's on the other. "For us."

Aaron latched on to Rita's free hand. And while the people they loved watched them from the shore, the Clarksons walked down into the unusually placid Atlantic. They didn't flinch at the cold, even as the freezing temperature stole the oxygen from their bodies, sent goose bumps prickling up their skin. When they were waist deep, Belmont nodded and they all dropped under at the same time, their grips tightening inside the greenish-blue water.

Belmont imagined they each thought of something different while they were under. As always, his mind strayed to Sage, but his mother needed to own the moment. She was the one who had brought them together and put them in the water together. Maybe he was missing Sage's presence, but a whisper in the back of his mind was growing stronger, telling him to go back to shore. It was strange, this sense of…incompleteness, when he and his siblings had come so far. But there it was. It wouldn't go away.

Peggy, Rita, and Aaron must have felt it, too, because all four of them were quiet as they walked back to shore, still hand in hand. They were wrapped in towels by Sage, Jasper, Elliott, and Grace, pulled close. All of them moved together for body warmth, but something caught Belmont's eye over the top of the group.

His name?

His name.

It was written in huge gold letters and emblazoned across the back of a man's robe. BELMONT. And underneath his name, the word PRESIDENT was embroidered in script. The shoulders occupying the robe were shaking with obvious mirth. Obvious even though the man was facing the opposite direction. He was speaking to a woman who'd also taken the plunge, but something caused that woman to look over at Belmont. When she did, her mouth dropped open and she pointed. Right at him.

That's when the man wearing his name turned around.

And it was like looking right into a mirror. One that showed him a quarter century into the future.

This man was his father.

Even as Belmont's throat closed up and he reached blindly for Sage, a thought floated past him on a breath of wind. *Miriam had a plan, after all.*

"Oh my God," Sage breathed, following his line of sight. "Oh, Belmont."

Just as they'd done in the mine, his sisters' and brother's hands found his back and supported him. Bolstered him. Made him who he was.

"I wonder why Miriam didn't just tell you where to find him," Aaron said, his voice unnatural. "Or who he was."

Belmont didn't have to think about the answer. "Because she knew I would need you guys with me when the time came. Before this trip... I would have come alone."

Rita squeezed his shoulder. "Well, we're with you now."

Taking his eyes off the man who continued to stare at him across the expanse of beach, Belmont turned to the group. "I know you are. You always were."

But a moment later Belmont crossed the sand alone, fully prepared to shake the hand of the man who'd given him life and ask for answers. Because that was the thing about gaining strength from the ones who loved you. You held on to it wherever you went.

* * *

Miriam Clarkson, January 1

If you're reading this, stop. Unless something bad has

happened, in which case, screw it. I'm obviously not there anymore to stop you.

I hope I didn't make a big deal out of dying. Hope there were no last-minute confessions or wistful wishes that I'd seen more sunrises. If I did succumb to those clichés and killed everyone's vibe, I'm sorry. If I didn't? Well, bully for me. But I'm succumbing now, in this book, because I've had too much bourbon.

Oh, come on. At least pretend to be scandalized.

So, here goes. I love my kids. I love that I didn't have to say it every day for them to know it. To be comfortable in it. But looking back—hindsight is more like 40/40 when you're about to croak—I know I only fixed minuscule problems and ignored the mammoth ones. I never cooked family dinners, which is pretty damn ironic when you think about it. I am—or was—a culinary genius, after all.

People make dying wishes and their loved ones carry them out. That's how it works, right? Well, I don't wish to put that weight on my kids. But I have no such qualms with a cheap notebook I bought at Rite Aid. So here it is. My. Dying. Wish.

Please be patient and try to remember that I often have—or had, rather—a plan.

When I was eighteen, I spent a year in New York City. On New Year's Day in 1984, I jumped into the icy waters of the Atlantic with the Coney Island Polar Bear Club. I was a guest of a guest of a guest, as eighteen-year-olds trying to make their way in New York often are.

Now here's where shit gets corny—apologies to my daughter, Rita, who of my four children, will likely find and read this first. See? I paid attention sometimes.

As I was saying.

When I walked back up onto that Coney Island beach, dripping wet and exhilarated, I could see my future. It wasn't perfect, but I glimpsed it. It glimpsed me back. I could see where I was going. How I would get there. Who would be beside me.

My life changed that day. If I had one wish, it would be for my four children, Belmont, Rita, Aaron, and Peggy, to jump into that same ocean, on that same beach, on New Year's Day.

Together.

Knowing I'm right there with them.

And no, Rita, I'm not joking. How dare you question a dead woman.

EPILOGUE

Six months later

Sage stared at her reflection in the mirror, tilting her head so she could admire the white flowers Peggy had woven into her hair. Her best friend had stepped outside to make sure everyone was in position for the wedding ceremony, and Sage was grateful for the few moments alone. This was her wedding day. She was marrying Belmont Clarkson.

"Sage Clarkson," she hummed, laying a hand on her swollen belly, feeling a brush of life against her palm. "If we'd waited any longer, you would have been a guest at the wedding."

When Sage and Belmont had returned from New York, she'd assumed he would want to get married right away. But he'd surprised her. He'd been doing that a lot lately.

One morning while they were listening to the tide break

through the open window of their apartment, she'd caught him staring at her. He'd laid a lingering kiss on her mouth while sliding a diamond ring onto her finger. "We're already as official as two people can get, Sage," he'd rasped. "But I'm so proud of you being mine, I'd be honored if the world knew."

"I want the whole family here."

Belmont had eased her down onto the couch and kissed her growing stomach. "Me too. I want them with us."

And then he'd lifted Sage's nightshirt and used his mouth between her legs.

The memory made her shiver, even in the summer heat.

Having the family present for the wedding meant waiting, so that's what they'd done. After all, it took some time to wrangle three hectic schedules and draw the Clarksons home from all over the country.

In New Mexico, Rita and Jasper were already expanding their restaurant, Buried Treasure, to meet the growing demand for Rita's cooking. By next summer, they would be finished with another new addition and be able to seat twenty more tables. Rita and Sage had announced their pregnancies at the same time during a Sunday morning phone call, leading to an embarrassing round of hormonal tears on both sides. In October, Rita and Jasper would welcome a son. They'd already asked Belmont to be the godfather.

Aaron and Grace hadn't picked a permanent home yet and Sage wasn't sure they ever would. After they'd gotten the new YouthAspire camp up and running in Iowa, they'd moved on to the next project. And the next. Calling themselves Four Ribbons, they'd created an online community where failing nonprofit organizations could petition for help. Based on Aaron's research and Grace's gut feeling, they would choose their next project and go. Aaron used his expertise to rally the local community around the chosen cause, and the differences they were making were nothing short of miraculous. A major television network had approached Aaron and Grace to do a reality show just last month, but they'd turned down the offer without hesitation.

Peggy and Elliott were a team that seemed to become stronger every time Sage saw them. Elliott appeared to be in awe of everything Peggy did and never failed to lend support to her ideas, even if those ideas were along the lines of a trust exercise in the desert. They also couldn't keep their hands off each other. Elliott's leave of absence from coaching had done wonders for their relationship as it allowed them to spend unlimited time together. Since arriving in San Diego for the wedding, they'd been sneaking out of dinners and dress/tux fittings, returning with guilty, but satisfied, expressions. "Must be the sea air," Peggy had murmured rather dreamily this morning, while fixing her askew ponytail. When Elliott returned to coaching next fall, Peggy already had plans to lead a booster community at the college. She would be the liaison between the university and alumni, creating mentorships for athletes and raising money for students whose families were in need, just as she'd done with Kyler Tate's family when their road trip had paused in Cincinnati. Peggy and Elliott's relationship was clearly flourishing, as was their bond with Alice, Elliott's daughter. She hadn't come to San Diego for the wedding, opting instead to attend theater camp over the summer. But the distance didn't stop Peggy and Alice from texting constantly.

Usually about boys.

As for herself and Belmont? They hadn't spent a night apart since returning to San Diego. They'd driven back to California in the Suburban, of course, which was parked in their designated space outside. Belmont's apartment, a two-bedroom overlooking the Pacific, had become their home, and while Belmont wanted to buy a house, they were putting it off for a while longer. There was something magic about the apartment. Maybe it was knowing he'd dreamed of her inside its walls. Maybe it was the gentle sound of rolling waves you could hear in every room with the windows open. Or maybe it was listening to the lapping of water and knowing Belmont was out there working on one of his three salvage boats, counting the hours until they were together again. But there was something about the place they called home. She could still remember how he'd followed her from room to room the first time she'd entered, as if taking mental snapshots of her in every square foot. "I love it, Belmont," she'd whispered into his neck. "It feels like forever."

Sage blushed to the roots of her hairline thinking about what followed. Belmont's hands parting her legs, palming her breasts, guiding himself between her thighs. She'd thought their lovemaking couldn't get any better than it had been in the church, their very first time together. And that night would always hold a special place in her heart. But...wow. As they'd grown more confident with intimacy, things had just...*ignited*. Belmont was barely in the door some nights before Sage was being stripped down and carried to the shower. Or bed. Or like last week, taken roughly on the entry table while sauce simmered on the stove.

She fanned herself with a fluttering hand. "Stop thinking about it or you'll walk down the aisle looking like a tomato."

And Belmont would know exactly what she was thinking. He always, always knew.

After two weeks back in San Diego, she garnered the courage to go get her old job back. Before the trip, she might not have been so brave. But after she'd faced down the town bully in front of God and man, there wasn't much that could scare her. She'd quit the wedding planning firm so abruptly, thinking she would be remaining in Sibley for the indefinite future, but in spite of her hasty departure, they'd welcomed her back with open arms. Planning happily-ever-after's for a living was even more rewarding now that she'd found her own.

The bedroom door opened and Peggy slipped inside. "Everyone is ready down on the beach." Peggy went up on her toes and squealed. "We're going to be *sisters*. Oh my God."

Sage's laughter came out in a watery burst. "We always were. But..." She stood and smoothed the white chiffon of her wedding dress, which ended just above the knee. "Now it's real. I'm marrying him. And I don't think it's possible to be any happier."

"Stop. You're going to make me ruin my makeup," Peggy wailed. "And let's face it, my makeup is perfect."

Sage picked up her bouquet of sunflowers. "Quick, what would Blanche Devereaux say?"

Without missing a beat, Peggy cocked a hip and adopted a Southern accent. "Wearing white on your wedding day, huh?" She tossed her hair. "They would laugh me out of the church in anything less than scarlet."

The two best friends were still smiling as they walked out onto the beach minutes later. But Sage's steps faltered when she saw who would lead her down the aisle.

Her father stood waiting at the beach's edge in a tuxedo, looking healthier than she'd ever seen him. From the many phone conversations they'd had since Sage departed Sibley, she knew the town—especially the church—had rallied behind her parents, supporting them while they attempted to stay sober and attend meetings. They were still inseparable, though. Bernadette, as usual, wasn't far away from her husband, in the small gathering of people waiting for her beneath a waving white canopy decorated with yellow and pink flowers.

Peggy patted her arm and handed her off to Thomas, going to join her siblings.

Sage knew without a doubt that Belmont was responsible for her parents being present, and she couldn't bring herself to look at her future husband just yet, lest she burst into tears. She could picture him standing, tall and proud, beside his best man, Aaron, and Rita, who would pronounce them man and wife. She could see Jasper and Elliott and Grace, their smiles genuine and encouraging. Libby was there, too. Come fall, she would be their daughter's nanny and she was going to be amazing at it.

Belmont's father was there, too. Their relationship hadn't been the milestone Belmont had been hoping for, mostly because Belmont had reached a very important milestone on his own. He'd reached down deep and found a wealth of inner peace and strength unlike the world had ever seen. So he'd become friends with Jonas Belmont instead. Good friends. Through Jonas, they'd found out he'd met Miriam the morning of a Polar Bear plunge in the late eighties. There had been a month of whirlwind dating and nonstop togetherness. Jonas had fallen head over feet for Miriam and thought she'd felt the same, so he'd proposed one night on the beach in Coney Island. But he'd wanted a wife who stayed home, content to devote all her time to a husband. So she'd turned him down. Jonas had taken it hard.

Like a typical heartbroken young man, he'd been stubborn. He'd closed himself off to the memories of Miriam and chosen to ignore that he was going to be a father. If she wanted to be on her own, so be it. And he'd spent a long time regretting it, but life and his own family had taken precedence. Belmont, being Belmont, had forgiven him and they'd slowly worked their way toward a relationship. One built on the mutual acceptance of each other's flaws.

A lot like Sage's relationship with her own father, whose eyes she looked into now, noting they were clear and hazel, just like her own. Was it too much to hope Thomas and Bernadette could still turn their lives around? No. Hope was overflowing. It was real and she would never stop having it. "Thank you for coming."

"Thank *you* for coming," Thomas responded, obviously referring to Sibley.

Finally, Sage blew out a breath and stepped onto the runner, arm and arm with her father, and locked eyes with Belmont. The baby kicked in her stomach. Hard.

Her fiancé was nothing short of striking in a black tuxedo, his hands folded at his waist. Although they let go and dropped at his sides when he saw her in the dress for the first time. His lips parted on a puff of air she swore she could feel against her neck... and he smiled. That same incredible smile he gave her on the beach in Coney Island.

Her limbs were temporarily paralyzed by the depth of affection in his expression. It reached out and held her close, sending her floating down the aisle toward the love of a lifetime. The greatest love she could have ever hoped for.

When the service was over, the siblings and their other halves went out on Belmont's first boat. They each took a position overlooking the water, side by side, shoulders brushing. Belmont cut off the motor and came up behind Sage, pulling her back against his chest.

"There's my heartbeat," he whispered in her ear. "I love you."

And everyone was silent in the sunlight as they drifted...drifted...

DISCOVER HOW THE
CLARKSONS' ROADTRIP BEGAN!

Rita Clarkson is stranded in
God-Knows-Where, New Mexico, with
a busted-ass car and her three
temperamental siblings. Then rescue
shows up—six-feet-plus of hot,
charming sex on a motorcycle. And
Jasper Ellis has only a few days to
show Rita that he isn't just for
tonight...he's forever.

Please see the next page for a
preview of *Too Hot to Handle*.

CHAPTER ONE

The roof! The roof! The roof is… literally on fire.

Rita Clarkson stood across the street from Wayfare, the three-star Michelin restaurant her mother had made a culinary sensation, and watched it sizzle, pop, and whoosh into a smoking heap. Some well-meaning citizen had wrapped a blanket around her shoulders at some point, which struck her as odd. Who needed warming up this close to a structural fire? The egg-coated whisk still clutched in her right hand prevented her from pulling the blanket closer, but she couldn't force herself to set aside the utensil. It was all that remained of Wayfare, four walls that had witnessed her professional triumphs.

Or failures, more like. There had been way more of those.

Tonight's dinner-service plans had been ambitious. After a three-week absence from the restaurant, during which she'd participated in the reality television cooking show *In the Heat of the Bite*—and been booted off—Rita had been determined to swing for the fences her first night back. An attempt to overcompensate? Sure. When you've flamed out in spectacular fashion in front of a national TV audience over a fucking cheese soufflé, redemption is a must.

She could still see her own rapturous expression reflecting back from the stainless steel as she'd carefully lowered the oven door, hot television camera lights making her neck perspire, the boom mic dangling above. It was the kind of soufflé a chef dreamed about, or admired in the glossy pages of *Bon Appétit* magazine. Puffed up, tantalizing. Edible sex. With only three contestants left in the competition, she'd secured her place in the finals. Weeks of "fast-fire challenges" and bunking with neurotic chefs who slept with knives—all worth it, just to be the owner of this soufflé. A veritable feat of culinary strength.

And then her bastard fellow contestant had hip-bumped her oven, causing the center of her divine, worthy-of-Jesus's-last-supper soufflé to sag into ruin.

What came next had gotten nine hundred forty-eight thousand views on YouTube. Last time she'd checked, at least.

So, yes. Pride in shambles, Rita had overcompensated a little with tonight's menu. Duo of lamb, accompanied by goat-cheese potato puree. Duck confit on a bed of vegetable risotto. Red snapper crudo with spicy chorizo strips. Nothing that had existed on the previous menu. The one created by French chef and flavor mastermind Miriam Clarkson. Had the fire been her mother's way of saying, *Nice try, kiddo*? No, that had never been Miriam's style. If customers had sent back food with complaints to *Miriam's* kitchen, she would have poured bourbon shots for the crew, shut down service, and said, *Fuck it...you can't win 'em all.*

For the first time since the fire started, Rita felt pressure behind her eyes. Twenty-eight years old and already a colossal failure. Not fit to compete on a reality show. Not fit to carry on her mother's legacy. Not fit, *period*.

In Rita's back pocket, Miriam's notebook burned hot, like a glowing coal. As if to say, *And what exactly are you going to do about me?*

A hose-toting fireman passed, sending Rita a harried but sympathetic look. Realizing an actual tear had escaped and was rolling down her cheek, she lifted the whisk-clutching hand to swipe away the offender, splattering literal egg on her face.

"Oh, come *on*."

Denial, fatigue, and humiliation ganged up on her, starting in the shoulder region and spreading to her wrist. Secure in the fact that no one could hear her strangled sob, she hauled back and hurled the whisk, watching it bounce along the cobblestones leading to Wayfare's entrance.

No more.

She felt Belmont before she saw him. It was always that way with her oldest brother. For all she knew, he'd been standing in the shadows, watching the flames for the past hour, but hadn't felt like making his presence known. Everything on his terms, his time, his pace. God, she envied that. Envied the solitary life he'd carved out for himself, the lucrative marine salvage business that allowed him to accept only jobs that interested him, spending the rest of his time hiding away on his boat. When Belmont sidled up beside her, she didn't look over. His level expression never changed and it wouldn't now. But she couldn't stand to see her own self-disgust reflected back in his steady eyes.

"They won't save it," came Belmont's rumble.

Her oldest brother never failed to state the obvious.

"I know."

He shifted closer, brushing their shoulders together. Accidental? Maybe. He wasn't exactly huge on showing affection. None of the Clarksons were, but at least she and Belmont had quiet understanding. "Would you want them to save it, if they could?"

They were silent for a full minute. "That's a million-dollar question."

"I don't have that much cash on me."

His deadpan statement surprised a laugh out of Rita. It felt good for two-point-eight seconds before her chest began to fill with lead, her legs starting to wobble. The laugh turned into big, gulping breaths. "Oh, motherfucking Christ, Belmont. I burned down Mom's restaurant."

"Yeah." Another brush of his burly shoulder steadied her, just a little. "What she doesn't know won't hurt her."

Exasperated, Rita shoved him, but he didn't budge. "And they call me the morbid one."

Belmont's sigh managed to drown out the sirens and emergency personnel shouts. "She might be dead. But her sense of humor isn't."

Rita once again thought of the journal in her jeans pocket. "You're right. She'd be roasting marshmallows over there. Starting a hot, new upscale s'more trend."

"You could start it yourself."

No, I can't, Rita thought, staring out at the orange, licking flames. She'd already started quite enough for one night.

* * *

Rita and Belmont were sitting silently on the sidewalk, staring at the decimated restaurant, when a sleek white Mercedes with the license plate VOTE4AC pulled up along the curb, eliciting a sigh from them both. Rita shoved a hand through her dyed black hair and straightened her weary spine. Preparing. Bolstering. While Belmont's modus operandi was to hang back, take a situation's measure, and then approach with caution, her younger brother, Aaron, liked to make a damn entrance, right down to the way he exited the driver's side. Like a Broadway actor entering from stage left into a dramatic scene, aware that eyes would swing in his direction. His gray suit boasted not a single wrinkle, black shoes polished to a shine. His golden-boy smile had made him a media sensation, but for once it was nowhere to be seen as he approached Rita and Belmont.

Aaron shoved his hands into his pants pockets. "Fuck. Right?"

"Yep," Rita said, swallowing hard.

Her politician brother did a scan of the dire scene, brain working overtime behind golden-brown eyes inherited by all the Clarksons. Except Belmont, whose eyes were a deep blue, on account of him having a different father. A fact that Rita forgot most of the time, since Belmont had been there—an unmovable presence—since the day she was born. Aaron had come later. *The second coming.*

"Are you all right?" Aaron asked her abruptly, a suspicious twinkle in his gaze. "You must have been in there a while with the smoke. The soot around your eyes—"

"Hilarious, dickhead." Her heavy black eye makeup

and general *fuck off* appearance were a constant source of amusement for her clean-cut younger brother. "You have a funny way of showing concern."

"Thank you. What do I need to handle?" Aaron adjusted the starched white collar of his shirt. "Did you make a statement yet or anything?"

Rita allowed the steel to leach from her spine. "I've been kind of busy just sitting here."

"Right." Aaron feigned surprise at finding Belmont on the sidewalk with them. "Jesus. I thought you were a statue."

"Ha."

"You smell like the ocean."

"You smell like the blood of taxpayers," Belmont returned.

"Well." Rita finally found enough presence of mind to yank the smoky apron over her head, chucking it into the street. "I think I just remembered why we haven't hung out since Mom died."

Truthfully, even before that rainy afternoon, the time they'd spent together as a family had felt mandatory. Organized by their mother and fled from in almost comical haste.

"Oh. My. *God.*"

At the sound of their youngest sibling, Peggy's, voice, all three of them cursed beneath their breath. *Let the family reunion officially begin.* It wasn't that they didn't love their baby sister. And in many ways, Peggy, a personal shopper to San Diego's elite, was still a baby at twenty-five. Her big Coke-bottle curls and cheerleader appearance guaranteed that she got away with just about everything. Including neglecting to pay her cabdriver, if the irritated-looking man following her with a receipt clutched in his fist was any indication.

"How did this happen?" Peggy hiccupped, playing with the string of engagement rings dangling from her neck, as Belmont wordlessly paid the cabdriver. "I just had dinner here two weeks ago. Everything seemed *fine*."

Rita battled the compulsion to lie down on the sidewalk in the fetal position. *Oh God.* Her mother had bequeathed her an award-winning restaurant and she'd burned it down. On Rita's *first day back*.

Aaron was busy scrolling through his phone, the screen's glow illuminating his perfectly tousled dark blond hair. "Look at the bright side, Rita. Now you can pursue your dream of being a Hot Topic register girl."

Rita barely had the strength to flip him the bird. "Jump up my ass."

When Peggy approached, Rita couldn't look her in the eye, so she focused on her younger sister's toes, which were peeking out of strappy silver sandals. "Hey. I'm glad you're okay."

Rita's throat went tight. "Thanks, Peggy."

"I'm sorry about the restaurant, too. I know how much you loved it. How much Mom loved it." Her youngest sibling nodded and cast a discreet glance over her shoulder, turning back with a charming half smile. A smile responsible for four marriage proposals over the past three years. "Mom probably would have wanted me to talk to those firefighters, though. Am I right?"

Rita groaned up at the sky.

Meet the fucking Clarksons.

© Nisha Ver Helen

New York Times bestselling author **Tessa Bailey** can solve all problems except for her own, so she focuses those efforts on stubborn, fictional blue-collar men and loyal, lovable heroines. She lives on Long Island avoiding the sun and social interactions, then wonders why no one has called. Dubbed the "Michelangelo of dirty talk" by *Entertainment Weekly*, Tessa writes with spice, spirit, swoon, and a guaranteed happily ever after. Catch her on TikTok at @authortessabailey or check out tessabailey.com for a complete list of books.

You can learn more at:
TessaBailey.com
Facebook.com/TessaBaileyAuthor
Instagram @TessaBaileyIsanAuthor
TikTok @AuthorTessaBailey